DISASTER IN SPACE

Marrows made a direct-dial call to Cocoa Beach, Florida, the news center just south of Cape Kennedy: "Les? Marrows here. Yeah, fine—just great. Look, I'm onto something. It's strictly off the record for the moment. I need some answers."

He talked for ten minutes. Another piece dropped into place. There was a flap at the Cape. Trouble with the S-IB booster at Pad 37. This was ordinary enough, but to have crews working around the clock was something different. Even more out of the ordinary was the Air Force working around the clock at the launch pads for the Titan IIIC. They didn't have anything scheduled for two months. But they were rushing a booster to the pad. Why? No one knew. NASA claimed it had no idea what the Air Force was doing, and the Air Force gave out a polite "classified." Crap. They'd never slapped the security label on a IIIC from the Cape before.

Slowly but surely the finger pointed to the space station. He had just enough information with which to speculate.

In his mind he saw the black headlines:
DISASTER IN SPACE

MARTIN CAIDIN

FOUR CAME BACK

Copyright © 1968 by Martin Caidin

A Baen Book

Baen Publishing Enterprises
260 Fifth Avenue
New York, N.Y. 10001

First Baen printing, September 1988

ISBN: 0-671-65433-0

Cover art by Miro

Printed in the United States of America

Distributed by
SIMON & SCHUSTER
1230 Avenue of the Americas
New York, N.Y. 10020

**To Nick Silverio,
who always
brought them back**

Chapter I

September 28, 1972
Time—2100 GMT

He studied the notations before him and then, at the top of the page, wrote in what he had forgotten:

Commander's Log, Station Epsilon
Position . . .

He left the space blank. He knew they were crossing over the east coast of Africa. The exact coordinates didn't interest him. When you made a complete orbit of Earth every hour and forty-four minutes, your position reports were academic. At nearly five miles every second, it didn't matter where you were but where you would be in the minutes to come.

Under the heading for status reports he made cryptic entries for communications, power systems, telemetry, scientific and engineering experiments. As he wrote, he knew he was avoiding what really mattered. He sought false refuge in the minutiae of

1

his report. On the face of things it was relatively unimportant. He hated to think of it as worthless. It wasn't, of course. *Hopeless is more like it*, he thought. The pen moved.

General Situation . . .

Again he stopped. With a sudden oath at his procrastination he forced the waiting to continue. *General Situation* . . .

In bold letters he wrote: *Critical*.

The pen made a rubbing sound against the paper.

I am imparting to this Log my personal thoughts and feelings, not only as Station Commander, but as a member of this group of people. I know I cannot separate the two roles and my words reflect the dual position. I do not know at this moment if I shall ever again walk on Earth. There is no way of telling who will be next. It behooves me, then, to place everything in this record, now a diary as much as the official Station Log. What is happening to us, and in what manner we respond to the tragedy, will be of the greatest value to those who will follow us here. As they must follow. It would be a calamity of the worst order if all this were to be wasted. The frenzied reactions now sweeping the world far below us must never be permitted to close the gates.

Perhaps I was eluding reality, but I know what I sought in my future after our return to Earth, now only a few days from our originally scheduled return. I have thought many hours about June and myself . . .

Suddenly he could write no more. There had been too many hours without sleep. Death had come out of nowhere. *Something* stalking them, striking without warning or pattern. It was the destruction of years of effort and planning. The awareness of the tragedy returned repeatedly as a black cloud to his mind. He felt as if tendrils were reaching into the convoluted folds of his brain, constricting his ability to think. He yearned desperately for an enemy with whom he might come to grips, something against which he could rain blows with his fists. But there was nothing—only an unknown force that struck without warning, swiftly and silently, but with ghastly effect.

He pushed the pen against the magnetic clip on his worktable and snapped out the light. He relished the soft gloom, watching with blank mind as the dim glow of instruments became visible to his eyes. On impulse he rose to his feet, moving in the exaggerated slowness of one-tenth normal gravity, and walked to the viewport facing "down" toward the planet. He undogged the hatch and stood quietly, seeking in the awesome spectacle before his eyes some measure of the strength this vista always supplied to him.

Four hundred and sixty miles below, the part of Earth visible to him was going through the exchange of night for day. The massive curve of the planet hid the sun directly but not its glowing, millions-of-miles-long wisps of light that sprayed across and beyond the world around which he rushed with frightening speed. He studied the scene, and part of his mind told him that what he saw was wrong. For it appeared as if he, in the space station, were suspended without motion, and that the globe itself turned. It was an optical illusion of exquisite beauty, watching the sphere that blocked out most of space rolling toward him.

In that portion of the world still huddled in darkness he picked out the glowing signposts of cities.

With the sun still obscured, he made out those metropolitan areas beneath clouds; their glow diffused the atmosphere like sprays of fog in a great sea of blackness. The curving edge of the planet sliced away an inverted crescent of stars. When you lost sight of the world itself, it signified its presence in this more subtle manner.

Dawn came with its usual whispering rush, with the irresistible fascination that always attended its passage. It appeared swiftly, a scimitar of rainbow hues slashing into night, unstoppable, a band of light glowing from within. Well ahead of the scimitar, preceding the blood-red hue of its glowing edge, fainter light rushed over the earth. He knew the twilight zone painted a false picture. The light he saw was reflected from high clouds; the land beneath still lay mantled in darkness. He was eager, in a detached sense, to watch everything that happened. He lifted his gaze to take in the velvet backdrop beyond the curving edge of the world. With the sun still obscured by the planetary bulk, he could see the needle points of starlight in their haphazard splash across infinity. Then the iridescent dawn was upon the world and reflecting, even where he studied the scene, a faint pink glow along the edges of the viewport. His vision, however, went far beyond, and two worlds leaped into view, one huddled in its dark blanket and the other awakening to what was now a violent slash of light.

Moving with the habit of experience, his hand dropped the dark filter across the viewport. At nearly three-hundred-miles-a-minute, he hurtled across space to meet the sun. It jumped up with a savage lurch from the horizon. For a long moment—his vision protected by the dark filter—he stared unblinking at the nuclear orb millions of miles distant. The flaming disc mocked him. No longer was there darkness, he felt, either outside or within himself. The light compelled his return to his desk, to the waiting pages of the Station Log. He read his last line. *I have thought many hours of June and myself.*

An angry gesture crossed out the last few lines. Now his concluding words read: *The reaction of panic and fear now sweeping the world far beneath us must never be permitted to close the gates.* Those words might yet be prophetic, he knew. There were terrible riots at launching sites throughout the world.

He resumed his writing. He felt the need to regiment his memory of what had taken place.

The onset of the plague—there seems no better word for it—has been swift. First among us to be affected was Bill Jordan. The rash appeared without warning on his face, and within only a few hours Jordan was seriously ill. His skin had a mottled appearance, an angry red color that deepened almost to a purple. With the onset of rising fever, postules appeared along his neck. Then the discoloration moved downward from his face and neck like a tide, the postules following several hours later. Apparently they caused Jordan acute discomfort, perhaps much pain. There was no way to tell because he became incoherent. These other effects have been the worst. As the fever increased, Jordan's eyes became glazed. That is the only expression that can be used. He lost his ability to focus properly.

Dr. Koelbe is convinced that Jordan had lost depth perception though this could not be confirmed because he was unable to conduct any tests under the circumstances. At different times Jordan underwent complete vertigo. The term "complete" is stressed, for Jordan, a veteran of zero-g, was found grasping violently at any nearby object for support. This happened even when he was sitting, or lying down, Koelbe says that everything points to damage to the brain.

Nothing could be found in the blood specimens obtained from Jordan. Not even the test animals injected with his blood produced any results. The manner in which Bill Jordan died, outside the station, has had a severe impact on the other members of the Epsilon crew.

His mind went back to the figure of Bill Jordan, rotating and tumbling slowly. He heard once more the insane sounds that had come through his helmet earphones. The memory made him shudder, and he forced himself to bend once more to the Log.

Conditions within this Station have deteriorated. From all indications, unless we can check the spread of what is loose among us, they will continue to worsen. It is all too easy to write about a condition of morale. Our present situation transcends that description. If the reader of this Log construes these words as representing fear on my part—he is right. If only we knew what we were fighting!

Dr. Timothy Pollard was the second victim. The onset of the plague (again I return to that term) differed from Jordan's case. There was the rash, the same discoloration, but a swifter spread. Within hours of noticing the rash, Pollard was suffering from brain degeneration. Koelbe is convinced of this. It was one of the most appalling things we have ever seen. Pollard is—was?—a brilliant scientist, and the destruction of his reasoning powers shocked us all. Pollard was changed almost before our eyes from a great mind into a raving maniac. He lost all reason, and was unable to control his bodily functions. He no longer recognized his friends, it must be emphasized. We had to drug and restrain him, both for his own well-being and the safety of the Station. Not one of us doubts that Tim Pollard's hours are numbered, and in this instance, death would be a blessing.

We are baffled by what is happening. Disorders to the skin and the bodily systems are common enough during long excursions into space. The problems of environmental control, waste management, reclaiming the unavoidable debris in the air from chemicals, machinery—all these things are within the scope of our experience. At one time or another, most of the men who have gone into orbit, or to the moon, have been afflicted—skin eruptions, eye inflammation, and other similar discomforts.

But this is unlike anything we have ever known, and already it has proved to be lethal.

I must record the status of Station personnel. Bill Jordan's remains have been interred in the vacuum-lock of the S-IVB. Tim Pollard is critically ill—to all appearances, a man who has lost his reasoning powers. His fever was reported to me as 105°, and rising slowly.

Dr. Page Alison, thank God, has been spared the trials of Pollard. Ever since she came down with whatever is stalking us in this Station, she has been in a coma.

Until Dr. Werner Koelbe was stricken, we still held strongly to our hopes for beating this thing. Jordan's death was not a cause directly of the plague, but a result of actions he took. We all believe in Koelbe. The man is brilliant. His breakdown was a terrible blow. When he suffered the attack (which manifested itself quickly in brain damage) and lost control, all of us were assailed by a feeling of despair. Dr. Koelbe is now under restraint, and has been given sedatives.

The rest of us are doing everything humanly possible to help those who have been stricken. Station routine is being maintained. Luke Parsons has assumed full engineering responsibility. The machine that has been our home for nearly six months continues to function well.

Henri Guy-Michel has caught us unawares. None of us realized to what extent he had become involved with Page. Now, of course, it seems evident that they both were serious about things. I mean that for a long time Henri must really have been in love with her. What we had assumed to be simply the same face of Henri, who has always tried so hard to live up to his reputation as the gallant among astronauts, turned out to be something none of us suspected. He moves about as if this new burden of pain could in some way alleviate what has struck down Page. His grief is real enough, yet he contains it extremely well. He is withdrawn but not morose. He is worth his weight in any three men, the way he attends to those who are ill, and he has shouldered additional burdens in station duties.

I never realized until this disaster struck to what degree I had come to associate my own future with June Strond. Aside from that, I must note that she has been a pillar of strength among us. As always, she is reserved and careful in her work, but decisive in her actions. We are seeing a different June these days. She works as if she had always been a nurse. She is positively remarkable in the way she handles Henri. She had always recognized his professional worth but treated Henri as if he were something of a

*playboy in need of remonstration. Now she is patient
and tender with him.*

*Despite the fact that the complement of this Sta-
tion has been reduced by half, all programs continue
to be monitored. We have, of course, sealed off the
Life Sciences Laboratory. Without Page Alison to
continue her personal attention to biological specimens, there is no need to attend that area. Most
monitoring is automatic, as is telemetry of accumulated data. However, the setting of equipment for
that period after we were to depart Epsilon can no
longer be conducted as planned.*

The pen stopped. There was no warning. But there
it was—a complete malaise suddenly sweeping through
him. He noticed, as if from a distance, that his
fingers had released the pen, that he was slumped in
his seat. He found it increasingly difficult to throw
off the feeling that everything with purpose had come
to an end. He thought briefly of Bill Jordan, mocking
himself with the pursuing thought that more bodies
would join Bill's in the S-IVB vacuum-lock. They
would keep moving the bodies. But who would move
the final one?

He pushed himself to his feet. The viewport waited
for him, but he didn't want to look at Earth. Not
now. The five hundred miles might just as well be a
million. Moving slowly, he made his way along the
curved panels that made up the walls of his quarters.
Halfway around the compartment he stopped and
undogged the viewport hatch. He stared out at the
splash of stars on velvet.

But he couldn't shake the image of Earth in his
mind. To do that he would have to be even more
than unconscious. It filled his mind just as it com-

manded his eyes whenever he looked down upon his home world. Now that he might never return, after six months in orbit, the yearning to walk on the ground again intensified until he was brought to the point of trembling.

When the hell had all this begun?

He knew the answer well enough. Only three weeks ago, outside the Station, when he and June Strond were assisting Tim Pollard with that clumsy telescope. It had been a time of high spirits. . . .

Chapter II

Dr. Timothy Pollard, Professor of Astronomical Sciences, shouted loudly behind his curving face-plate and whirled head over outstretched heels, a pressure-suited mannikin rotating giddily in the middle of nothing.

"There!" he exclaimed. "It's all very unscientific, but for half a year I've been trying to get up the nerve." As he moved his gloved fingers, small thrusters spat in vacuum to bring his ungainly tumble to a halt. He was only partially successful. He gasped for air. "I wonder what the Board of Directors would say about this!" he cried.

Mike Harder and June Strond laughed with their friend. The sudden air of jubilation in the gaunt and usually stoic Pollard was a fresh tonic, reflecting their own mood. The scientist worked his thrusters clumsily, spinning about as he struggled to reach the body of the nearby telescope. Harder extended his arm and Pollard grasped at him with anxious futility.

11

"Never get the hang of this bloody nonsense," the scientist gasped anew. He let his body remain limp as the sure hand of Mike Harder reeled him in as he would a fish. Pollard pulled himself up to a handhold on the body of the telescope.

June helped steady him. "You're the quiet hero type, Tim," she said.

Pollard recoiled slightly from her arm. "Hero type? Me?" He made a rude sound.

"But of course!" she replied quickly. "You'll see when we get home." They glanced at the darkened Earth far below. June gestured to Pollard. "You'll have to get used to all sorts of dreadful things. Parades, welcoming speeches, the acclaim of your fellow scientists."

"With a bit of knife-twisting, I'm sure," he added.

"We'll never see you again," she went on. "Drowned in a giant testimonial bowl of chicken gumbo soup."

"But a hero to the end!" he shouted. He tried to mimic a drowning man by pinching his nose between thumb and forefinger and succeeded only in banging his gloved hand against his faceplate. "Damn! I'm always doing something like that!"

Mike Harder glanced at the timer on his left wrist. "Let's get this thing back in its hole," he said. "We'll have sun in a few minutes."

Pollard nodded, realizing immediately that they couldn't see the gesture. He looked toward the horizon where the advance glow of the sun intruded on the star-flecked blackness. "Right," he said. "We're all done."

He looked with open affection at the massive optical instrument to which he clung tightly. The great telescope had paid a hundred times over for its exorbitant cost. Drifting high above the muddy atmosphere, stabilized perfectly to track any particular target of the heavens, the machine had placed him in the enviable position of the man who has made history, around whose efforts unnumbered scientists would be revolving for years to come. The astronomical plates he had taken were of a clarity and depth unlike any ever seen in the long history of the oldest science known to man. He was the one who had been chosen to snap its atmospheric fetters and open up new reaches of the universe.

He thumped the dull-gray metal, indicating the vital photographic plates within. "It's a nice feeling," he said aloud. "Those will be the final plates we'll send home by cassette."

They shared his sense of accomplishment. This was to be the last time he would package the negatives, watch the cassette retrorocket flare in vacuum to send the blunt-shaped vehicle on its long fall back to the planet—there, to be snatched from its drifting parachute by a recovery plane. The months of photographic experiments were all completed. He looked again at the brooding assembly of metal and glass, feeling a closeness for the equipment that had served him faithfully over a long period of time.

"Only three more weeks to go," he said brightly. He could not disguise his feelings. Not one among their company could do so. More than five months lay behind them as they had sped around the planet nearly five hundred miles below. Home had assumed a new meaning, and isolation from the world a different context. The compulsion to return to Earth had become almost a living force within them. "Home" was no longer a country. It had become a world.

"Back off!" Mike Harder warned.

They thrusted away to a safe distance. Harder adjusted the small radar controls at the base of the telescope, and with a tweak of his backpack thrusters drifted away from the hulking shape. Pushing against the equipment would only have thrust him in the opposite direction. It was much simpler (and more effective) to use automatic devices to return the telescope to the space station. Thrusters adjusted the aiming attitude; flame needled into being. The telescope glided eerily toward the station, completely attuned to electronic commands. It would come to a halt several feet above the S-IVB tank and from there they would nudge it gently into its storage cubicle.

Harder glanced at the station. Only a part of the huge form, visible in reflected starlight, showed dimly against the blackness of the planet. All open lights had been shut down during the time Tim Pollard carried out his photographic work.

Harder thumbed his radio switches. "Bill, are you reading me?"

Bill Jordan's voice rattled tinnily in their headsets. "Five-by, boss. You want the lights?"

"Yeah," Harder replied. "Wave your magic wand."

"Stand by stage center," quipped the engineer. Within the station Jordan tripped the switches.

Epsilon came eerily back into existence. A thousand feet away, now silhouetted against the earth, the great space station took on form and shape. Two huge cylinders, each ninety feet in length, formed the extreme ends of the eight-man assembly. The cylinders lay along a single line, connected by thick cables and a tubular passageway that extended from the end of each giant cylinder. Each end part of the station was a tank, ninety feet long and thirty-three feet in diameter. Equidistant between the two long tanks, at a right angle to the others, was a single tank of smaller dimensions. This was the S-IVB, serving as a hub to the cabled extremities of Station *Epsilon*.

The two outer cylinders—the whole assembly linked by cable to form a station four hundred feet long—rotated slowly. Rotation gave the centrifugal force men felt as gravity. It kept soup in its cup and butterflies out of the stomach.

The first of the three major elements to come alive beneath the lights was the converted S-II tank denied forever to them. The thick cylindrical shape contained within its rounded flanks a nuclear reactor hooked up to remote controls. Cabled power lines fed energy to the manned station components. Lights placed strategically along the reactor tank were necessary to manned operations outside the station. Since *Epsilon* rotated about its center, it was necessary always to have a clear perception of the entire assembly. This was essential, not only for men in pressure suits but for spacecraft from Earth that—in order to dock with the manned S-II tank—must "chase" the rotating cylinder. This required skillful maneuvering on the part of the man behind the controls. Losing perception could mean getting "zapped," as the astronauts said wryly, by the great nuclear reactor. Bright floodlights, facing toward the outer end of the tank, kept it garishly conspicuous when illumination was required. Right now they weren't necessary. But Bill Jordan considered himself a virtuoso with his master controls, and he'd been outside enough times to realize the tremendous show he could put on with those lights, bringing them to life in controlled sequence.

Mike Harder warmed to the scene unfolding before his eyes. There was no question that the drama was real enough. He knew he should have offered the scene no more than a passing glance; he'd been out here like this a dozen times before. But he could never let this moment pass without the cascade of emotion that slipped ghostlike through his mind. Down there floated a miracle unlike any other in existence. Harder watched the lights of the S-IVB wink staccato-fashion into life. And then, along cables gleaming like silvered webbing, the station itself appeared. *Epsilon*—the greatest scientific project in history. Harder watched the red and green running lights, saw the yellow glow of lights behind the protective glass of the viewports.

Epsilon—a damned good name, thought Harder. It represented the five nations behind the great scientific laboratory rifled into its orbit 470 miles above Earth. Four Americans made up the hard core of the station. The United States had absorbed the bulk of the cost, and though there was an outward semblance of international cooperation, the United States really ran the show. But the effort was real and the intent sincere. England had sent Dr. Timothy Pollard as its first astronaut; Pollard was its stargazer, keeper of the mysteries of the universe. And a damned good man, Harder knew.

From West Germany came Dr. Werner Koelbe. At first Harder had thought they had made a wrong choice in Koelbe. Pollard was reserved, as one might expect an English scientist to be. Compared to Pollard, however, Koelbe was a brooding introvert. It wasn't that at all, Harder learned after some months. Werner Koelbe, despite his extraordinary qualifications, was a man carrying a cross. *To hell with that nonsense,* Harder chided himself. *Koelbe's carried all his weight, and more.* And he had. As personal physician to them all, and a medical research scientist of unmatched skill, he had earned their respect and their gratitude. Work performed by Koelbe was regarded "down there" as tangible payoff for the staggering cost of *Epsilon.*

Whoever was responsible for the thinking behind the political front of *Epsilon*, mused Harder, had done a hell of a job in selecting the scientist to run their communications and navigation programs. The French government had been playing footsie with the Russians for a long time with their well-publicized mutual space effort. Russian boosters sent heavy French payloads into space. Russian Molniya satellites in high orbit formed the basis for a Russian-French communications satellite network that had snared most of Europe as customers.

The walloping success of the Russian-French space partnership left the United States out in the cold. But you can't beat the personal touch, and some unknown genius in Washington, acutely aware of that fact, came up with the answer that toppled Russian popularity in France to yesterday's news. The answer was Henri Guy-Michel, a scientist of no small ability. That was important. But it didn't hold a candle to Guy-Michel's dazzling smile, broad shoulders and *savoir faire* that had already made the first French astronaut the unparalleled darling of France.

Henri Guy-Michel in an American space station warmed and thrilled the hearts of his countrymen. *And women. Christ, we must never forget the women,* Harder thought with a sudden grimace. *Every time they look at that smiling son of a bitch they're ready to come. Half the country's females are eager to tumble into the sack with Henri . . .* Harder shook his head in wonder at it all. *Epsilon's not that important to the devout, but he's the first phallic symbol in orbit. I suppose the way they feel about this station goes hand-in-hand with Henri. And now we're also heroes to the French. If Big Charlie were still around he'd have a fit to end all fits. . . .*

Another stroke of genius had resulted in the selection of one of the small nations of Europe to be represented in *Epsilon*. There was England, and West Germany, and France. Size isn't everything, some-one had realized. What about tradition in explora-tion, courage, excellence in science? The American finger of selection pointed to Norway, and the Scandinavian lands blossomed out with a fierce pride in that choice—Dr. June Strond, geophysicist, ex-plorer, skilled researcher, master of a dozen allied sciences and technologies. She was responsible for *Epsilon*'s Geophysics and Earth Sciences projects. And she was more qualified in her area of work than most scientists who put their pants on one leg at a time.

And she has a body and a face and an aura about her that has you ready to crawl up the walls, Harder told himself. Harder looked long at the pressure suit concealing June's face and body, then with a grimace forced his eyes away. He wanted June so bad it was tearing at him inside. Jesus, you could take cold showers only so long, and still the desire gnawed at your vitals. He had to remember that June was a woman, beautiful and responsive, from a land where physical love was carried on as casually as teenage petting in the States. His eyes traveled mentally over her form, her full breasts and thighs, and in-wardly he cursed. He thought of Guy-Michel and couldn't help the anger that spilled into his mind. *The bastard isn't satisfied with what he's got. He's on the make for June, and if I ever catch him trying to—*

Light stabbed through his visor without warning. Within the station, Bill Jordan had brought to life another array of the brilliant beams. Curving metal flanks with surfaces dulled from long exposure to meteoric dust glowed against the darkened planet.

The silent detonation of light brought to Mike Harder the scene of Jordan before his control panel.

Epsilon's First Engineer never touched the station systems without intrinsic awareness of every action that resulted from his use of the controls. Bill Jordan, and Luke Parsons with him, were intimately familiar with every part of *Epsilon*. The project needed their genius. No one can assemble anything as exquisitely complex as a huge space station without building in all the bugs and hair-tearing problems attendant on its operation. Millions of interrelated parts made up the critical systems; it was the reliable functioning of those systems that kept them alive, and prevented *Epsilon* from being a massive white elephant rather than the huge scientific and commercial success they had made of the station. That success was a matter of record. No one knew better than Mike Harder, who commanded the effort, that Jordan and Parsons, as station engineers, were responsible for the many nations now standing in line, money in outstretched hands, to get into the act. *Nothing succeeds like success.* The old cliché was the keynote to a long life for *Epsilon*.

Two other Americans made up the crew of eight who manned the station and ran its scientific and engineering experiments. Life Sciences, under the sure control of Page Alison, had given biologists the world over a staggering wealth of data to confound old truths and establish a host of new theories. The biological laws pursued so faithfully on Earth lost validity under conditions of raw space radiation and prolonged weightlessness. Page controlled bizarre laboratories, both in the main part of *Epsilon* and under the zero-g environment of the S-IVB tank. Harder thought of those labs, and his lips formed a smile.

It had taken them all many weeks to accept the

riotous minor jungles Page tended in her space chambers; one just didn't expect botanical wonders nearly five hundred miles straight up. That wasn't so bad, however. But canaries and parakeets . . . well—blonde hair, saucy manner, and all—Page had done a tremendous job. Harder was well aware, as were the others in the station, that Page Alison and Henri Guy-Michel were more than casual friends. Much more. But what the hell. Harder was tough in the clutch but he didn't believe in being a stiff-backed martinet when the station ran smoothly. Such things were inevitable, and Page and Henri *were* circumspect. Although, God knew, Guy-Michel didn't give a damn one way or the other. It was his casual air that needled Harder when it came to Guy-Michel's personal relationships with the women in the station.

He accepted a woman coming to him and shucking her clothes as if it were the most natural thing in the world. Accepted, hell. He *expected* it! Harder tried to be fair with himself as much as with the Frenchman. It wasn't too difficult to do when he thought of Page and Henri. But somehow, Harder felt, Guy-Michel was crossing a line when he also tried to make out with June. Harder felt the anger sweep through him, all the more heated because the Frenchman would laugh in his face. He knew Henri's standards. No one had spoken for June Strond, and she hadn't spoken for anyone else.

Goddamnit, stop mewing around like a lovesick puppy, Harder! You aren't that clean right down the line, are you, Colonel Michael Stevens Harder, United States Air Force? How about that big scientific front you're putting up, and the way you disguise the real nature of your affairs up here?

The Russians have been right as rain in their accusations, haven't they? Everyone knows the sta-

*tion is loaded with military surveillance equipment,
that the scientific label is strictly a cover-up as far as
you're concerned. What's the rock-jawed veteran of
space got to say about that? At least Guy-Michel
doesn't try to hide what he is or what he wants! Hell,
he's honest about it, if nothing else. Right?* The
thoughts that burst through his mind astounded
Harder. He wasn't accustomed to such free-wheeling
inside his skull. And there was work to do—

Yeah, Colonel. Get the lead out.

Harder laughed aloud at his command to himself,
as if an alter ego were expressing dislike for his
procrastination. The burst of laughter boomed through
his own headset and startled the others. From behind their faceplates they stared at him.

"What was that, Mike?" Tim Pollard voiced the
question for himself and June Strond.

"Nothing, nothing," Harder said with a touch of
impatience. "Just stargazing. We're wasting time."
He looked at the swiftly brightening horizon. "Let's
get with it," he said brusquely.

Body thrusters spat, turned the suited figures about.
More bursts of gas appeared, frozen instantly into
glittering ice. Like three armored denizens of a bot-
tomless ocean they drifted toward the light-splashed
S-IVB tank.

"I can't help thinking every time I see this how
beautiful it is," June Strond said. They studied the
impressive sight of the station expanding in view as
they closed the distance.

"You're right, you know," Pollard answered. "It's
like something out of Christmas, the way the lights
surround all that."

"Christmas!" Harder said in surprise. "Does that
look like a Christmas tree to you, Tim?"

For a moment the astronomer was silent, watching

the S-IVB tank growing in size. The great telescope, so familiar to him, waited several feet above the yawning clamshell doors of its storage cubicle. "I suppose so, old man," Pollard said finally. "It's all a matter of view. Like what Christmas is to a man, how he feels about it."

"You're going to feel something else if you don't slow down," Harder warned in response. Laughing at his own preoccupation, Pollard thrusted hurriedly with the others to halt his movement. They hovered about the telescope. "June, get the guides, will you?" Harder directed. The woman thrusted gently to within the clamshell doors and grasped the handholds. Bracing her legs for resistance, she extended two rods upward from the doors. "Okay, got 'em," Harder said. He hooked the guides to receptacles in the telescope, examined the links, and nodded to himself. You had to do these things just right in zero-g. Even a slight movement out of line wouldn't be stopped without bending metal. Harder pushed himself back from the telescope. "Okay, you can reel it in now," he called to June.

"Right," she said, stabbing the control button.

An electric motor began to retract the guides, towing the telescope along with them. Several minutes later, the great instrument was secured within the top level of the S-IVB. Harder and Pollard drifted to the side of the tank, waiting for confirmation of the storage locks.

"Mike, she's all set," June said.

"Good. Close the doors," he replied.

They watched the clamshells coming together like huge flower petals, lit brightly from within. Harder made a final inspection of the doors.

"She's in the barn," he said. "How's it down there, June?"

"All done, Mike."

"Okay, come on out."

June floated from a hatchway in the side of the tank. She judged her movement and body position carefully. The tank itself was turning slowly, and any careless move meant that she would drift into the path of the cables linking together the station assembly.

"You all set, Tim?" Harder asked.

"All set."

"June?"

"Right as rain."

"Let's go. I'll trail," Harder directed the others.

What came next appeared easy enough but they were in a moment of deception. The trick was to pull themselves, hand over hand, along the cables to the "up" section of the S-II tank that made up their quarters and working areas. It was deceptive because their bodies possessed angular motion. So long as they compensated for this motion, and absorbed its effect through a careful change of direction—"down" along the cable to the S-II tank—handling their own bodies was little problem. But if they were careless, the effect was like trying to walk on ice that wasn't there, while an invisible force dragged them away from where they were, along an invisible curve. It could be exasperating. To Mike Harder, the corrective body motions were as natural as walking.

They lowered themselves along the cable with their feet pointing in the direction of rotation. This gave them the effect of sliding, feather-light, down to the airlock.

"You know, I'm damned well going to miss this sort of thing!" exclaimed Pollard. "There's nothing in the world really like it."

"How could there be?" retorted Harder. "You're not on the world."

"I know that, you nit," Pollard joshed back, clamping his boots to the cable to slow down his motion. "But I fear I am going to spend time looking up from down there and wishing I were back up here."

Harder grinned at the scientist. "The hell you say," he laughed. "Six more months up here and *Epsilon* would start to look like a nut farm to you."

"Nut farm?"

"Sure. Where the funny people live."

Pollard turned to June. "What *is* he talking about?"

Her laughter was light and free. "Ignore him, Tim," she said in his defense. "He is only making with what he thinks is funny. It is a characteristic of Americans to talk in parables."

"The devil it is," Harder snapped back at her. "That's a Russian talent from way back."

"Then it's true," she answered sweetly.

"What's true?" he demanded.

She planted her feet solidly on the airlock hatch, flexing her knees and bending her body to take up the sudden stop in momentum. "That you have stolen everything from the Russians," June said with a smile. "You yourself admitted they invented the parable, and then you stole it from them."

Pollard turned to face her and bowed from the waist. For the moment he forgot where he was. Instead of his upper torso bending forward, his posterior and legs lifted from the airlock hatch. The others burst into laughter as the scientist hung suspended, unable to secure a handhold, starting to drift away. At the last moment Harder grabbed the squirming Pollard by the ankle and drew him down to the hatch. Pollard clamped a glove onto the nearest cable and mumbled his thanks.

Harder kicked several times against the hatch.

Luke Parsons winced as the sound of booted feet

thudded through the suit room adjoining the airlock. A final glance verified green status for the lock.

"I hear you, I hear you," he complained. He stabbed the verification button. "Come on in."

Outside, in vacuum, the light flashed green. Harder pulled the handle and the hatch swung open to receive them.

Chapter III

"Oh, my," she sighed with eyes closed. Luke Parsons grinned as he lifted the cumbersome pressure suit from June Strond.

"Feel better?" he asked.

She arched her back to release muscles that had been cramped for hours. Parsons looked at her with admiration. The woman had an extraordinarily catlike grace—that extra something that makes a woman beautiful. June was oblivious to the impact of her stretching movements. Abruptly she opened her eyes and favored Parsons with a flashing smile.

"Much better, Luke, thank you," she said. She rubbed her shoulder where the suit had chafed. "I never like wearing those things," she gestured as Parsons hung the suit in the drying rack. She moved her hands over her jumper where it had darkened, clinging to her body. "I always get so clammy," she said with a grimace. "I feel I haven't had a decent shower in weeks."

He laughed in agreement. "Think of it as an occupational hazard, June," he said, sliding the cubicle door shut. Moving around under zero-g was a tougher job than people realized. Even with experience, a man sweated like a horse when he lacked friction and body leverage for his movements. You knew you couldn't do a thing, squeezed into a pressure suit and drifting in the middle of nothing, but you tried anyway. It was instinct, pure and simple. Sweat ran through your pores like water pouring from a hose. Parsons set the controls for thirty minutes of warm drying air to circulate through the pressure garments.

Mike Harder stood just behind them. "Just like a woman," he said.

June turned to him. "What's just like a woman?"

"You," he said easily. "Got a wardrobe that costs forty-thousand-a-suit, and still you complain about what you wear."

She gestured casually to dismiss his words as nonsense, smiling at him. Michael, she knew, expressed his pleasure with her in this bantering kind of criticism. She had come to look forward to these exchanges.

"Are you going to stand here all day?" a voice demanded. Tim Pollard sagged against the curving wall of the airlock service room. His hair was matted and his jumper dark with perspiration. "Christ, I'm bushed," he went on, wiping his face with a towel. "Working in those devilish things always does me in."

"Tim!" June exclaimed. "How can you say such a thing! You're supposed to be a hero, remember? The dedicated scientist dashing around space in your—"

"—handy-dandy star-spangled boxtop-special glittering space suit," Mike Harder added.

"With your trusty needle-nosed laser-ray gun ready to repel all boarders," Luke Parsons tacked onto

Harder's words. Parsons went into a crouch with an
imaginary ray gun in his right hand. "Don't fire until
you see the whites of their eyes!" he cried.

"Whites?" Harder asked. "Space monsters don't
have whites of their eyes. Where did you get *your*
science fiction?"

"I forgot," said a chastened Parsons. "Yellow okay?"

Harder shook his head. "Uh-uh."

"Orange?"

"Better."

"There he is!" Parsons shouted, dramatizing his
words and gestures. "Admiral Pollard of the Intergalactic Fuzzy Corps with his trusty laser-ray gun."

"Don't forget needle-nosed," Harder interrupted.

"Yeah. Needle-nosed laser-ray gun! Repelling all
boarders! Protecting innocent victims against preda-
tory space monsters!" Parsons spun around and stuck
his forefinger against the nose of the startled Pollard.

"*Zaaaap!*" cried Parsons.

"Good Lord!" said Pollard. "You're mad, you know."

"Don't you want to be a hero?" Parsons muttered
with an angry scowl on his face. He stood nose-to-
nose with the bemused Pollard. "Don't you want to
be Grand Admiral of the Intergalactic Fuzzy Corps?"

"All I want," Pollard said with sarcasm, pushing
gently against Parsons' chest, "is to get some sleep.
I'm not as strong as the weaker sex." He added a
gesture of open respect to June Strond. "She's been
out there as long as I have and likely has worked
harder than I have. But look at her," he said, pointing. "She doesn't show even a sign of it. Me—I am
practically done in. In your own idiom, Space Cadet
Parsons, I have bought the farm, and I wish to sleep.
I'm going home."

Pollard twisted open the airlock door leading to
the central passageway of *Epsilon*, a hollow tube,

five feet wide, that ran the length of the S-II-Tank.
Where they stood in the airlock room was the "up"
end of the station. By moving through the tube they
gained access to any part of *Epsilon*. Airlock hatches
within the tubular passageway opened into each compartment level of the station.

Along its ninety-foot length *Epsilon* was divided
into thirteen levels. The "up" airlock, through which
Harder, Pollard, and June Strond had just gained
entrance to the station, formed Level 13. Level 12,
immediately below, was the Life Sciences Laboratory used by Page Alison, the single largest compartment of *Epsilon*. Like the other levels, it extended
thirty-three feet in diameter, but gained great volume through the twenty-foot span from floor to ceiling. It had seemed empty, almost cavernous, when
they first occupied *Epsilon*. After several months in
orbit, Page's green thumb had produced a small
jungle of creeping, climbing things that filled the
compartment level and gave the air a sweet, heady
smell they found much to their liking.

Beneath Page Alison's "jungle room" was Level
11, the Medical Section for Dr. Werner Koelbe.
Wall panels subdivided the level into different laboratories for Koelbe's research activities, and for monitoring the physiological condition of the station crew.
Astronomical Sciences and Geodetics shared Level
10. Below them, Level 9 divided into sections for
Geophysics and Earth Sciences. Insulated wall panels made Level 8 into the living quarters for Pollard,
Guy-Michel, and Koelbe, and, for the two women,
June Strond and Page Alison. The next compartment
downward, Level 7, was divided into the Commander's Quarters, the Conference Room, and Mike Harder's Command and Monitoring Section.

Communications and Navigation, within Level 6,

made up the working area for Henri Guy-Michel. Level 5 contained the Engineering Section for the station; here monitoring boards gave Bill Jordan and Luke Parsons, whose quarters also were on this level, a constant survey of all station systems. Electronic sensors enabled them to know what was going on anywhere within the station; "making a fix," of course, demanded direct application of the engineering skills.

Level 4 comprised what the *Epsilon* crew had named their "People Room." Here, subdivided along the circular floor were—on one side—the galley and dining area, which served also as a motion picture projection room; divided equally along the other half of the level were the showers and exercise room.

Despite its size and mass, the space station needed the balance of a tightrope walker. It was a "living structure" rather than a solid mass, and the heaviest parts went into its outward, or "down" area. Level 3 contained tools and equipment storage, water supply, and other dense materials. Immediately below, in Level 2, were batteries, pumps, pressure systems, emergency fuel cells, generators, oxygen and gases storage, environmental-control and other systems that required heavy equipment. Just as a water-filled bucket swung around at the end of a rope provides stability and mass during its swing, so the heavy mass assembled along the downward end of *Epsilon*'s swing made sure it would not become an unbalanced and quivering assembly. Level 1, the "basement" for the space station, made up another airlock system. There was both a personal airlock and a complex docking arrangement for spacecraft.

From top to bottom, end to end, *Epsilon* was a compactly-assembled mass of equipment, controls, electronics, and functional systems. At the same time, its thick cylindrical form provided for its occupants the luxury of ample room; no one felt cramped for space. Were it necessary, *Epsilon* could absorb another fifty scientists, but such a move would have been self-defeating. With only eight people making up the station complement, there was no need to maintain a flow of supplies from Earth. For the six months they were scheduled to remain in orbit, Mike Harder and his team remained independent of their mother world.

Tim Pollard opened the airlock door to the tubular passageway and looked down. Immediately, his stomach wrenched. Ninety feet of gleaming light reflecting through the silvered tunnel hit him like a blow. He had accustomed himself to floating in zero-g where he didn't have an ounce of weight. He'd beaten that. But the tube was a personal challenge every time he slipped within its confines. One time Pollard had frozen in the tube, drowning in vertigo. His universe had reeled wildly about him. He had whimpered and clung like a frightened child to the guidepipe that ran through the tube. Then he'd heard a voice. "Just take it slow, Tim. I'm right beneath you." Pollard shook with fear and grabbed at Mike Harder's voice. "Take a deep breath and let it out slowly," Harder said, calm and soothing. "That's it. Breathe slow and deep. You're not the first one to experience this reaction and you won't be the last. Breathe slowly. That's the way."

Harder waited for a few moments. Then he had told Pollard to move. He didn't advise him or recommend it. It was an order, and Pollard knew it. He moved—one hand at a time, easing his way upward through the tube. When he reached Level 10, he was able to walk through the airlock hatch without any visible sign of fear. He had turned back to Harder, but the man was gone. Mike never said a word, then

or later, about the incident. But Mike knew. And
that helped.

Pollard opened his eyes. The gleaming walls seemed
to stretch away forever, diminishing with distance to
a small aperture. He forced himself to study indenta-
tions along the tube walls that served as foot rungs
and handholds. *Look for details, you bloody fool!*
That was the secret. Take it one part at a time. In
the direct center of the tube, running the full length
of the station, was the teflon-lined guidepipe. To
move "down" through the station you slipped on a
thermal mitt and let go. Up here in orbit the artificial gravity kept a man's weight to only a tenth of
what it was on the earth's surface. But weight wasn't
as important as acceleration. A man's body acceler-
ated with only a tenth of the speed he experienced
when falling near the surface of the earth. When he
released his grip on the teflon pipe he began a gentle
floating descent, guiding himslf with his hand around
the pipe. To slow down or to stop, he tightened his
grip. The thermal mitt prevented friction burns. Coming "up" through the tubular passageway required
muscle energy, but it was more of a strong swim-
ming motion than a strenuous climb. Tim Pollard
weighed 170 pounds, reckoned in Earth weight.
Within *Epsilon*, he "weighed" only seventeen pounds.

He didn't mind going "up." This demanded performance from his body. There was a cause and an
effect. But the trip down, for Pollard, was almost
always a vertiginous experience. It seemed to take
forever to *know* that he wasn't going to fall helplessly
down that long tube.

Pollard leaned out into the tube. Crouching, he
grasped the teflon pipe and swung his body into the
passageway. He braced himself, cursing his weakness. He forced himself to relax. He looked back

through the hatch, a self-conscious smile on his face. Mike Harder nodded with a barely perceptible motion. Slowly Pollard relaxed his grip on the pipe. He gasped for air until his slow, sinking movement reassured him that there would be no heady plunge down the circular corridor. He watched the lights drifting past him, showing his gentle acceleration.

Forty feet down from the airlock level, Pollard clenched his fist. His descent eased. As he came abreast of Level 8, he squeezed tighter and came to a halt. He swung over to the recessed foothold, checked the airlock warning lights and opened the oval hatch that led into the compartment. As he prepared to leave the tube, he looked up. He saw Harder watching him. Pollard smiled and waved as he disappeared from view.

Mike Harder studied June's face. Her expression yielded her obvious pleasure in the sensation of the moment.

"Hey, you still with me?" he asked, a trace of annoyance in his voice.

She watched the light reflections playing in his eyes as they drifted downward through the tube. For a long moment she did not respond. She emerged from her preoccupation and made a face at him. "You're impossible," she said.

His sudden laugh echoed through the tube. "Why? What did I do?"

"You didn't *do* anything," she said, piqued. "It's the way you think, *Colonel* Harder."

He glared at her. "Get to the point, Princess. You've lost me."

She motioned impatiently. "Don't you ever *feel* this, Mike?" She closed her eyes, the dreamy look reappearing on her face. Her voice fell to a whisper.

"Marvelous. It's the only time I ever feel completely free." She sighed. "I wish I could do this forever."

Mike didn't answer. For the moment he preferred silence. He never was able to put into words what he felt. It stayed inside him, bottled up. He knew about his feelings. Hell, he responded to them. But only to himself.

He looked again at June. He knew how she felt about this effortless, slow-motion glide through nothing more substantial than air. They might have been two creatures of some deep ocean, drifting downward through a medium that could be neither seen nor felt but accepted their passage with infinite gentleness. Not even weightlessness compared to this. Of all June's experiences during her long months in space, it was this soft, sighing movement through the gleaming corridor she would most remember. Being outside was an experience both thrilling and exciting. But there was always that cursed pressure suit, always the knowledge of lethal danger no further distant than the thickness of the suit material. Here, feathery light, she was like a fairy with cool air to caress her skin. Here was the childhood dream in reality.

Harder slipped his arm about her waist. With his other hand he squeezed the thermal mitt on the teflon, slowing their descent. Ah, his arm about her. There was something she desired even more than this feathery motion. . . . She opened her eyes slowly, her lips smiling at him.

"Nightcap?" he asked.

"Umm, yes," she nodded. "I could use one."

He released the airlock hatch, held out his arm for her, and followed her into his quarters. Behind her she heard the hatch being locked. She smiled to herself at the thought of the door being locked, containing her. On Earth, the move would have been significant. Not so within *Epsilon*. Living in space was a matter of reflex actions, and one of those reflexes demanded the sealing of all hatches and doors. A single slice of stone coming in at a hundred thousand miles an hour would produce a dazzling flash, followed by the inrush of vacuum. *Epsilon* was like a ship with its airtight compartments. She appreciated the concept, was at home with it. Who wouldn't be, after a childhood in Norwegian waters?

She slipped into a wide chair and kicked off her sneakers. They bounced with exaggerated rubbery motions, like shoes in an animated cartoon. She snuggled into the chair, seeking the pressure against her body. One-tenth gravity was wonderful, but there were times when she missed the feel of Earthside, the touch and pressure of things about her.

Harder looked over his shoulder. "Are you that tired?" he asked, surprised.

"Uh-uh. Not tired, Michael. Just seeking the comfort of a friendly chair, I suppose."

He waited before answering. "Hidden meaning there, Princess?"

She left his question unanswered. With an angry gesture he crossed the room and slid open a wall compartment. She watched his hands, the motions of his body. By not responding to his question she had angered him. He was a strange man. She sensed—she *knew* his desire for her. Yet she did not seek out his affections. Her own emotions were confusing. She wanted Michael, knew they stood together on the brink of love. Yet a wall rose between them.

She hated the unseen divider. Sometimes she admitted its name. Peter, she thought. Peter Fyresdal. But he was in another world, and they were here. She wondered why Michael went only so far with

her and then stopped, almost as if he were pulled up
short by an invisible string. So many times he had
opened the door. And then it closed with a bang,
inexplicable and frightening. Was she supposed to
respond more than she did? What did Michael want?
A verbal announcement? She was not equal to the
demand. Nor could she herself press for what she
knew they both sought. She wanted Michael to come
to her. *To take me.* The thought startled her. *But he
won't. Something stops him. Is it Peter? Because he
is not here, and Michael has knightly feelings about
another man's woman?* She clenched her hands until
she felt her nails biting into her palms. She forced
herself to relax.

Harder removed the plastiglas bottle from the wall
cabinet. Her eyes followed his every move. She
watched the care with which he poured the brandy
into the glasses, closed the snapdown lids. Memory
of wine in crystal slipped into her mind. A fireplace,
the moon icy-white on snow. Not here. She felt the
frown on her face and quickly erased the signs. Here
you did not handle wine carelessly. Romance demanded discipline. Damn! Those glasses—practical
for drinking but impractical for two people together.
Snapdown lids. Otherwise, an inadvertent move would
send the liquid bounding in quivering globules through
the room.

He offered the glass. She rose from the chair,
standing quietly. "The lights. Turn them off, please."
He reached out and his hand closed over the switch.
They were on the down—Earthward—side of the
station. The world loomed before them.

She would do it. "Sit here, Michael."

He took his seat slowly without replying. She
slipped onto his lap, curled against him, her head on
his chest.

The urge to relax swept against Harder. It had been coming with increasing frequency these last few weeks, and he had fought against it, as he must. Yet he could not dismiss the feeling that no harm could be found in relaxing station discipline. Despite their easy manner with one another, their sense of closeness in the true friendship they had found, he had always maintained rigid standards. Harder preferred to apply pressure in a subtle manner, through open need and voluntary response, unless the situation demanded steel. When necessary, he could be a stiff-backed son of a bitch. But it hadn't been necessary on *Epsilon*. The crew members were adults with extraordinary intelligence and well-founded responsibility. They worked so well as a team that no disciplinary measures were required. They performed their tasks with the skill expected of them. But now there was that unspoken need to do more than passively accept what they had given him. There was the call, he sensed, to join the others in the unspoken but surging feeling of triumph for what they had accomplished all these months. The implications of *Epsilon* were profound; they touched on diplomatic and geopolitical affairs. The space station—it was being said, Earthside—signified a whole new era in international relationships.

Harder was less certain of his thoughts when he returned to the woman who curled warmly against his body. Did he love her? He suspected this was so but he lacked the criteria with which to make a sound judgment. June had a bewildering effect on his emotions. He wished he could enjoy the same clarity of reflection about himself and June that he did with everything else.

What he found in June was more than comradeship, or a sense of familiarity due to their being thrown together in the close confines of the station. He was accustomed in his military career to spending long periods of time without women. It didn't bother him; it was all a matter of mental conditioning. He had enjoyed women, made love to them, had embarked on wild physical adventures. But he could take them or leave them. It wasn't the same now, with June. Besides, personal proximity in the station was a flaw in reality, and it did not often lead to moments conducive to intimacy. There was the need to be constantly aware of every aspect of the station, to perpetually monitor the requirements of survival. One mistake out here in space could bring about a terrifying disaster. Accordingly, not for an instant could he turn his back on the responsibilities of his command.

Of course the others shared in this task. But, in the last analysis, he was the Commander, and thus bore the brunt of all decision-making. This fact naturally militated against his having much time for purely personal considerations. *Epsilon* was a beautiful machine, and she was also a bitch to him in this respect. There were occasions when he could be alone with June, but he was never able to forget the all-pervading presence of the station. June meant more than a brief affair to him. If that had been the extent of their relationship, no problem would exist.

The constant physical and psychological monitoring of Dr. Koelbe, necessary though it was, also put a thorn in their collective sides—a psychological pricking of their individual sensitivities. Koelbe one day, after an examination of Page Alison, had been uncharacteristically vague in his meeting with Harder. Harder sensed this and was annoyed. There had been a small scene when Harder had picked up the mantle of his command and demanded that the doctor stop beating around the bush. The history of this station, the base for all future projects, was absolutely critical. Every aspect was critical. There was the need to record *everything*. Billions of dollars and years of effort were involved in *Epsilon*, he reminded Koelbe.

Koelbe leaned back in his chair and sighed, as if Harder's words had relieved him of a personal responsibility. Approaching the matter warily, Koelbe said, "There has been an assignation between Dr. Alison and Herr Guy-Michel." The use of the German startled Harder, but not nearly so much as Koelbe's choice of words.

"A *what?*" he demanded, his voice unknowingly harsh.

Koelbe took on the demeanor of the professional scientist. He coughed in apology. "I have just completed an examination of Dr. Alison," he said slowly. "There is no question," and he motioned awkwardly, "that there has been physical intimacy between Page and Henri." The doctor's hands fluttered as if he were trying to find some place to rest them.

Harder burst into laughter. His mirth doubled at the expression on Koelbe's face. "You're just finding that out? Hell, man, that's the worst-kept secret in this station." He was amazed at Koelbe.

The doctor didn't think the matter humorous, and kept a steely distance between them. "There is a difference, Colonel," he said coolly. "This is not a matter of 'finding out,' as you put it. I am a doctor. I have made an examination. I have records to keep."

"Of course, but for all concerned, it would be best to keep this within the psych records, don't you think? The medical reports will receive dissemination, Werner, but the psych sheets will remain under strict secrecy."

Koelbe nodded, accepting the way out. He disliked a role in which he would be a meddler. He preferred to keep such matters strictly on a professional level. "Yes," he said at last. "That will attend to the possible—uh—ramifications."

A smile appeared on Harder's face. "There's just one thing, Werner."

Koelbe looked up at him.

"You've fallen victim to the oldest trap there is," Harder said.

Koelbe's eyes narrowed. "What do you mean?"

"You said there wasn't any question, didn't you, of Dr. Alison having engaged in a sexual act? Isn't that the gist of it?"

The doctor nodded. "Yes. But I don't understand what you're getting at."

"Bear with me," Harder replied. "Your knowledge comes to you entirely through your professional relationship. It's a matter of a required physical examination, and—"

"Yes, yes," Koelbe interrupted impatiently.

Harder was amused and didn't hide it.

"How do you know it was Henri?"

Immediately Koelbe saw the thrust. He smiled, as much at his own weakness as at Harder's ploy. "Of course," he said. "That I do not know." He motioned to prevent Harder's response. "You are correct," he laughed. "The assumption on my part is beneath me."

Harder nodded. "That's right, Werner. We don't know. Nobody knows. And as far as I'm concerned, no one will ever know." He looked carefully at the doctor. "Will they?"

Koelbe shook his head. "No," he said. "They won't."

I wonder, Harder thought, how much of my accepting this thing with Page and Henri is simply my being objective—or is it because I'm emotionally involved myself? He tried to be honest. Where he might otherwise have expressed official disfavor, he was inclined to look the other way. Only with the greatest self-control had he managed to avoid the same situation with June. He stroked her hair gently, content with her presence. Again his thoughts drove at him. How much longer could he walk the fence? When would he assert himself as a male? Where were they going? Where would this lead to?

Damn, I wish I knew. . . . But he didn't know. Was he in love with her? What the hell *was* love? Perhaps if he could answer that question he might be able to answer the others that plagued him. He had never known anyone like June. With his emotional hangup he held an enormous respect for her as a person. He had always thought of meeting a woman who would be more than a physical and emotional mate. To him, the woman with whom he would gladly spend the remainder of his life had never really existed—until he met June. Physically attractive, she was even more exciting in the idealistic relationship he had always secretly imagined.

June Strond was a minor heroine in a nation not noted for its adulation of scientific figures. In a land where seafaring men and arctic explorers of great strength and fortitude were renowned, she was an exception. The raven-haired thirty-one-year-old woman scientist always caught off balance those who had heard of her work, and then encountered June Strond. On such first meetings more of the woman than the scientist created the impact. June stood five feet six inches tall and wore her black hair cropped short. Against her fair skin her brown eyes were warm and friendly. She cut a stunning figure, but there was none of the fashion model nonsense about her; her body was that of a well-conditioned athlete. In every sense of the word June Strond was a beautiful woman, her presence characterized by a flashing smile and evidence of a quick wit and intelligence. Those who met her were impressed with her, physically; very quickly they were enchanted with the person who emerged from that meeting.

By the time she was twenty-six, June had earned her Ph.D. She had taken her Master's at the University of Oslo, and then had gone on for her Doctorate at the Institute for Advanced Studies in Rjukan, specializing in the geological sciences and in earth resources. Eager always to support field trips when her laboratory work so indicated that need, June Strond showed her mettle as a skilled mountain climber, and proved equally adept in the expert handling of boats, small and large.

This was hardly unusual in a Norwegian; it was this skill (imparted by several older brothers) plus her merits as a research scientist that isolated her from her female contemporaries. She had engaged in several pioneering expeditions to the Arctic, had crossed the North Pole by dogsled, and had made one long stay of eight months at the Norwegian scientific camp in the Antarctic. As Dr. Strond, representing the Institute for Advanced Studies at scientific conferences in Europe and the United States, she had gained an enthusiastic following. Already mildly famous within the scientific community for her astonishing looks, she merited the respect of her peers because of her revolutionary proposals for food production, on a widespread scale, from plant and animal life within the sea. When the United States began a satellite-survey research program for tracking animals and insects on the earth's surface from space, she was assigned by her government to participate with American scientists in the project.

Norway's invitation to join in *Project Epsilon* produced heated controversy within that government as to whom they should submit as a crew member for the space station. The decision was based on June Strond's work on natural-resources surveillance through space systems. Astonished when the proposal was first extended to her (she had flown in bush planes and in airliners but was not a pilot and had never entertained the thought that she might ever go into space), she soon became excited with the prospects—and accepted.

Rumors had circulated through Europe that after the number of Russian female cosmonauts sent into orbit, the United States would relent its hard stand on male-astronauts-only, and arrange to have an American woman scientist aboard *Epsilon*. Dr. Strond, explained NASA, would not be required to fulfill the duties of an astronaut in the sense that she would be a pilot-member of a spacecraft. On this basis, facing only intensified jet training to prepare her for the sensations of flight, and to determine her reactions to the physical punishment imposed by such flight, Dr. Strond was submitted by the Norwegian government as a member of the *Epsilon* team.

The attention showered upon the raven-haired beauty was overwhelming, although her preoccupation with her training, and NASA's skill at insulating its space heroes, kept her reasonably well cocooned from an onslaught by the press—to whom June Strond was the greatest package to have come along for many a month. Considerable attention was given to comparing the Norwegian woman with Dr. Page Alison, the American woman scientist who had been accepted for *Epsilon*. Unquestionably June Strond offered a marked contrast to the blond, pert appearance of Page. Even their backgrounds, aside from the scientific effort, were greatly dissimilar; in her own right, Page Alison was a skilled flier, and June Strond had little desire to master the demands required of a pilot.

The two women became fast friends. June spoke English fluently, as she did German, Swedish, and French—and, of course, her native tongue. This eliminated a barrier that might otherwise have proved difficult to overcome.

The press, as might be expected, took undue notice of the fact that June was not married. Dr. Alison had been divorced after a youthful and blind plunge into matrimony. Her story had glutted the pages of the sob-sister magazines and women's columns. She had been engaged when she was twenty-seven. Six months later, her fiancé plunged to his death on a mountain-climbing expedition. There were stories that linked the name of Peter Fyresdal with June. Were they engaged? How long had they been going together? There was a loud cheer from the office of Ben Blanchard, who ran the public affairs office for the Manned Spacecraft Center in Houston, when June demurred that her personal affairs had no place in the press.

Mike Harder knew the details of her life well before they met. As Commander of *Epsilon* it was his business to know exhaustively those people with whom he would commit the great experiment. And as Commander he could exercise a final veto power. No matter what governments willed or beseeched, he had the final say on selection. Integrating the affairs of eight human beings was as much a challenge for the six months in orbit as assuring reliability of mechanical and electronics systems. Before he passed his final judgment, Harder put each person through his own grueling inspection.

It was Harder who had taken June Strond aloft for her orientation and training flights. Initially, he broke her in gently in a jet trainer. When she knew the facts of life, he took her aloft in an F-4C jet fighter, a brute of a machine with bone-bending performance. Harder was not gentle. If anything, he did his best to punish his passenger, and when it came to punishment on wings, Harder was one of the best in the business. He knew June had made the grade after one flight in which he had blacked her out first and then, coming out of battering g-forces, had flung the airplane into a great soaring arc that rendered them weightless for more than a minute. The transition was particularly cruel. Harder meant it to be just that. He was successful. She was sick in the airplane, and sick again after they landed.

He had looked at her with a humorless grin as she dry-heaved. "Ready for more?" he growled at her.

Slowly she straightened from her spasms. Her hair was unruly from the jet helmet, and she was pale from the flight and its consequences, but she looked him straight in the eye. "You son of a bitch," she said quietly. "I only hope that one day I can get you in a fishing boat." She turned to the hulking shape of the airplane. "I'm ready," she said. "Let's go."

Harder couldn't believe it. Roughly he thrust out his hand. "Welcome aboard," he grinned, and she knew she had made the team.

There had been times, after those first two months in orbit, when routine had settled into the station and they had found occasion to be alone together. Something alive and tangible sprang to life between them. He cursed himself for what he believed to be the emotional response of a youngster; nevertheless, the feelings remained.

June herself could not help but retreat before the awesome remoteness of where they were . . . nearly five hundred miles above the planet, hurtling through space at a speed close to five miles a second. Every so often it got to you. There were moments when you were receptive, and your guard was relaxed, and you looked down at the tremendous curve of the earth, and you thought: *My God, is all this really true?*

At such times the sense of remoteness was appalling. Instinctively June wanted the comfort any woman would seek. The attraction between them had been there for a long time. It became more evident in the cautious sparring of emotions, the wary judging that there would not be summary rejection.

Harder was a man unlike any other June had known; despite her being drawn to him, despite their association and sharing of moments in which life hung in the balance, she could not be precipitous.

Gradually, the image of Peter had faded in her mind, becoming a phantom of another existence. The moments with Michael had come, almost of their own making, and finally, willingly, she yielded. So now, at this moment, she experienced a warm sense of comfort in the shield of Harder's arms.

He held her close, embraced her fiercely, felt the warmth of her breasts pressing against him; they kissed, long and tenderly, their bodies clinging together, the heat rising between them. But always, when they released one another she remained silent. No word escaped from her moist, parted lips, and her eyes remained unfathomable to him.

Those were the moments when the desire swept over him and he wanted her desperately, when the ache knotted deep in his belly. Yet he always encountered the same barrier holding him back. He believed absolutely—he *knew*—that she would yield completely to him, but that he must take, rather than be offered. And he could not bring himself to that final step. Something was missing, and whenever he left her, he felt frustrated, a white heat pulsing deep inside him. With that heat was a flaring sense of anger, the nature of which never failed to elude him.

And, all the while, he remained blind to the desires that surged through June's young body.

What Mike Harder failed to understand, Henri Guy-Michel saw with a natural instinct. Where Harder was blind, the Frenchman was wise and experienced. He knew women, and he knew Europeans, and, most of all, he knew European women. He knew of June's engagement and of her fiancé's death. He knew they had made love. They *must* have loved as would two healthy young animals—joyously, freely, and completely. To have done otherwise would have been madness.

Mike Harder was a fool, thought Guy-Michel. A proud, puritan fool who fought the urging of his loins, who could not recognize a woman's desire even when she murmured almost helplessly in his arms. The idiot! Could he not see two feet in front of his own face?

June Strond was a scientist, but she was first a woman—a beautiful warm creature, her body made for love. Guy-Michel waited with impatience, finally incredulous when Harder did not take what he was offered. He knew the idiot American had not lain with her. He could tell with a glance at a woman's eyes; he could tell from her mannerisms, the soft tone of her voice, when she had made love. And the more violently, the more completely a man took her, the happier, the fuller, she would be.

Guy-Michel relished his sexual affair with Page Alison. Why not? It was a beautiful affair. Page was a lithe animal, responsive and completely abandoned. The Frenchman thought of June and his eyes narrowed with anticipation. It would be even more satisfying with the Norwegian woman. She would not just make love. There would be so much more! That one went deep; she would drain a man emotionally as well as spend his body. And if Harder wished to continue being a fool, well—Guy-Michel shrugged.

He had bided his time, plotted his moves beautifully. He made certain to be with her after she had spent several hours with Harder—after she had returned to her compartment, her body aching, almost shaking from the frustration of her loins, both loving and hating Mike Harder. He knew she would endure a suffering within her. The woman had loved and been loved. One day Guy-Michel called June on her intercom. Could he see her? He wished to talk with her. No, it could not wait. He went directly to her quarters. Page was on a project. She would be occupied for hours in the S-IVB tank.

Guy-Michel made small talk. He had to talk with a woman who would understand how he felt, someone from the continent. It was utter nonsense, and normally June would have seen right through him. Perhaps she did, but he cared nothing about her perception—only her reaction. He sat beside her on the couch in her quarters, and didn't hesitate to bring their bodies together.

When he made his move it was totally frank. Guy-Michel had never made a pass at a woman in his life. Boorishness lay beneath him. He said her name softly:

"June." When she turned, he touched her face lightly. His kiss was gentle, deep, sustained. He felt the tremor sweep through her convulsively. He felt the heat through her lips, her body arching instinctively. When a woman demands love, only a fool stops to think. He crushed her in his arms, slid down to a position with his body crushing hers, her tongue darting into his open mouth.

The heat came swiftly between his legs and he pressed his hardness against her thigh. The response was immediate. She gave a slight cry, half-moaning. Always gentle, never still for a moment, his hand went inside her jumper, found her breast, caressed the nipple. Her head fell back and she closed her eyes. Quickly Guy-Michel opened her suit, started to fondle her more intimately.

Mike Harder found them that way. He had knocked on the compartment hatch but they had been too engrossed in each other to hear. Harder stepped around the corner partition. Guy-Michel knew everything had gone to hell when her body stiffened. He looked at her eyes, rigid and wide, and before he heard Harder's profane exclamation he knew who it was.

The Frenchman sighed. The man was idiot enough not to pluck the flower offered him, and he was also a clumsy dolt who didn't know enough to stay away. With his body still obscuring June's form from Harder, Guy-Michel managed to bring the zipper back up to her waist. He climbed to his feet to face the American.

"You miserable son of a bitch," Harder muttered. "I ought to break every bone in your body."

Guy-Michel rolled his eyes. *"Mon dieu!* A hero. Spare us!" He grinned lecherously at the enraged man before him.

"You've gone too far this time, Henri. I've tried to look the other way where Page was concerned, but—"

The humor faded from Guy-Michel. "You've done what, Colonel?"

"You heard me!"

"I heard a pompous fool speaking, yes," Guy-Michel said quickly. "Whoever gave you the authority to forgive or condemn, or to have anything to say about what I do in my personal life?"

Harder gaped at him. "You're forgetting yourself, mister."

"I've forgotten nothing," Henri snapped. "What I do personally is none of your damned business."

"Anything you do in this ship is my business!" Harder roared.

"No, it is *not*," Guy-Michel said softly. "I am not in your silly Air Force, Colonel Harder. I owe no allegiance to you in my personal life."

Harder turned to June. She was still on the couch, her legs drawn up, her chin resting on her knees as she watched them and listened to their growing hostility. Mike was being a fool, and he didn't know it. "What have *you* to say about all this?" he shouted at her.

She kept silent.

"God damn it, June, *answer* me!" he shouted.

She looked up at him. She knew what to do with the moment. Instantly she was aware that Henri understood everything. Maybe this was exactly the right time to set things straight.

"You should knock louder, Michael," she said.

Her words left Harder speechless. After several seconds he found his voice. He looked at her coldly and the word spilled from his lips before he could stop it.

"*Slut.*"

Instantly he was contrite, hating himself. He started forward. "June, I'm—"

"Leave her alone, Harder." Guy-Michel stood suddenly before him. "Leave her alone and get out when you're not wanted."

Harder ripped a wicked right to the Frenchman's stomach. The blow started of its own volition. Harder hadn't consciously willed it. Once started, his hands moved by reflex. He brought his left up in a looping blow that tore at Guy-Michel's face. It would have landed square except for the light gravity. Harder's first punch had doubled up the Frenchman and hurled him backward. By the time he had thrown himself in blind rage after the other man, Guy-Michel had regained his balance.

A foot came out of nowhere and slammed into Harder's mouth. Had the Frenchman been wearing shoes, rather than the soft sneakers they used in the station, Harder would have lost some teeth. As it was, the blow spun him around, splitting his lip. The next moment they were at each other in close combat, each striving in the strange light gravity for a commanding position. In the long run it must be Harder who would win; he was a top wrestler and well versed in hand-to-hand combat training.

It didn't go that far. June threw herself from the couch between them, screaming. "*Stop it! Both of you, stop it!*" She forced herself between them until they held back their blows for fear of striking her.

"You fools!" she said with a sudden, explosive anger that startled them both. "Get out, both of you!"

"June, I'm sorry I said what I did."

"*Get out!*" The words stabbed like knives into Harder. He looked at Henri Guy-Michel, who stood quietly, still breathing with difficulty. Harder wiped blood from his lip with the back of his hand, and left without another word.

Guy-Michel waited only a few moments longer. He looked at June. "I'm sorry, June." He said the words with a soft smile. She didn't answer.

It was bad for several days afterward. Harder fought his pride with all his strength. He kept reminding himself that the station came first. He also learned something—how much June really meant to him. He'd been blind with fury, but he had no right to unleash his anger in violence. He knew well enough that Guy-Michel lived by his own code. If June had been spoken for, if she had been Mike Harder's girl, the Frenchman would have kept his distance. But Harder hadn't put up any fences around the woman. He'd acted the fool. Finally, he called Guy-Michel to his office. He laid it on the line, and apologized, and offered his hand.

Guy-Michel took it, but didn't say a word. He shook hands, turned, and left Harder's quarters. From that moment on, their conflict lay far beneath the surface. They got along, they worked well, and Guy-Michel made no more attempts to climb into the sack with June. As far as the Frenchman was concerned, it was all up to June. He wouldn't touch her. But the moment she let him know . . . well, then it would be to hell with Colonel Harder!

But she didn't offer the welcome mat. To himself, Henri Guy-Michel shrugged. Who could understand women?

Now, gratefully, Harder was with June in his quarters, content in their silence with one another. The feeling of constraint that had marked their relationship since Harder's fight with Henri had gradually dissipated with the passage of time, and the proximity of working together in the station. Actually, as far as June was concerned, the flare-up between the two men was a blessing. Michael had erupted from his shell. His anger—his explosive reaction to Henri—bespoke his feelings for her. For the first time in days they had found the opportunity to be alone and there was suddenly a magic aura of warmth and controlled passion drawing them close.

Together they looked out on a lovers' world, watched the stunning sweep of blazing light usher darkness across a planet. June slid against him, and he felt her unzip his jumper, her hand gliding across his chest, moving with her silken touch across the flat of his stomach. The heat stirred within him and no longer did he think only of June. His thoughts fused June and himself into a single entity. The thought wisped through his mind that there was someone else back on Earth waiting for her; then angrily he thrust the thought aside and banished everything from his mind except themselves.

He knew. There was no more waiting. She was his, to have and to love. He cast aside his hesitations, lifted her face, kissed her passionately, bruising her lips. Her hand reached down along his stomach. She yielded her body.

The intercom rang.

Chapter IV

He started so suddenly in the chair that June fell sprawling off his lap. "*Son of a bitch!*" he cried in a voice of anguish. What was happening? She rose to her feet and saw the blinking red light on the intercom panel, and she understood.

"Who the hell can that be?" he shouted uselessly. No need for her even to comment. She really didn't care. Not now. Deep within her she sighed. It had taken so long to reach this moment. Finally Michael was going to commit himself.

Rudely he pushed her aside. He stared at the offending light flashing on the intercom panel. He muffled a string of oaths. As if in response, the intercom sounded again, its melodious tone mocking.

"It's my own goddamed fault," he railed, his anger offering an explanation.

It wasn't necessary, even if Michael wished to kick himself mentally. *Add one for me for good measure,*

54

she thought spitefully, but kept her silence. When they had come into the room and he had poured their drinks, he had neglected to switch on the *Sleeping* or *Do Not Disturb* signals. With any one of the signals lit up, the crew would have left him alone, respecting the need for sleep or privacy. Only a dire emergency would have caused someone to hit the alarm for general quarters. But he had not switched on any lights to guarantee his privacy. And it was his "own goddamned fault," as he had so succinctly remarked.

He leaned over his desk and hit the transmit switch. "Go ahead," he said with anger still in his voice. June stifled a giggle; Michael was snarling into the speaker.

"Colonel? Henri here. I hope I have not disturbed you?"

An inarticulate sound came from Harder's throat. June couldn't contain herself, and turned to smother her laughter. Harder glared at her. "What? I could not understand," Guy-Michel's puzzled voice. "Mike, do you hear me?"

Harder took a deep breath and let it out slowly. "I hear you. What is it?"

"Ah, I am sorry. I can tell from your voice. But—"

Harder could almost see Guy-Michel shrug as only that uninhibited Frenchman could perform.

"—there is a message. It is marked for priority attention, and I did not see a light on your board."

Harder grunted, not trusting himself to speak.

"Apparently there is a time factor involved," Guy-Michel went on. "I have not read it all, but it concerns an experiment."

"Uh-huh," Harder said, still kicking himself for not having turned on his light.

Guy-Michel did not respond at once. As the pause

lengthened, Harder knew what the Frenchman was doing. He had checked the board by June's name. No lights. Aha! She is not in her compartment. Hmmm. And the colonel, he is disturbed, yes? *The son of a bitch*, Harder thought. Despite himself he began to grin.

"This message—it is too long for the speakbox," Guy-Michel said suddenly. Speakbox! That, too, was Henri. "Are you perhaps free for the moment?" Harder swore he heard the man chuckle. "I am not interrupting anything?"

Harder turned to glance at June. She was making a careful study of the brandy glass in her hand. He thought her shoulders were shaking. Harder jerked his attention back to the intercom.

"No, you're not disturbing a damn thing," he barked. "C'mon down."

"Good! Page is with me," Guy-Michel said with excessive enthusiasm. "Oh, by the way, Mike—I have been looking for our star-gazing friend. He didn't answer from his quarters."

"He's sacked out, Henri. We got in not too long ago and Tim was bushed. You know the way he sleeps. A bomb couldn't get him up right now."

"Of course," Guy-Michel laughed. "All right, then, we shall be right there."

Harder switched off. He raised the compartment lights and looked carefully at June. "Damn you, woman," he grated. "Are you laughing at me?"

She struggled to answer him without open mirth. "What would you like me to do? Cry?"

He growled deep in his throat.

"Is that an answer?" she prodded.

He waved a hand wearily. "No, no, of course not. I'm sorry."

She moved quickly to his side and kissed him on the cheek. "I know, Michael. Thank you."

Her words left him speechless.

Muffled sounds coming from deep within the station saved him from an answer. He could hear and feel the movements of Guy-Michel and Page Alison as they worked their way to his quarters. The opening and closing of hatches carried to him on Level 7. Even their movement into the tube, working their way down from the Life Sciences Laboratory on Level 12, imparted its effect to the station. *Epsilon* was alive, quivering with movement, the shifting of mass. From experience you could tell what was taking place in almost any part of the station, and could follow the movement of the crew. Harder and June Strond felt the compartment floor vibrate slightly as the two figures in the tubular passageway slowed their descent and stopped just beyond the compartment airlock hatch. Harder signaled airlock clearance to enter. The warning light went on as the outer hatch opened. As soon as Harder saw the green light—Guy-Michel and Alison were now in the airlock compartment—he opened the inner hatch for them.

For a moment Guy-Michel hesitated. With a single experienced glance he took in Harder's ill-concealed impatience and the slight flush on June's face. Henri missed nothing. He smiled broadly and moved aside for Page Alison. Harder motioned to the brandy on his desk and looked the question.

"But of course!" Guy-Michel answered with a gallant wave.

Harder wanted to whack him over the skull for his exuberance. Instead, he reached for two more glasses while the French astronaut chattered on breezily.

"Ah, to turn down such an offer would be unthinkable. Are we celebrating something?"

Harder ignored him. "Here." He extended glasses to Page and Henri. "Fill your face with that," he said to the Frenchman. "It's got to be better than your conversation."

Guy-Michel raised his eyebrows. Before he could reply he saw the slight motion by June. The Frenchman rarely could resist a riposte. He thrived on them. But the signal from June stemmed his words. After all, he thought, it was true. You could push a man only so far. And in such a delicate matter as this! Guy-Michel curbed his response but chuckled to himself. He did not fail to notice Harder gulp his brandy in a single swallow.

Harder put his glass down slowly. "What's the special flap, Henri?"

The French scientist reached into a pocket of his jumper. He waved a message form. "It is something about dust, I think."

"Dust?"

Guy-Michel nodded. "I think they are all crazy," he shrugged. "It says here—"

Page Alison snatched the message from his hand and gave Guy-Michel a disapproving look. He shrugged again and found a comfortable chair, sipping at his brandy.

"It's for Tim," Page said, "but it's not that urgent to get him out of bed."

"What's the dust business?" Harder asked.

Page scanned the message form. "Apparently *Epsilon* will be passing through a region of heavy dust," she answered. "This doesn't tell much, only that there'll be more complete details coming through in a few hours. It may be dustlike debris, or perhaps the remnant of a comet. I don't know yet."

"And?"

"We're to get samples," she said.

"May I see that, please?" He extended his hand for the paper. The dust, he knew, was heavy only in a relative sense. It wouldn't alter the vacuum through which they rushed, but probably there would be meteoric particles as well. They might even take a few hits on the station, although the meteor bumpers would insulate them against any real danger. During the period that Earth would be swept by the "clouds" of dust there would be some spectacular meteor displays.

The dust might prove of immense interest to science. It might be part of a comet, perhaps even debris from the planet that had once existed between Mars and Jupiter and then been shattered by some cataclysm long before man had begun to walk the surface of his own world. Dust could contain secrets of the solar system.

He looked up at the others. "Any ideas?"

Page answered quickly. "Not too difficult. We'll need containers we can seal before we bring them back inside. That sort of thing."

He nodded, picturing a cable-sling relay. "I'll get Parsons and Jordan to rig up a system." He thought for a moment. "Luke will be on duty for a while yet. He can get started right away."

"Good," she said, "I believe the experiments will involve me to some extent."

"But why should you be interested in dust out here?" Guy-Michel broke in. "Shall you plant things in it?"

"Dolt," she said with open sarcasm.

He raised his brows to beseech help from the others.

"There may be organic compounds in the dust, Henri," June said.

"This is most interesting," he lied blandly.

"Microscopic life forms to you," Page snorted.

"I am fascinated," he said, sipping his brandy.

"I'll bet," Harder growled.

A secret smile appeared on the face of Guy-Michel. For the moment he had forgotten their interruption, and stole a glance at June. She looked back with her eyes unblinking. Henri's smile broadened. His grin spoke torrents of words. Harder scowled. He didn't like asides, and Henri's amusement was wearing thin. *What the hell are you so touchy about?* he demanded of himself. He knew the answer and scowled some more.

As aware as Guy-Michel that they had blundered in at a bad moment, Page Alison rose to her feet and placed her glass on Harder's desk. She gestured with the message form. "I'll save this for Tim—for later," she said. "I'll talk to Luke and get things under way." She motioned to her companion. "And Cheshire Cat, here, can do some of the manual labor."

He finished his brandy. "What is this Cheshire Cat?"

"Never mind, Smiley. Just come along."

Guy-Michel rose to his feet and performed a mocking bow to Harder. He wondered if the colonel would lose his temper and hit him. The thought was entertaining. There was no time to pursue the matter as Page almost dragged him to the airlock.

No sooner had the hatch closed than Harder slammed a fist angrily into his palm. The sharp crack of sound echoed in the compartment.

Subdued laughter came from June.

"What the hell is so funny?" he demanded.

"Forgive me, Michael. But you were—ah, how shall I say it? Wearing your emotions on your sleeve?"

"And that is so goddamned funny?"

Immediately she sensed her error. "No," she said

quietly. "It is simply not like you . . . in front of the others." She knew she had said the right words, and barely in time. Had he believed there to be mockery, she would have lost him—right at that moment. But her remark had protected them both.

He looked at her cautiously, wondering about what she had said. His voice was low and husky. "We can pick up where we were before they interrupted us."

She shook her head quickly.

"I suppose you're right," he said with a touch of weariness. "You just don't turn it on and off like a light switch."

"Thank you," she said with a smile. "There is that . . . that something, yes?" She looked through the viewport at the stars. "It was there," she went on. "It will be there again." She ran her fingers through her hair. "I am tired," she admitted. "More than I thought." She rose to her feet and crossed to him quickly. Her lips brushed his cheek. "I will see you for dinner?"

"About an hour," he said, nodding.

Through the resonance of the station he heard her enter her compartment on the level above his own.

Henri Guy-Michel and Page Alison slipped through the airlock hatch into Level 12. The oxygen-cool smell of massed plant growth swept against them. Guy-Michel closed the airlock and chuckled.

Page lifted her head, her eyes quizzical.

"No, no," Henri said quickly to her unspoken question. "Not you. I was thinking of our esteemed leader."

"What the hell do you find so funny?"

His surprise showed. "There is heat in your words, *cheri.*"

"Well, damn it, you were pushing pretty hard,"

she snapped. "And there wasn't any reason for it. You know we walked in at a bad moment."

"Yes, yes," he admitted. "That is true." His hand brushed her hair. "I will tell you something else," he said with mock gravity. He rolled his eyes. "A crime! I am guilty."

"I don't know what you are, but I think you're losing your marbles."

"Ah, but it is a crime for a Frenchman to have interfered with a moment of amour."

"Mike . . . and June?"

"For such a delightful lover, *cheri,* you are sometimes a foolish girl. Are we talking about De Gaulle and Queen Elizabeth? Do you think they were merely holding hands with one another?"

She held his gaze. "That is precisely what they were doing."

He looked at her shrewdly. "You seem confident."

She tossed her head in a gesture of disdain. "I am."

"This time I *am* fascinated," he said quickly. "Tell me, how do you know this?"

Her laughter came easily. "Women know, Henri. They just know. After all, we do live together. And I am. . . ." She faltered.

"Not inexperienced in such matters?" he said kindly.

Color surged to her face. "Nothing has happened between them," she repeated with emphasis.

"But it was about to happen." He chuckled. "The moment, ah, critical," he said with a French accent, "was almost upon them."

"Not old granite-head," she persisted. "That's the whole problem." Then she said, as much to herself as to Henri, "Jesus Christ, some men are blind. She's done everything but pull down his pants."

"I know."

She studied him carefully for several moments. "What happened between you and Mike?"

He smiled at her.

"Aren't you going to tell me?" she demanded.

He kissed her lightly on the lips and drew her close. "Ask *mon colonel*."

"Fat help you are," she pouted.

He didn't answer. Abruptly he shrugged as if to dismiss the subject. His hand slid down her back across her bottom, caressing her. They kissed fiercely and she rubbed her thighs against him.

One day we must make love in the center tank, he thought. *The positions we could have while we are weightless—!*

He laughed to himself as he felt her hand caress him.

Chapter V

India and Ceylon nestled beneath a wide pressure area—speckling clouds that obscured the lush land framed by the deep reflecting blue of the Indian Ocean and the Bay of Bengal. Beyond the sharply curving horizon the universe loomed black, its stars invisible. Harder thought idly that people believed you could always see stars in space, that the celestial panorama waited inevitably for the spectator. But it was not so if you were looking down on a planet inundated with dazzling sunshine, reflected by turbulent atmospheric seas and clouds. It was like staring into bright lights in a room and then walking to a window and looking up into the night sky. For a while you couldn't see a thing except the registry of light against your own eyes. At the moment, looking upward from Earth, not a single star was visible.

He really wasn't paying much attention to the sight that had thrilled him so deeply the first time.

His gaze was vacant, his mind preoccupied. Anger still diffused his thinking—anger with himself for displaying emotion in front of the others. He couldn't remember the last time he'd done that. He'd become mildly famous among test pilots for his imperturbable manner, no matter what flap might be going on. He'd ridden flaming jets down to the ground and scrambled away with his clothing scorched, and the rescue crews always found him with the same unchanged expression on his face. Certainly he would have agreed with and been pleased by Page Alison's description of him as "old granite-head."

June was right. He'd worn his emotions on his sleeve and he had no call to be pissed off at Henri. The Frenchman had simply applied the needle, and if Mike Harder wanted to be oversensitive about it—well, he could always complain to the chaplain. Harder did his best to remain honest with himself. He knew his shortness of temper with Guy-Michel was nothing more than a compensation for his own hesitation with June. In a distant way, he forced himself to make the admission: he envied Henri. The personal objectivity with which he weighed his actions was characteristic of Harder, but he didn't like the conclusions. He had never envied any man. He knew that what fascinated him was Henri Guy-Michel's freedom with anyone and everyone around him. Henri had a laughing easiness that made life—even as restricted as it was in this station hundreds of miles above the planet—a delight.

No, Harder reprimanded himself, there's more to it than that. He knew—without proof, if proof were needed—of the relationship between Henri and Page. Yet neither of them displayed any embarrassment about a situation that was common knowledge to *Epsilon's* crew. He knew—and he couldn't stay the grin accompanying the thought—that Henri Guy-Michel could never return to Earth without honestly laying claim to having made love to a woman nearly five hundred miles above the world. That was really making the Mile High Club the hard way! With the thought of such liaison the grin faded, for Mike Harder did envy the ease with which Guy-Michel pursued his desires. The reason was not because of the relationship with Page, of course, but because he had been unable to unlock his own desire for June Strond. What the hell was the matter with him? He shook his head, the anger again spilling through him at encountering the same old wall.

Goddamn the Frenchman, Harder thought, and then burst into laughter, remembering how Henri had become a member of the *Epsilon* crew. As much as he tried to find fault with Guy-Michel, it always came back to the same thing. He liked the son of a bitch. In fact, he was greatly pleased to have Henri consider Mike Harder his friend. Certainly they had started off their relationship with fireworks. . . .

"You are Colonel Harder, no?"

Mike Harder looked up from the papers on his desk. For a long moment he didn't answer the man standing in the doorway to his office. He wasn't sure he believed what he saw. His visitor was attired in a dazzling red flight suit. The boots were white. Harder noticed that, as soon as his blinking eyes became accustomed to the blazing red of the suit. But it wasn't only that the boots were white. They were jump boots. In itself this wasn't unusual: most pilots preferred them in the event they might have to eject. Jump boots kept a lot of ankles from snapping. But *white* jump boots? And with a red parachute on the outside of each ankle? Was this apparition before him a pilot or a skydiver?

Harder was not a man to be fazed by a garishly-attired pilot or a charging bull elephant, although the elephant would be easier on the vision. Around the neck of the man in his doorway was a silk scarf of rich green. It draped casually. Under his left arm he carried a jet helmet. No mistaking that. Harder's glance took in the visor, the umbilicals. But the helmet was painted a burnished gold. It was all too much. Harder leaned back in his chair and stared.

"What—I mean, who the hell are you?"

The stranger accepted this outburst as a sign of positive identification. "Ah, you *are* the good colonel, then!" he said with open enthusiasm. He strode quickly across the room to the desk where his body stiffened and he executed a brief, formal bow. His hand shot out to grasp Harder's hand firmly.

"I am Colonel Henri Guy-Michel," he said, "and I am at your service."

Harder motioned to a chair and resumed his own. He didn't believe it. *This* was Guy-Michel? This was the French "scientist" who had been programmed for Project *Epsilon?* Harder looked anew at the eye-stabbing figure seated across his desk. Guy-Michel had placed his flight helmet at the edge of the desk and was extracting a cigarette from a jeweled case. Inwardly Harder groaned. What the hell had they done to him?

He accepted the cigarette and took a light from the flame held by Guy-Michel. "I wasn't expecting you," Harder said after a pause. "And while we're on the subject, how did you manage to get past my secretary? She's known around here as Bulldog Drummond."

"Marcel!" At the call of his name a giant appeared

magically in the doorway. "Colonel Harder, may I present Major Marcel Dufour, my copilot. Major, this is Colonel Michael Harder." Six feet six inches of giant Frenchman, dressed exactly like Guy-Michel, snapped to attention, clicked its heels, and ramrodded a salute to the startled Harder. He vanished as quickly as he had appeared. Guy-Michel waved his hand. "Marcel is entertaining your secretary. You said her name was—" He leaned forward.

"Bulldog Drummond," Harder said in a flat voice. "Ignore it. Never mind." He flicked ashes onto the floor and studied Guy-Michel with more care, looking beyond the resplendent garments. What he saw on second glance was more pleasing to the eye. A man who would match his own height, not quite six feet, with broad shoulders, barrel chest and thick, wavy blond hair. The wide face was marked by a solid jaw, quite unlike the initial impression. Immediately, Harder altered his thinking. The quality in this man came on slowly and Harder was convinced that here lay hidden strength. He didn't know what drew him to that conclusion but he was abolutely certain of it. Harder, as a judge of men, could never recall having made a mistake in such matters. This one had it.

"Meaning no discourtesy, Colonel," Harder said, "but I am taken unawares."

The Frenchman cast a dazzling smile at him. "My government—it is fond of secrets. We were waiting for favorable winds. You understand?" Harder didn't. Not yet—but he waited. "We have been waiting for a long time for conditions just right for the record. Last night they were perfect." Guy-Michel shrugged. "We—Marcel and I—took off immediately. It was a nice trip. We were able to fly here with only one refueling."

"From where, Colonel?" Harder's patience was evaporating swiftly.

"Why, I thought you knew." The surprise on Guy-Michel's face was genuine. "From Paris, of course."

Recognition dawned. He had forgotten all about it. There had been reports filtering down from Washington that the French were going to attempt a new world speed record, nonstop from Paris to Houston, flying their new Mirage VI bomber. The craft was a swingwing type like the F-111, but more advanced, which meant that this peacock before him had just cracked wide open a world record for speed, from Paris nonstop to Houston, Texas.

"We came here directly from the airdrome," Guy-Michel was saying. He became aware that Harder had known nothing of his impending arrival. Instantly the Frenchman was on his feet. "Colonel, it would seem I am intruding. I will cut Marcel's throat for not having made the proper arrangements."

"The devil you say," Harder responded quickly. "My apologies to you. And my congratulations, I should add." He knew how to bring things back to normal. "What did you maintain on the way over?"

A quick smile met the question. "Ahhh, it was beautiful," the Frenchman replied, instantly expansive. "We managed to avoid the winds by remaining at about sixty-eight thousand feet, and—"

"You *held* sixty-eight?" Harder was impressed.

"The new Mirage—she is a . . . how you say? A beautiful bitch?"

"That'll do."

"Yes. And the mach, that was even prettier. It was a good feeling. The needle stayed at point seven all the way."

"Not bad," Harder mused aloud. "That's a long haul for mach one-point-seven, all the way from Paris."

"Not *one*-point-seven," Guy-Michel corrected. "It was *two*-point-seven."

Harder looked up with open respect. Nearly three times the speed of sound all the way from Paris. He smiled at his visitor. "That sounds like quite a machine you have there."

"It is," Guy-Michel nodded. Then, making an instant decision: "Would you like to fly it?"

"Very much."

"Well, then it is done!"

They shook hands on it.

Henri Guy-Michel was the most unlikely individual ever to come into the American space program and, had his qualifications not been so extraordinary and the political climate so ripe for exploitation, it is doubtful whether he would have even been permitted within the holy inner sanctum of the Manned Spacecraft Center in Houston. A brilliant pilot, a capable engineer, and a scientist of no mean ability, he was the idol of Paris and the rage of France.

Guy-Michel came from a family of wealth sufficient to permit his indulgence in outrageously expensive tastes. Official doors opened to him as if by magic. To his credit Henri Guy-Michel backed up this freedom and astonishing government sanction. To all appearances he might have been nothing more than a spoiled playboy. To those who knew otherwise, he was dedicated to his work, cognizant that he could sustain his singular status only through delivering the goods in whatever endeavor he found himself. That he continued to have the opportunity to accept the challenges he found so much to his liking stemmed from an even rarer, happy circumstance—not only was he capable, and his family wealthy, but the latter also figured prominently in French industry and politics. Henri Guy-Michel had it made.

He had learned to fly as a youngster, careening around grass fields and demonstrating to his instructors the natural flair of a born pilot. Early in his flying career had come an association with skydivers, who enjoyed an immense popularity in France. It was to Guy-Michel's credit, and indicative of the manner in which he pursued his tastes, that the first his family knew of his prowess in the art of parachuting was when his friends carted him home in the back of an open truck, grimacing and cursing a leg quite neatly broken.

"It was most unusual," the jumpmaster had explained to his startled parents. "Henri—he jump perfectly. But the wind—it shifts." The inevitable shrug accompanied this news. "Henri—he work his lines to avoid a tree. He is unaware of the cow . . ."

The story had made front pages all across France. Henri Guy-Michel had fallen victim to a cow. Those who knew him best smiled. "What else? Did you think it would be a bull?" Three months later he went out of a plane at ten thousand feet for a satisfying free fall, "—only to be certain I have not forgotten what to do," he explained to his raging father.

But if he was incorrigible in such affairs he was also unquestionably qualified to meet the challenges of life. The moment he came of age his father ordered him into the French air arm. To the surprise of all, Henri did not protest this plunge into harsh discipline: indeed, he ran with open arms to the agile trainers and sleek fighters awaiting him. For three years he served as a fighter pilot with commendable, if flamboyant, skill. He resumed his skydiving activities, but this time as a member of the contest-winning military team of France. The episode of the cow was forgotten with the sight of Henri and his teammates standing in the winners' circle of international competitions.

The winners' circle appeared to drive a hard truth home to the young Guy-Michel. There were two ways to do the things he liked. One was simply to do them and ignore the shock waves that rippled outward. The second choice was to put to his advantage the actions he carried out. He was a devotee of skydiving who sought the vicarious thrills of jumps from higher and higher altitudes. Soon he was tumbling out of planes so high that he found himself no longer engaged in a sport but in a serious business. Oxygen, pressure suit, electrically-heated clothing—the works. Did not the air arm have research programs for pilots who were forced to abandon their machines at very high altitudes?

Inevitably Guy-Michel moved into the thick of the action. Financial status and political contacts got him what he wanted. Not *out* of danger, but facing the bull in the middle of the arena. He went higher and higher. He tested small stabilization parachutes, oxygen survival equipment. Powerful rockets exploded him out of fighters and bombers at low altitude and high, at slow speed and into the teeth of supersonic blasts. He made more than four hundred jumps before he realized he had reached his saturation point. Perhaps he was aware of his search. Perhaps he didn't give it a moment's thought. But Henri Guy-Michel was running hard after the excitement beckoning to him from his personal rainbow of challenge.

He startled even his close friends when he showed up among the enthusiastic supporters of free-ballooning. To him this was heady excitement. You accepted the elements in the wicker baskets slung beneath the pregnant cows of the air. Henri took his license and embarked on voyages of splendid scenery across the Alps. He drifted over mountains and through valleys, and stared down at seas and lakes. Wisely he brought along with him the measuring apparatus of various scientific groups. He helped chart air currents and streams, served as a medical guinea pig, delighted his peers, and, finally, after disappearing in the mountains of Italy during an unexpected but particularly violent snowstorm, showed up nine days later—cold and hungry, but eminently victorious in having survived the worst of the elements.

After a long rest for his nerves—certainly it was not for a physical rest that he performed magnificently in one bed after the other on the Riviera—he returned to active duty in test-pilot school. At the close of his intensive training he had his master's degree in aeronautical engineering and was studying keenly the best of new worlds to conquer. The opportunity came without prologue—through the back door.

For several years the French and Soviet governments had cooperated in mutual space ventures. France had launched her own satellites and, in using boosters built in France by French technicians, had spoonfed the populace with this stirring demonstration of Gallic ingenuity. But when it came to the serious business of hurling heavy payloads into orbit, Gallic ingenuity was a sop rather than a solution. The Russians offered France a partnership. Molniya satellites would establish a Russian-French monopoly of television communications over Europe. Giant Russian boosters would hurl heavy French-designed and French-made satellites into orbit. "Big Charlie" curled a disdainful lip at the scientific battlements lining the shores of Cape Kennedy, and embraced the Kremlin.

Guy-Michel's chance at the stars came from Moscow when the Soviets made much of their largesse by inviting France to submit to them a French cosmonaut who would become a member of a Russian space crew. Henri Guy-Michel? He was the natural selection; no one considered that any other would represent La Belle France. Was he not a splendid physical specimen, as well as a test pilot, an engineer, and a scientist? Guy-Michel crammed in the Russian language, boned up on the sciences, and, with the cheers of his countrymen ringing in his ears, flew off to the cosmonaut training center at Baikonur. There he went through eight months of refined torture. His skydiving and physical stamina brought him through the worst of it with little difficulty. He passed all the tests with open praise, even from the Russian veterans. Praise was all he received.

A five-man Soyuz cracked into high orbit to rendezvous with a waiting monster of ungainly appearance but spectacular performance. Henri Guy-Michel tramped in the woods for want of anything better to do and cursed his singular lack of success in enticing a Russian lass between the sheets—*any* sheets, his or hers. The Soyuz boomed out of parking orbit and sailed around the far side of the moon while Guy-Michel brooded. The Frenchman joined the others in the victory celebration in Moscow. There he assayed the facts as they were, peered shrewdly into future possibilities, and went home to Paris.

Then came the first tentative proposals among the governments of Europe concerning an exciting new venture by the United States that would be known as *Project Epsilon*. . . .

The French didn't know it but a small group convening in Washington was determined to capitalize on the resentment still smoldering over what the French considered the shabby treatment of their national hero. Word went out through diplomatic channels that if agreement could be reached secretly, beforehand, the United States was prepared to accept Major Henri Guy-Michel as a member of *Epsilon*. The French evaluated the proposal and saw it as a means of saving face. They also looked long and hard at the man who would be the commander of the space station, and announced proudly the assignment to *Epsilon* of *Colonel* Henri Guy-Michel.

The national hero so honored had to be rousted from bed to receive the exciting news. "At four o'clock in the morning you interrupt me?" he roared into the phone. "It will wait!" Since his response was made from the side of a charming young companion, most Frenchmen agreed with his retort. After all, there are some things that do not brook interruption. Besides, Guy-Michel had to make up for eight months of drought in the U.S.S.R.

Chapter VI

Dr. Emanuel Garavito clipped the end from a long, thin cigar which he placed neatly between strong white teeth. It was his ritual for beginning a meeting, and he avoided none of the gestures for which he was well known at the Manned Spacecraft Center. Mike Harder waited as the cloud of smoke billowed about the head and shoulders of *Epsilon's* Project Director. The cigar lighter made an audible click as Garavito snapped it shut. Everything in order, he inhaled deeply and pointed the cigar at the man seated across his desk.

"You understand this meeting is entirely off the record, Mike?"

Harder nodded. "I figured it that way."

The director raised his brows.

"You're acting much too nice, Manny." And Harder laughed.

Garavito glared at his cigar. "I thought I covered it better than that," he said candidly.

Harder was silent.

Garavito rested his elbows on the desk. "You're right, of course," he said. "So I won't beat around the bush." He looked carefully at the colonel. "Have you made your decision yet about Guy-Michel?"

Harder reached for a cigarette and returned the unblinking gaze of Garavito. "If I didn't know you better I'd say you were pushing me," he said quietly.

Garavito raised his hands in mock alarm. "Perish the thought!"

"You're just anxious, huh?"

The director nodded slowly. "I am more than anxious," he admitted. "And if I *could* lean on you, Mike, I would. But the policy is sound, and you have the last word."

Harder sighed. "This is too big for pressure," he said. "The wrong choice down here could blow everything all to hell and gone, up there."

Garavito looked unhappy. "I know, I know," he said. "That is why, despite the screws from the top, I haven't bugged you."

Harder thought about that. They must really be pouring it onto the *Epsilon* director if he was this open about it.

"You know the bit," Garavito went on. "Someone got overly enthusiastic and made the invitation to France official."

"And if I say no," Harder concluded, "that puts you in a sticky situation, doesn't it?"

"All wrapped up in flypaper," Garavito said sourly.

"But the final decision remains mine, right?"

Garavito didn't look happy about it, but he nodded.

"I won't keep you in suspense any longer, Manny," Harder said. "I made my decision a few days ago."

Garavito couldn't bring himself to speak.

"He's in."

"Thank God!" Garavito cried, spilling cigar ashes over his suit. "This calls for a celebration." He peered through lidded eyes at the colonel, then took a bottle and glasses from his desk drawer. "Also strictly off the record, of course."

"Of course," Harder smiled, accepting the Scotch. They toasted one another and swallowed slowly. "What made you decide?" Garavito asked.

"Hell, there's no question that he qualifies. That wasn't the problem. I was trying to figure it for upstairs, how he would take to six months with no place to go."

Garavito nodded in agreement. "Obviously you're no longer concerned."

"Sure I am," Harder said. "I don't know if he'll be able to last until then."

Garavito laughed. "I know what you mean. He does have a propensity for the public eye, doesn't he?"

"Give the devil his due," Harder said. "He doesn't go around looking for it. The public eye, I mean. He sure as hell looks for the other thing, though."

"I understand," Garavito said with care, "that he has had, ah, an abundance of amatory adventures since he arrived here?"

"You can call it that. I think he's in a contest with Marcel to see who can outlast the other." Harder emptied his glass and waved off seconds. "And that big son of a bitch is inexhaustible, from what I hear."

Garavito smiled. "The, uh, grapevine has been pregnant with all sorts of rumors. There is even a story that he is a second Rasputin."

Harder chuckled. "I wouldn't doubt it. He spent a

weekend with my secretary and she walked around in a daze for a week."

Garavito arched his brows. "Bulldog Drummond?"

"The one and the same," Harder said.

Garavito drummed his fingers on the desk. "Well," he said finally. "To change the subject." He shuffled papers. "We have made a tentative selection for Life Sciences," he said at last.

Harder appreciated the emphasis on the word tentative. It had damned well better be.

Garavito glanced at a folder. Abruptly he laid it aside and picked up the bottle.

"What's that for?" Harder asked as Garavito poured.

"Oh, nothing, really," Garavito said innocently. "I just think you should be prepared for the latest addition to the *Epsilon* crew. Provided," he added hastily, "you approve, of course."

"Of course," Harder mimicked.

Garavito turned to his desk intercom and called his secretary. "Miss Johnson? Please ask Dr. Alison to come in."

Harder turned the name over in his mind. "Dr. Alison? I don't recall anyone with that name."

"No, perhaps not," Garavito agreed. "But you'll spend a long time forgetting her, I dare say."

"*Her?*"

Page Alison's appearance spared Garavito a reply. He rose to his feet to introduce a striking blonde.

"Good Jesus Christ," Harder whispered under his breath.

The rumors had been strong for months that in Project *Epsilon* the United States would commit to space its first woman astronaut, or "astronette," as the press was so fond of saying. The pressure for the move had been growing for a long time. Ever since the Soviets had sent the first woman into orbit in 1963, with the flight of Valentina Tereshkova, and followed up this initial mission with other female cosmonauts, demands in the United States for equal achievements in space had reached clamorous proportions. Until now, the space agency had turned a deaf ear to its critics; NASA stood secure behind its oft-repeated explanation that there was no real or demonstrated need for females in orbit. *Epsilon* changed all that. Having a female in space for a period of six months would provide an unequaled opportunity for medical research. On the woman, of course. Besides, a female scientist could perform certain tasks in orbit as well, if not better, than could her male counterpart.

"There's another factor to consider," Dr. Garavito said darkly to a closed meeting of his project council. "We're not exactly winners of the popularity poll. Most people have climbed down from the bandwagon of space flight. They frankly don't give a damn. A long time ago it was said that the true hero of the space age would be the character who gets full public and financial support behind the program. *We need that support.* And," he emphasized unnecessarily, "we ain't got it." He rolled his cigar from one side of his mouth to the other. "What we ain't got we got to get," he said in clipped fashion. "It's as simple as that. One way we can get it is to get behind us the support of half the population that hasn't really cared one way or another about what we're doing."

A long silence followed his words. One brave soul ventured forth upon the stormy waters. "You mean—"

"Uh-huh," Garavito said.

The others looked at them blankly.

"Fill us in?" one said hopefully.

Garavito glared at him. "In one word, gentlemen. Broads."

"*Broads?*" they chorused.

"In space?"

"In the station?"

"We're not running a subway line," Garavito snapped.

"But—"

"But *what?*" Garavito snarled. "If you have any comments with any meat to them, okay. Let's hear them. But don't come to me with moth-eaten clichés and platitudes about how this is a man's world." He chewed his cigar. "The women have most of the dough." He glared at them. "Remember that fact. And they've got influence. One more thing I want you to all remember. Every congressman and senator goes home to a broad. Maybe it's his wife or his mistress, but it sure as hell isn't another congressman or senator. It's a female." He smiled nastily. "I want those females to like us. That's your job."

First there were the statistics. Science notwithstanding, no one wanted to hear the professional qualifications or the scientific background. "We ain't going to sell her degrees," one of Garavito's staff smirked. "What we're going to sell is what she's got."

Another member of the staff looked askance at this disburser of public affairs wisdom. "Which is?" he queried.

A photograph appeared on the conference table. "She's got it, all right," they murmured approvingly. They were right. Dr. Page Alison had it. Five-feet-five inches in height. Dark blond hair, shoulder length. Green eyes. One hundred and twenty-six pounds.

"Get with it," another staff member murmured.

"Thirty-five, twenty-five, thirty-five," was the final pronouncement.

"We're in," someone said with relief. "That we can sell."

"We could maybe get her on the cover of *Time*. After all, she's a *scientist*."

"And a pilot," someone added.

"Done some skydiving, too," said another.

"Screw *Time*," another snarled. "We want her on the cover of *Life*, like Schirra."

"Think we can do it?"

"Well, we can always get a picture of her in the showers with the rest of the boys."

"*Very* funny."

"I hear her old man's a top screenwriter in Hollywood." The group paused to hear this new fount of knowledge. "She could make it anytime she wants."

"Never mind that. Is she married?"

"Past tense."

"I'd marry her. Christ, now there's a real—"

"Nobody asked you."

"*All right*, all right! Let's get back to business. Let's see the biog material. . . ."

Dr. Page Alison, thirty-two years of age, assembled in the manner that delights men young and old, had been active in space technology and science ever since her college days. For several years she worked for the Life Sciences Division of North American-Rockwell. This was a fact vital to her professional career.

North American-Rockwell was the prime contractor for Project Apollo. They built the engines for all three stages of the huge Saturn V. They also built the Command Module in which Apollo astronauts flew on their way to and from the moon. North American-Rockwell, even more to the point, designed and built the giant S-II fuel tank which, once in orbit, was to be converted to the *Epsilon* space station. Dr. Page Alison had been in the program from the ground floor up. She worked on the facilities that would be used in space for life sciences research during the lifetime of *Epsilon.*

Her professional qualifications were even more impressive than her physical attributes. She was a graduate of the University of California and the California Institute of Astronautics where she earned her master's and her doctorate in the life sciences. Her thesis dealt with the growth and development of plant and animal life under conditions of weightlessness. Once her associates settled down to her disturbing—in the physical sense—presence, they accepted her for what she was: a brilliant, hard-working, and accomplished scientist.

She lived in Beverly Hills with her father, a screenwriter with meaningful prominence—which meant that for a long time he had made money hand over fist. This afforded Page the blessings of pursuing both her career and a full personal life, which to her meant "try everything." She was a superb athlete (a factor not considered lightly in her selection for *Epsilon*): she pursued skiing, skindiving, boating, skydiving, and flying. Virtually everything to which she had applied her skills had been rewarded with success.

Except marriage. She had tied the knot of alleged bliss when she was twenty-two, while still pursuing her degrees. Four months later she divorced her husband. Mighty hero on the gridiron, he was a spindling in bed with a wife who—her natural passions aroused to fever pitch—found his inadequacies appalling. She could not tolerate a male, hulking in physical stature and properly endowed to give marital bliss its fullest meaning, who had a hangup that went far back in his past. She didn't really give a damn what his mother had done to him in the bathtub. Page preferred the bed.

She had tried holy wedlock and it had proved an unholy bore. Now she was free. Sexually uninhibited, she was also too wise to plunge into affairs without critical selection of those who would share her naked embrace. Quick and impatient with male friends in everyday life, she was equally swift to discover fault with them on rumpled sheets.

"He's got to have something between his ears as well as between his legs," she'd told a friend in exasperation.

Despite a coolness bordering on contempt for most men with whom she came in social contact, Page Alison remained in great demand. More than rumpled sheets were involved. A dozen qualified suitors had asked for Page's hand in marriage since her divorce, but she found herself unable to yield completely. And to Page marriage was just that. She didn't want to rule her spouse—Page sought a man.

During the formative period of Project *Epsilon*, Dr. Emanuel Garavito made the decision that avoided for NASA an intolerable grief of spurned females. Rather than a public search for and examination of those women who felt they were qualified (most of them believed they could meet the essential qualifications, that is—to keep satisfied the male members of the *Epsilon* crew), Garavito set up a survey team that quietly studied those women who might truly meet the severe qualifications for *Epsilon*.

Page Alison was among the thirty-seven women who met the initial qualifications and who came to Houston to be subjected to weeks of tests that ranged from the intellectual to the bone-jarring. Six of the thirty-seven survived and went on to more intensified examinations. Page's eleven hundred hours as a pilot came to her aid. Her skydiving proved invaluable. She was the only one of the six who did not return gasping from flights with smiling astronauts who took little pity on this invasion of their domain.

From the six, one emerged as unquestionably superior to the others. Dr. Garavito and other NASA officials had no question in their minds that Page Alison must be assigned to *Epsilon*.

Mike Harder was the question that couldn't be answered. Harder accepted the fact that Page Alison met all requirements. She had passed every grueling physical test he himself had met. Intellectually and professionally she was as deserving as any astronaut to be counted among the *Epsilon* crew.

But—a woman!

That was the only hitch, the only stumbling block. And because there existed no other reason—Mike Harder was a man honest with himself—he acquiesced. Not with boundless joy, it must be admitted. But elation on the part of Harder wasn't what Garavito and the others sought. Just a slight nod of the head would do.

Garavito turned out to be a prophet with honor. Lagging public interest in space affairs soared to unparalleled heights with the announcement that the attractive woman scientist had become the latest addition to the *Epsilon* crew. Garavito huddled in a meeting with Ben Blanchard, who ran public affairs at Houston, and with Stan Tyson, his contemporary at NASA headquarters in Washington. They bided their time, and at precisely the right moment notified the Norwegian government to make its announcement of June Strond.

Epsilon was front-page news everywhere. Garavito

and his team had catapulted the space program into a popularity unknown since the days of John Glenn.

"There's just one thing," Stan Tyson said to Garavito and Blanchard at a private dinner celebration. The others looked at him and waited.

"We've got some healthy people in that crew, right?"

They nodded.

"Who chaperones whom?"

Chapter VII

Mike Harder flapped his wings. Air thrummed audibly as his arms pinioned in a circular up-and-down motion.

"Faster, faster!" Bill Jordan cried.

Harder dipped one wing, stuck his feathered foot out at a sharp angle and began a graceful turn.

"That's it!" Jordan shouted happily. "Keep it up!"

Harder gritted his teeth and threw all his strength into his arms. He knew the motions. The arms went up and down, but as they did so, he kept curving them. The trick was to angle the plastic feathers just right. Get the right angle of attack into the movement of the wings, then, downthrust! Beat the hell out of the air, put some muscle into it! The air moved past his face—reward for his frenzied flapping. The side of the tank slid toward him. Expertly he started to shift his body. He twisted his arms so that the palms of his hands faced forward. The sudden increase of pressure stabbed into his shoulder muscles. But he'd timed it just right. As his center of gravity changed, he brought his legs forward, coasting at an angle to the wall. He let his sneakers absorb the shock, flexed his knees, and the instant the pressure slipped away he leaped outward. His legs propelled him with greater speed than before.

Harder grinned hugely. In the center of the tank he twisted his arms, drew his feet toward him, and went into a wide loop.

"Split S!" Jordan shouted. He focused the motion picture camera on Harder's gyrating body.

Harder came out of the loop, flapping madly. He dropped one arm and a leg and felt his body rolling. The moment he was inverted, facing the top of the tank, he arched his body and drove his feet like a scuba diver in hot pursuit of a shark. He twisted his arms again, beating the air, and when he had just enough speed, changing the angle of the feathers jutting from his feet, he curved through the air to reverse direction.

Jordan removed his eyes from the camera sight. "That was great, Mike!" he exulted. "Got every bit of it." He patted the camera fondly.

Exhausted for the moment, his body soaked in sweat, Harder drifted like a hummingbird in the center of the tank. But without effort. He didn't need any in the S-IVB tank where zero-g prevailed. "You through for a while?" he called to Jordan.

"Yeah. Take ten," the astronaut replied. "I want to put in a new roll of film."

Harder flapped his arms gently, a soft and easy beat that repositioned him. Relaxing his arms, he moved his feet up and down with the same motion he had learned long before, in scuba diving. He eased to the side of the tank where Dr. Werner Koelbe helped remove the wings and handed Harder a towel. The skintight sneakers Harder wore, shaped like ballet slippers, were constructed of metallic fiber. The platform where Koelbe stood was magnetized to provide a sure footing. Harder pressed his feet down firmly, wiping off his body.

"Your right arm, please."

Harder extended his arm while Koelbe wrapped the blood-pressure cuff expertly, pumped, and then checked off the gauge readings. Koelbe went through a swift medical check of Harder's heartbeat, pulse, temperature, and other items he jotted down on his record sheets.

"Everything okay?" Harder asked idly.

"Mmmm."

"Very concise, doctor."

"Well, it's not every day I have the chance to examine a bird."

"Hey, Mike," Jordan called across to them. "Ready any time you are."

Harder reached for a plastibottle with iced tea. He inserted the flextube in his mouth and squeezed the bottle gently. Koelbe dutifully noted the quantity of liquid absorbed by Harder.

He extended the wings to Koelbe, and pulled his feet free. A moment later he was again in full-feathered regalia. He lifted his feet to the edge of the platform and shoved away, floating gently to the center of the big tank. He had an area slightly more than thirty feet high by twenty feet wide in which to cavort.

Dr. Koelbe watched him with more than idle interest. Harder made an impressive sight. The ancient Aztecs would have considered him the physical embodiment of a god. He wore only the skintight slippers and boxer shorts. His skin was bronzed deeply from scheduled exposure to the ultraviolet lamps; no spaceman's pallor marked this crew. Sweat glistened on Harder's body, accenting his rippling muscles. Harder was just short of six feet. There wasn't an ounce of fat on his frame; at 182 pounds (Earth weight, Koelbe thought with amusement), Mike Harder was one of the finest physical specimens he had ever studied in motion. He was unusually sinewy for his size-weight ratio. Stripped to brief shorts, he showed whipcord musculature. More impressive was the flow of strength as he moved—a physiological rhythm affirming a body well-disciplined and durable under stress. Despite their long tenure under one-tenth g, Harder had made certain to sustain his physical conditioning. Not a day went by that he wasn't working out in the gym on Level 4: tension springs, isometric exercises, body-contact wrestling. These kept his frame as fit as it would have been under normal gravity.

But among all of Harder's occupations he enjoyed this most of all. Had there not been a medical program to determine human orientation under zero-g, Mike Harder and the others would still have turned the S-IVB tank into their uproarious adult playground. Nothing could quite compare with their flying like birds. Only here, in the weightlessness of space, could a man join the bird in true feathered flight. The extraordinary construction of the terrestrial bird, of course, endowed it with flight. Under the crushing pull of surface gravity a man could never hope to fly without the manipulation of air pressure through artificial devices. On earth the bird was master; here men could join the feathered flock and cavort wildly.

The "feathers" were ingenious. Made of lightweight plastic, they produced the greatest lifting and thrusting force commensurate with the muscular energy of a man. The S-IVB tank was pressurized to only six pounds per square inch, rather than the fifteen pounds found on the earth's surface. The lower pressure meant the equivalent of nearly tripled muscle power.

When Harder flapped his wings he did so with meaningful effect. Weightless, he had only to accelerate his body mass, a task easy enough with his scientifically designed wings. They did more than flap up and down in response to Harder's arm motion. He wore wings with glovelike appendages. By bending or extending his fingers, which operated tubular control rods, he was able to control the positioning of the "feathers" at their trailing ends. In effect, he had a limited aileron action—precisely that enjoyed by the feathered creatures of the home planet. With experience, Harder had obtained a dexterity and control Koelbe would never have believed possible had he not personally been witness to the colonel's free-flying antics.

Normally a man floating within the S-IVB tank would have been helpless to gain the curving walls, or to reach the overhead or the deck that was their arbitrary position of "down." A man floating weightless lacked friction for movement, and hung up in the air. They had tried all kinds of experiments under these conditions. Henri Guy-Michel proved out an old theory. Floating in midtank, ten feet from the nearest surface, he breathed in deeply and then exhaled in a controlled pattern, his lips shaped for maximum effect. It nearly winded him, but he definitely began to move, a hilarious light-air pressure parody of the squid.

Serious physiological experiments they might be, but the crew—the women as well—eagerly joined in these sessions. Because of safety considerations, Harder refused to permit more than four people at any one time in the S-IVB tank. One of the four was always suited up, equipped with a body thruster, and ready to get emergency suits to the others in the event of a meteoroid penetration of the tank. It had never yet resulted in an emergency, but Harder believed implicitly in his precautions.

Koelbe himself had engaged in these weightless antics. When one was freed of the cumbersome pressure garment, the effect was so heady as to be almost overwhelming. Their favorite pastime was free flight. The trick was to position the body against a curving wall, with the legs bent and tensed, the body restrained by the arms. Then, a controlled leg-straightening kick from the wall, much the same as a swimmer completing a lap, spinning around, and kicking off from the side of a pool. During the floating passage from one side of the S-IVB tank to the other, there was enough time to do twists, rolls, and all kinds of body contortions. A long time ago no one had believed it possible that weightlessness was anything but no-friction, no-freedom. How ridiculous, mused Koelbe. Hadn't anyone ever watched a diver spring from a board, or an athlete bound upward from a trampoline? They didn't need air resistance or body-positioning friction. What they did in the way of body movement took place after they were free and airborne.

Of course there was a difference. If you kicked off with too great a thrust you didn't diminish your speed, and you could hit the opposite side of the tank in a clumsy crash. Balance was everything, and it came only with time and practice. Koelbe smiled to himself. He had never expected to need liniment in a space station. But there had been plenty of sprained ankles and wrists and sore muscles. Tim Pollard had come a cropper after one ungainly smash into the insulated tank wall. He lost control during his cross-tank passage, arms and legs akimbo as he struggled to regain a sense of body balance. He overdid it and became tangled in his own limbs.

When he thudded against the wall, a knee whacked
him solidly in the eye. The British astronomer had
the dubious distinction of being the first man in
space to sport a black eye.

Mike Harder performed for the camera. In response to Bill Jordan's shouted exhortations, Harder
went through a series of intricate maneuvers. These
were for the record, a test of agility and control,
although Harder warmed to the challenge personally
as much as he performed for science. *That man,*
thought Koelbe as he observed Harder's extraordinary skill, *is truly one of the new humans. He is
adept—no, the term is inadequate. He is more than
catlike. He is fully adaptable. . . .*
Harder was flying backwards, his feathered arms
scooping air and thrusting it before him. Abruptly
there was a flurry of plastic feathers as he drifted to a
halt, breathing deeply. He looked across the tank at
Koelbe, and laughed. "One damn thing I know," he
said. "Birds don't sweat, do they?"
Koelbe thought about that. "I suppose not," he
replied. "Why do you ask?"
"Because they don't carry towels to dry themselves. I'm soaked." Floating in midair he removed
his right wing. Koelbe wadded up a towel and tossed
it to him gently. It floated within reach of the astronaut's hand. As comfortable as he might be in a gym
on Earth, Harder dried himself thoroughly, and flipped
the towel back to Koelbe. A moment later he had the
wing back in place and prepared to resume his
maneuvers.
A flash of yellow streaked through the air and
clamped onto Harder's short hair and one ear. The
others shouted with laughter at the sight of the canary that had joined its giant feathered friend. Nor-

mally they kept the bird in a large cage. During their tenancy of the station the canary was released to join their antics. As it had now; the small feathered creature had flown at Harder as though mocking him for his attempts at flight.

"Fly like the bird, Mike!" Koelbe directed him with a smile. "He is a very good teacher."

Jordan zipped in with his zoom lens for a closeup of the canary gripping Harder's ear. Finished, he lowered the camera. "I know what's missing!" he shouted. "Just hang loose for a few minutes and we'll pin some feathers to your ass!"

Harder turned with a slow beating of wings to fix Jordan with a cold stare. "You ready for yours, motor-mouth?"

Slowly Jordan lowered the camera. A grin appeared. "Ain't you learned your lesson yet?" he asked.

By way of answer Harder flapped his way to the platform and divested his arms and legs of his feathered garments. He turned to look at Jordan. The astronaut had secured the camera and was removing his jumper, stripping to the same attire of shorts and slippers. Jordan rubbed his hands briskly. "I'm gonna cream your ass, boss."

Harder extended his hand with his middle finger raised. Jordan kicked off from his platform and drifted to the curving wall opposite Harder. There he set his balance with one hand and his feet, half-twisted toward the colonel. "You ready?" he called.

"Yeah," Harder growled. "What's the rules today?"

"The same," Jordan said. "No biting, no fingers in the eyes, no kicking in the balls."

Harder laughed. "Just a friendly game."

"Let's get with it, big man," Jordan sneered.

"Werner—you timing us?"

Dr. Koelbe nodded, his thumb poised over a stopwatch. "Any time you are ready, gentlemen," he said with mock severity. "Three falls, or five, today?"

Harder jerked a thumb at Jordan. "Let him get a real workout," he grunted. "Five."

"Look who called who motor-mouth," Jordan jeered. "You gonna talk all day or do you wanna wrassle?"

"Start counting, Werner," Harder ordered.

The doctor called, "Five . . . four . . . three. . . ." The two astronauts aligned themselves to confront each other in what was surely the strangest body-contact sport known to man—zero-g wrestling. If you couldn't grab somebody, or something, you spun about helplessly, hoping to drift within reach of a wall so that you could kick off again. Sometimes, Koelbe thought, they went at their sport just a bit *too* eagerly. Jordan had once caught Parsons in a cruel hammerlock, his feet twisted expertly around those of his adversary. Jordan kept up the pressure while Parsons wriggled madly, relinquishing the hold when Parsons gasped "Uncle! Uncle, goddamnit!" Parsons had had a stiff neck for a week.

". . . two . . . one . . . zero!" Koelbe shouted.

Instantly they sprang from the walls like two barracudas rushing toward each other. First contact was critical. Two skulls meeting head-on meant king-sized headaches, or worse. But they were both too skilled in this business for that kind of sloppy mistake. The intent was to incapacitate the other man with a locking hold.

The peculiarities of movement under zero-g meant that the first one to gain a hold usually won the fall. Today the match was the best three-out-of-five. With the energy expended in twisting about like cats, both men would be exhausted by the time they called it quits. Harder was the stronger of the two, and with just a shade more skill in weightlessness. Jordan met these problems with the mat skill he'd developed as an intercollegiate wrestling champion. It evened the odds out rather well.

Koelbe burst into laughter as he saw what Jordan had planned. As their bodies came together, Jordan pulled himself into a tight ball. Harder grabbed at his adversary but couldn't get a grip on bare skin, as Jordan had anticipated. The moment he felt Harder's hand scrabbling against him, Jordan unwound like a giant spring. Instantly he grasped an ankle, and with his other hand, a fistful of Harder's shorts. Before the colonel, unable to twist around, could block the other, Jordan had literally scrambled along Harder's back. In a flash he had a bowstring-hold clamped on Harder: one hand gripping an ankle, the other under Harder's chin, and—this was everything—his foot planted solidly in the small of Harder's back, bending the colonel like a bow, rendering him helpless.

"Give up?" Jordan shouted.

"*Unnngh.*"

"What?"

"*UNNNGH!*"

"He says he gives up," Koelbe translated.

"Oh." Reluctantly Jordan released his grip. "First fall for Bill," Koelbe called to them.

Harder pressed his hand behind him, against his back, groaning. Instantly Jordan pulled around to where he could see Harder's face. "Christ, Mike, you okay?" Harder's face was screwed up in pain. "Jesus, I didn't mean. . . ." Jordan's voice faltered.

Harder pointed to his side. "There, over there," he grunted. Koelbe looked sharply at them. He didn't think Harder had been hurt.

"You sneaky son of a bitch!" Jordan bellowed. The instant the "suffering" Harder had brought Jordan where he wanted him his arm whipped around and clamped Jordan in a vicious headlock. It was perfect. Harder positioned his body exactly. It was the only way he could hold the headlock without foot leverage, his upper arm and forearm exerting tremendous pressure on Jordan's face.

With all his skill Jordan twisted and wriggled. To no avail. Without friction or leverage, he couldn't pry loose. His face began to turn red as Harder relentlessly kept up the pressure, knowing that if he slipped even once Jordan would be free. Jordan's arm came around and his fingers locked onto Harder's jaw. But he couldn't apply the bending pressure that would release him. Each time he tried, his body worked against him, moving in a direction opposite to that of his arm pressure. When he grasped Harder's face and squeezed his fingers into the colonel's cheeks, Harder immediately tweaked Jordan's nose.

"Cut it out!" Jordan cried.

"Can't hear you," Harder grunted.

"Leggo!"

"Speak louder, man," Harder chuckled.

Jordan's hands signaled frantically.

"Time!" Koelbe shouted. "Second fall to Mike," he added as Harder released the hold. Jordan floated freely, rubbing a bright red ear. "You bastard," he complained.

"The chaplain's on leave," Harder retorted. "Tell it to Jesus."

Jordan glared at him and laughed. "Okay, okay, we got one each. Off the wall for the next?"

"Good enough," Harder said. "Let's go."

Each man half-curled his fingers, and they clasped hands in this manner. They flexed their knees, bending away from each other, and brought the bottoms of their feet together. "Ready?"—a moment's pause.

"Okay, cut out," Harder said. They released their hands and kicked. There was enough force in their movement to send each man drifting in opposite directions. Once they had floated to the wall, facing each other across twenty feet of space, they repositioned themselves for another head-on opening.

"Let's go, Doc," Jordan called impatiently. Koelbe started counting down, wincing as they collided in midtank and did their best to pulverize each other.

To Werner Koelbe, this was the best time of all in *Epsilon*—when the restraints and the cautious courtesies were thrown aside, and two grown men could become like children wrestling in the dirt. He never ceased to be amazed by their dexterity, and the instinctive moves they made to compensate for the myriad problems of body control under zero-g. The films he had made of such scenes kept television audiences around the world in a delighted uproar. It was proof, too, Koelbe thought, of man's uncanny and instinctive ability to adapt to any situation or any environment.

Once again the phrase *new human* slipped into his thoughts as he watched Harder and Jordan practicing controlled mayhem against each other. Of the two, Harder was the older by four years. Despite the difference in age and Jordan's wrestling experience, Harder was the master. These astronauts, mused Koelbe, stood out among other men, and of this unusual breed, Mike Harder stood apart even from his contemporaries.

Michael S. Harder was forty-two years old when he rode a Saturn V into high orbit. Three other men went with him to bring to life the waiting components and assemblies of what would be Station *Epsilon*. Two of these astronauts, Bill Jordan and Luke Parsons, would remain with Harder in their orbit 470 miles above the earth. The space station raced around the planet once every hour and forty-six minutes. As the months went by, their orbit would decay slightly; in six months' time it would be lowered by ten to thirty miles. But the giant station would be available to manned crews for several years.

Harder lacked the marks that distinguished the oldtime pilots who pioneered the early space flights. He didn't have the characteristic crows' feet at the corners of his eyes that came from squinting into bright sun at high altitude. Harder didn't belong to the "old school" of flying. Tearing up a piece of sky in an old biplane was something he had done several times as a lark. That kind of activity was in the same category as hurtling around a racetrack in a souped-up sports car. It was fun—not necessity. Mike Harder, as a pilot, gained maturity and skill under the auspices of modern technology. His world was one of screaming jets and steel-slabbed wings sharply swept, of strict attention to the slide rule demands of precision flight. He wasn't good. That would never have carried him to his present heights. He was extraordinary. His record, his skill, his calm under exploding emergencies, all made it clear that he was the best—a member of the ultimate few in pilots deemed capable of shouldering the burden, not of merely pushing beyond the atmosphere, but of leading the way. It was knowledge, skill, and technical competence—as well as his demonstrated personal attributes of leadership and command—that marked the sandy-haired man as outstanding. The hard lines in his face caused by oxygen masks and crash helmets, were an indelible signature on his features. Even in a room filled with pilots, he was one of those men the newcomer recognized as unique. He had a deep voice, and spoke with a mastery of self and environment that gave to him what many are quick to explain as a magnetic personality. Some called it the sign of the natural leader. Whatever it was, it distinguished Mike Harder.

Ten years before Project *Epsilon* became a reality, Mike Harder would have been looked upon as one of a handful of men capable of pioneering space flight. But that was in the early days of mastering orbital adventures, and since that initial decade of soaring into the radiation-lashed vacuum beyond Earth, the ranks of those who sailed the seas of space had grown swiftly. Men lofted into the new domain in Vostoks and Voskhods and Soyuz, in Mercury and Gemini and Apollo, in the X-15 and the Gemini B-MOL, and in new oddly-shaped lifting bodies. Dozens of men had breached the space barrier. Men and women in ships bearing the hammer and sickle. Many more were in trainig to follow. There were, literally, hundreds of astronauts and cosmonauts, not only in the United States and the Soviet Union, but in other lands as well. What made Mike Harder stand out was not the fact that he was an astronaut, but that among his own special breed he was still a man apart.

Harder considered his background as ordinary as any that might be found among the modern military test pilots. Once again history had caught up with men who were once so rare as to be counted on the fingers of both hands. Now they were only a part of the expanding numbers to whom space beckoned as naturally as had the higher atmospheric reaches to their fathers. Steve Harder, Mike's father, had been a bomber pilot. The life of his son was one military base after the other, each fading into an olive-drab anonymity of the passing years.

In 1929, Mike had come into the world in the base hospital at old Kelly Field just outside San Antonio, Texas. When he was eight years old he fell in love—not with pigtails and freckles and a wide smile, but with a great silvery-metal machine with four thundering engines. Steve Harder was assigned to the elite group within the 2nd Bombardment Wing at Langley Field, Virginia, that flew the first B-17 bombers. The awe Mike felt for the roaring giants was shared with others his own age, and older. The early Fortresses came and went, and the silver disappeared under green-brown camouflage. There was a war, and Mike's father faded into the darkness of the eastern horizon. Avid interest kept Mike pursuing the sound of battle trumpets high over the European continent, and there came a familiarity with Fortresses and Messerschmitts, with Focke-Wulfs and Mustangs, Spitfires, and Thunderbolts.

The drums of war carried across the Atlantic as Mike took fierce pride in his father's deeds, and the names Schweinfurt, Berlin, Hamburg, and Dresden became more than lettering on a map. Early in 1945, Mike saw his father for the first time in years when Steve Harder, bemedaled and promoted to the rank of colonel, returned from his forays over the shattered Reich. It was only a momentary respite. Soon his father disappeared again, this time into the western horizon. There was another huge, silvery giant—the B-29, and another war, ten thousand miles away. Steve Harder disappeared for the last time in a flaming gasp over Tokyo, the night turned into day by the shrieking flames. The father he'd never really had time to know became a cipher.

A year later his mother died. The next several years passed in an Ohio college, the young man somewhat at odds with himself and the world in the jangled aftermath of war. He lived with an uncle who was fond of the boy and tolerated him easily, who also wore Air Force wings and had fortunately escaped the fiery end of his brother during the same raid over Tokyo.

Late in 1948, nineteen years old and increasingly restless, Mike Harder shucked his books, stood with a group, right hand raised, and took his oath. Ground school, flight school, commission. Like many other young hot rocks with shiny wings on proud breasts, he flew Sabres in Korea.

Instantly he came to know how good he was. Four Migs burned or exploded or careened crazily into the barren mountains beneath his guns, and Mike Harder returned from the first jet air war to accept his pick of advanced Air Force schools. The pattern was necessary and predictable. Two years at Michigan State, his degree, back to the cockpit—now with a burning ambition to get into test flying. But first there was another tour of active duty.

Harder and a select group of fighter pilots wore a rare insignia: a grinning wolf's head. Not many people realized it meant the exclusive fraternity of the wolfpack—aircraft with flaming engines and swept wings. Seeking to overcome the problems of range and bristling Soviet defenses until new bombers and ballistic missiles might become available, the Strategic Air Command created its wolfpack team. Each team was made up of three fighters stripped of guns and armor plate, all weight not critical to their mission. Each fighter carried long-range tanks slung under the wings. Each mounted a probe for aerial refueling, and carried a one-megaton bomb.

Their mission was cut and dried. Each tanker would take its three fighters as far as possible into Soviet territory. Tanks filled, the fighters would break from their shepherd and go for the deck, pounding at maximum power just above the treetops, scattering in all directions for their targets, too fast and too low for radar to be effective. The Russians would have gotten perhaps a third of their number, and the others would have rammed through to their targets.

There was only one problem. Each mission was almost guaranteed to be a one-way deal. They didn't have fuel enough to get back to friendly territory. The wolfpack pilots were hot, eager, and aggressive. They were also damned relieved when the big jet bombers made them unnecessary. No one wants to write insurance for one-way pilots.

"Suicide service" opened doors, and Mike Harder took off at a dead run to the coveted test pilot school at Edwards Air Force Base in the California desert. Like many others of the Air Force and Navy elite, he tested new fighters and bombers, and did his best to cut the feet out from under his friendly competitors to get at the strange new shapes with tiny wings and mighty rocket engines. Mike Harder bullied and pushed and worked and flew his way into the cockpit of the stub-winged torpedo called the X-15.

The Air Force pinned astronaut wings on his tunic for flying the X-15 to sixty-three miles and coming back home in one piece. He now qualified for the rocket-powered lifting body, a bathtub-shaped monstrosity that had no wings, flew on channeled lift, and landed at a blistering 280-miles-an-hour on the hot desert sands. Mike Harder was looked upon as having a charmed life when he made six landings in the bathtub and walked away from each dust-spewing controlled disaster.

With all this behind him, Mike was a natural for the space pilot school. The Air Force assigned him to the Manned Orbiting Laboratory program, in which two astronauts in blue would ride the Gemini-B into polar orbit, crawl through a hatchway into a big cylinder, and spend the next thirty days spying on the Soviet Union—and anything else of interest. But the program dragged out. Project Mercury was history, and Glenn, Carpenter, Schirra, and Cooper were becoming the "old men" of space flight, although the way Schirra and Cooper ran things at Gemini belied their status as old veterans.

Project Gemini passed into history, and Harder was chafing at the MOL bit when the shock rippled outward from Cape Kennedy. Grissom, White, and Chaffee had burned to death high above Pad 34, and Apollo suddenly was in deep trouble. MOL would be the first new spacecraft in orbit. It wasn't. The Air Force fought bitterly against dollar cutbacks from Washington, and Apollo picked up steam. Late in 1967, Harder stood at Complex 39 on Merritt Island and watched, stunned, as three thousand tons of monster lifted from pad A and slammed a record 285,000 pounds into orbit.

The first Saturn V made it patent to Harder that playtime was over. Yet MOL frustrated its engineers and astronauts as they stayed chained to the ground and watched the Russians put up one new Soyuz after the other. The Apollo team whipped the first three-man ship into orbit in the late summer of 1968, tested the ugly but effective lunar lander, and sharpened their launch efficiency with a salvo of Saturn Vs drilled neatly into high orbits. Finally, late in 1970, Mike Harder and George Ormsbee cracked into polar orbit with the first MOL, swinging around the planet along a north-to-south path 150 miles over the poles.

Mike Harder was unaware of the manner in which Fate turned its wheels, but at the height of his success with MOL, his days with that program were numbered. Ever since 1967 the civilian space agency had been fighting a losing financial battle with Congress. Despite a ringing success with the first manned Apollo on the moon, NASA had fallen into disfavor. The staggering cost of Vietnam, international monetary problems, and little to show for Apollo except for some lovely film and a few hundred pounds of lunar rock, had given the once-great program a precarious financial lease on life.

The Russians tore up their agreement restricting space for peaceful purposes and tested a new series of orbital weapons; as might be predicted, this kept Pentagon and White House lights burning long into the nights. Military space funds doubled, and NASA peered apprehensively into a murky future. The greatest single technological asset the country had was about to be squeezed into near-nonexistence.

NASA officials huddled in order to come up with a major coup that would restore the operational status of the agency. Once their top engineering teams had broken up, they knew it would be difficult if not impossible to weave together again these critical assemblages of talent. The idea was conceived to utilize existing hardware, in the form of the Saturn V, to assemble a great space station. Not simply the scientific outpost originally envisaged. This one, to utilize to the fullest the commercial payoff, as well. The expense staggered the space planners. No matter how they scraped, shifted, altered and pleaded, the NASA officials found that their coffers remained too slim to support the project.

"It won't work," one said with a glum face.

His associates agreed. "We'll have to pass it by."

There was a realist among them. "Let's make a deal," he said.

Heads turned. "A deal?"

"*Yes*, damn it!"

"But with whom?" The new speaker was bewildered.

"With anybody who'll come in with us!" shouted the realist.

Thus Project *Epsilon* was born. Four nations would be invited to each send along a scientist to serve aboard the space station—for a healthy part of the tab, of course. That still wasn't enough. NASA huddled secretly with the Air Force to enlist still further financial and engineering aid. The behind-the-scenes agreement was cut and dried. The Air Force would pick up forty percent of the tab and this would put *Epsilon* neatly over the financial hill. But there was a price, of course.

"Of course," NASA chorused. "*Anything* to get the damn thing off the ground."

The people in blue suits made the most of the situation. An Air Force astronaut would be top dog. For the first time NASA balked. The Air Force assured the space agency they'd follow the old pattern. The officer would be placed on inactive status and become (ostensibly, at least) a full-fledged member of the NASA team. To the world he would be NASA. Heads nodded and the rest of it was detail.

From the beginning, Mike Harder knew the score and the role he would play. He would be station commander; he would fulfill his role as a NASA astronaut; he would test and experiment with scientific instruments and devices for Earth surveillance. At the same time, and without public knowledge, he would also carry out surveillance of certain critical areas of the planet beneath them with the same equipment he had used from the MOL. NASA didn't like it, but they kept their gripes within their own four walls. They had a winner on their hands with

Epsilon, and if they went along with it, their bread might be well-buttered on both sides.

The public found in Mike Harder one of its more enigmatic and fascinating heroes. Unlike his predecessors, Harder didn't take kindly to contracts with national magazines and newspaper syndicates. He refused to be dissected for some Sunday supplement articles that would extol his virtues and confine him to a stereotyped image. In his own way, Mike Harder followed in the footsteps of another Air Force officer-turned-astronaut, Colonel Gordon Cooper, who had driven newsmen to distraction with one-word answers to voluble questions.

Of course there was a public image. Mike Harder was brilliant, tough, skilled, and imbued with the wisdom that comes only from extensive experience. He was ruggedly handsome. He would command a great space station of six men and two women.

And Mike Harder wasn't married.

That made more news copy than anything else combined about Project *Epsilon.*

At the moment, Harder couldn't have cared less. He had a beautiful leg-scissors around the ribs of Bill Jordan, and was doing his best to twist one of his adversary's legs into a pretzel.

Jordan's cry of "Uncle! Uncle, goddamnit!" rang through the S-IVB tank.

Chapter VIII

They saw the flashes in the atmosphere from a thousand miles away. At that distance, great tongues of lightning flickered like giant electric bulbs. Clouds spawned from the terrible flames tearing the ground, and tumbled upward to seventy thousand feet where the jetstreams carved them into huge gray sheets. At five-miles-a-second, *Epsilon* rushed toward the fearful scene. Even their great distance barely minimized the horror they saw raging along the California hills.

"*Good Jesus.*" Luke Parsons spoke in quiet sympathy. "Can you imagine what it's like down there?" In the darkened compartment, with others of the *Epsilon* crew, he stared at the blazing maelstrom that roiled high above the western shoreline of the United States.

The distance closed swiftly, and details became more obvious. Page Alison looked planetward through powerful binoculars. The scene leaped into focus.

"Here," she said, handing the binoculars to June Strond. "I'm not that anxious to look."

June looked at her with surprise.

"My home is down there," Page said, turning away.

Tim Pollard looked through his binoculars. "I understand more than three hundred are dead already." He made the statement simply, repeating what they all knew from the newscasts. At any time they could study live television from the ground. No one felt the urge, least of all Page Alison, who feared for the safety of her father. MSC Houston had a query out to learn what they could.

Now they were directly above the coastline, seeing clearly the ominous clouds boiling between the Pacific and the high peaks to the east. The clouds were a mixture of water vapor, dust, smoke, and ashy debris—a sooty plague already covering hundreds of thousands of square miles. They were not entirely dark. Their upper reaches showed jagged tears from the heat lightning. Below the clouds pulsed tall columns of leaping red flames. The tinderbox of the Los Angeles area hills and valleys had burst explosively in every direction. The conflagration consumed entire hills in an irresistible sweep. Homes, stores, entire apartment buildings and complexes were sucked into the fiery maw. Thousands were missing, tens of thousands homeless. A state of disaster had been declared.

"They're going to be a long time getting that under control," Parsons said. "Anything on your father?" he asked Page. She shook her head.

"Damn it all to hell!" They turned to look at Pollard. "All that sort of thing could be avoided, you know." He gestured angrily at the inferno far below. "There's a whole bloody ocean right on the edge of all that fire, and no known way to get rain where it would put out that mess."

"All you need is money," Parsons said.

"Money!" exclaimed Pollard. "If we had what it costs to run that idiotic war in Vietnam for only one month, *one month*, mind you," and he stabbed a finger at Parsons, "inside of two or three years we could create rain whenever it was needed for something like that."

Parsons held up both hands. "Hey, I'm on *your* side, remember? I'm up here, not setting villages afire."

They joined in the laughter that followed. "Sorry, old man," Pollard muttered. "It simply gets through to me every now and then. When I think of how we're on the very edge of doing so much. . . ." He let the sentence hang. There wasn't much use in lecturing those around him. They felt the same way, and were working for the same goals.

Pollard looked around the darkened room. "Where's Mike?" he asked.

"Sawing wood," Parsons replied. "He and Bill tried to tear each other to bits this afternoon in the tank."

"Not another of those silly wrestling matches?"

"Yes," Parsons nodded. "Werner said they were like two animals. Enjoying the hell out of themselves."

"Who won?" Page asked.

"Guess."

"Mike again?"

"Yeah. Werner said he expected Mike to start chewing on Bill's leg at any moment." He grinned. "It must have been a good one. Bill was still limping when they came downtube, and when you're limping at a tenth-g. . . ." Parsons didn't need to finish. They'd all seen the wild struggles in the S-IVB tank between Harder and Jordan.

California and its blazing hell slipped out of sight behind them. No one was sorry to see it vanish over the curving horizon.

Pollard glanced at his watch. "How are we on time, Luke?"

Parsons studied his own watch. "Umm. We're on the downswing now. We'll fire as we come up past Cape Horn," he said, thinking aloud. "About twenty-five minutes or so. I'd better get things started."

"Thank you," Pollard said.

Parsons slipped through the airlock into the tube. Several minutes later the intercom sounded. "Parsons here," he called from engineering on Level 5. "You reading me?"

Pollard switched the intercom to "open-transceive." "Very clear, Luke. I'm on open line here," he said.

"Roger and the same," came Parsons' voice. "I'll call the sequences as they come up."

"Right."

Pollard, June Strond, and Page Alison moved closer to the viewports. Commanding their attention was a bulbous cylinder drifting two hundred yards beyond the station. Within the bright yellow cassette were the last photographic plates taken by Pollard in his astronomical research. At this moment, Luke Parsons was counting down to the moment of retrofire, when a stubby, solid rocket with a flaring chamber would explode into life. In a brief episode of fire the cassette would have its speed reduced by several hundred miles per hour, breaking its careful orbital balance, curving into the atmosphere far below. Afterwards, deceleration parachutes would trail behind, and a waiting recovery plane would swoop in with airsnatch cables to retrieve the valuable cargo.

The intercom came to life. "Ten minutes."

Pollard put the binoculars to his eyes to study the

cassette. He felt wretched at such moments and
would continue to be apprehensive until they received the signal acknowledging safe recovery. Every one of those photographic plates was extremely
valuable. With an effort, he forced himself to ignore
the gnawing in his stomach. He'd done his job. The
rest was up to Parsons and the crew of the recovery
plane.

He looked around the compartment. June and Page
were together at one viewport, talking earnestly.
Pollard smiled. Get two women together, no matter
what the circumstances, and there would be occasion
for furtive conversation. Housewives, fishwives, or
scientists—their colors didn't change.

The station was quiet. Harder and Jordan were
sleeping off their earlier combat. Koelbe was up to
his armpits in medical reports, driving himself to
sustain the efficiency he felt so necessary for a German scientist. Pollard made a wry face at the thought.
He greatly admired Koelbe and was fully aware of
the man's qualifications. But he overdid it, really.
His efficiency was more than that. Koelbe went after
his reports and records and charts in a manner Pollard felt was ruthless. It seemed immoral to attach
such intense emotion to paperwork. The British astronomer suffered a twinge of conscience. He knew
he was being unfair, that he couldn't judge the work
of others by his own standards.

Where was Henri? Of course—the California holo-
caust. Guy-Michel would be in contol on Level 6,
monitoring live transmission of the debacle. Video-
sound coverage of the greatest fire of its kind ever
recorded in California. Transmitters beamed their
picture-sound signals into space, kicked them to another satellite that power-boosted the signal, flashed
it to receivers around the planet. Europe, Asia, Af-

rica, South America . . . research groups, huddled beneath forty feet of snow in Antarctica, could look at the disaster if that was their desire. Just flick a switch, twist a dial, and you were there. Live. When it was happening.

Pollard glanced again at the two women. Just what the devil was so important that demanded all their attention? He shook his head. He couldn't understand his own wife, to say nothing of complicated females like these two.

"Five minutes."

"You know, I'm sorry about what happened."

June looked at Page. "Sorry? I don't understand."

Page twisted the binocular straps, avoiding her gaze. "I mean, the other day when Henri and I blundered into. . . ." She looked up finally. "You know, when you and Mike—well, damn it, it seemed as if old granite-head was going to rejoin the human race."

"Oh, that." June's voice was so low Page barely heard the words.

"We're the only two females in this oversized tin can. What's that supposed to mean?" Then, realizing her intent might be mistaken, Page said coolly, "Forgive me. I'm intruding."

"No, no," June gestured, showing a quick smile.

Page felt relief. This wasn't the place and/or the time for her to stick her nose into June's emotional life, yet she and June couldn't be closer.

June laughed self-consciously. "It *was* badly timed, I suppose."

Page showed sudden interest. "That's Henri for you. He enjoys nothing more than bad timing. Where someone else is involved, of course," she added.

"Of course." They laughed together.

"Henri thought Mike was mad enough to take a swing at him," Page said.

June looked up with her face showing no expression. "Did Henri say that?"

"Uh-huh," Page nodded.

June remained silent for several moments. "He did once, you know."

Page looked at her with intense interest. "So that's what happened!" she exclaimed.

"What do you mean, Page?"

"Look, I'm leveling with you, honey," Page said quickly. "I know that *something* happened between them." She laughed lightly. "But I didn't know they had come to blows. Was it bad?"

June nodded. "It was very bad."

Her tone was so serious Page sobered immediately. "Going to tell me?" she asked.

June studied her carefully. "I think, perhaps, you do not want to know."

Page leaned back, thoughtful, her lips pursed. She leveled her eyes and took a deep breath. "You mean about Henri trying to put the make on you?"

June couldn't conceal her surprise. "But—but how did you know? Did he tell you?"

Page threw up her hands to stem the flow of startled questions. "Of course not," she said, quick to allay June's apprehension. "He never said anything. He wouldn't."

"Then how did you suspect?"

"Honey, I know him pretty well. It was written all over him." Page showed a half-smile. "Did it work?"

"I won't lie to you, Page. It would have. I was so—so—"

"Frustrated?"

June took a deep breath and exhaled slowly. "Yes," she said, her eyes lowered.

"Did it help?"

June looked up suddenly. "Oh, but—you don't understand. We didn't—"

"I don't get you."

"Michael walked in on us."

Page nearly choked with laughter.

June couldn't help smiling. "So it's not only Henri who has bad timing." She rested her hand on Page's arm. "I'm sorry. I never meant to pry."

Page waved aside any apologies. "Don't be silly. Henri is what he is, and we've made no promises to each other."

She leaned forward, her voice almost a whisper. "What happened? You *must* tell me."

June shrugged. "I told you it wasn't good."

"Did old granite-head go after him?"

"Yes," she said quietly.

"Bad?"

"I think they might have killed each other if I hadn't stopped them."

Page whistled, delighted. "That explains the rest of it, then," she said.

"I don't understand," June prompted her.

"The other day," Page began, "I was in the tube, going past the dining area. The two of them were in there—alone, I guess. They were having it out—pretty badly. Just words," she said with a grin, watching June's expression of relief. "But they were pretty good words."

"What about?"

"Henri told Mike he was acting like a Prussian son of a bitch," Page said. "Something about minding his own damned business."

"Yes," June said quietly. "I've heard him say that before."

"I bet you have," Page said, chuckling. "Well,

they were going back and forth, and Mike was telling Henri that either he toed the mark or there'd be hell to pay."

"What happened?"

"Henri said he had a job to do and he would do it, and he wasn't interested in anything else that Colonel Harder had to say on the subject. He said something about what the hell could Mike do about it?" Page became serious. "You know, he's right, too. What could Mike do?"

June didn't think it funny. "He's a very proud man, Page," she said. "He is quite liable to do something drastic. Do you think there will be trouble between them?"

"Haven't we got enough for starters? Henri makes a pass at Mike's girl—Mike gives Henri rules on how to behave himself—Henri tells Mike to go to hell—and from what you've said in just a few well-chosen words, they tried to tear each other limb from limb. Then they square off at each other and start over again."

"Did they—?"

Page shook her head. "Uh-uh," she said. "I figured it had gone far enough, so I made a lot of noise coming in through the hatchway. I really didn't want any coffee, but I figured if I was there they'd cool it."

"That was wise of you."

"What the hell, June, they're all we've got."

"Do you think there will be more trouble between them?"

"I doubt it. They're both suffering from cabin fever," Page said. "Just healthy young boys with their dander up."

"It's difficult to think of Michael as a young boy, as you put it." June smiled.

Page suddenly became serious. "What happens

later," she asked, gesturing, "when this is all over? We've only got another week or so up here."

June didn't answer.

Page pressed the point. "Is it Peter?"

June shook her head. "It's almost as if he no longer existed."

"Does Mike know that?"

"I think so." June was silent for a moment. "Oh, I don't know, Page," she said fretfully. "It's all so confusing."

Page looked directly at her friend. "Don't lose him, honey."

She hadn't thought of it like that. June felt a stab of fear. "Do you think—?"

Page squeezed her hand gently. "I haven't spent my life picking flowers," she said. "I've learned a few things along the way. When you run across someone like Mike Harder, and you want him, you don't sit around waiting for things to happen. One day you'll look up and he'll be gone. You *do* want him, don't you?"

June averted her gaze. "Of course," she whispered.

"Then go after him."

They pressed closer to the viewports. A puff of vapor appeared, then another, and several more, as the thrusters of the cassette adjusted attitude to precisely the right angle.

"Ten seconds," Parsons announced. He counted down to zero. Faster than they could follow the sequence, a howling sheet of flame leaped into being, sprayed back. There was absolute silence. They saw the violent flame only for a moment. The cassette never seemed to move. One moment it was there, then flame appeared and the cassette vanished, hurled out of sight. It left behind a huge plasma, coruscating from within, chemicals and vapors still aglow with life. This, too, began to fade and finally fell behind the station. The show was over.

Tim Pollard felt a quiet sense of jubilation as the glowing plasma faded swiftly from view. A study of the tall and lanky scientist would have shown little of the emotion diffusing his thoughts. Yet he was deeply affected. The culmination of a great research program had been reached; Pollard knew his name would rest forever in the halls of astronomy. But it was more than that. Pollard was a simple man, yet despite his cautious methods he had become known as a brilliant, outspoken maverick of the new generation of astronomers.

An unquestioned genius, he had nevertheless earned the castigation of his elders for a lack of restraint they felt necessary for a member of their profession. Undaunted by what he considered superfluous criticism, Pollard continued on his own path, flinging about theories recklessly, and proving distressingly destructive to long-established and cherished beliefs. Some called him a second Fred Hoyle. Whatever the description, Pollard remained true to himself. He believed it necessary to venture past the range of the viewing scope and the photographic plates of the observatories that were the hallowed ground of astronomy. He had proved to be as adept in his work as he was with his heretical theories.

After a brilliant scholastic career, during which he had accumulated honors much as an outstanding athlete would accrue letters, Pollard had ventured into the interrelated disciplines of optical and radio astronomy. Again his associates insisted he should pursue one or the other of the two spheres. To such criticism Pollard maintained an air of massive indifference. "The only proper manner in which one should treat the harping of those cemented in their fossilized ideas," he proclaimed, "is quite the same manner with which the ancient Greeks treated migraine headache. With contempt."

Pollard spent much time at Jodrell Bank Observatory, using the world's most powerful and sensitive radio telescope with daring concepts and brilliant results, which led him to produce heatedly disputed statements and theories on the nature of the universe. During his tenure with Jodrell Bank there was a more practical and immediate aspect of his work. Pollard and other British scientists participated in deep-space tracking both of Russian and American spacecraft. To Pollard this was immensely satisfying.

He was not sanguine about the accuracy of optical telescopes in determining details and characteristics of even nearby bodies in space. Certainly the photographs taken by the 100- and 200-inch telescopes of the Wilson and Palomar observatories could not hold a candle to the spectacular pictures televised back from the moon by the comparatively crude Ranger spacecraft of the United States. The Luna and Surveyor pictures taken on the surface of the moon, the Orbiter panoramas of the front and invisible sides of that lifeless world, the astounding pictures sent back by Mariner from Mars, the stirring achievement of the Russian soft-lander on Venus—these, he felt, constituted true meaning in tangible, vital knowledge.

The space beyond Earth fascinated Pollard because he believed fervently that only from that vantage point could the astronomer really be able to study the universe. He was not concerned with the piddling lake formed by the solar system, but with the great depths beyond. He was drawn magnetically to galaxies and nebulae, to star clusters and nova. He spent half his thinking life millions of light-years from the tiny planet on which he stood. He was obsessed with the idea of astronomical instruments placed beyond the atmosphere where they would be free of the maddening distortions inherent in the turbulent gaseous ocean.

He accepted invitations to carry out research work at Lick, Wilson, and Palomar observatories in the United States. It was a fortuitous acceptance on his part, for it thrust him directly into the hardware center of the American space effort. His exposure to the aerospace industry, which sprawled across southern California, whetted his appetite for astronomical studies from the vantage point of deep space. Tim Pollard, to the dismay of his wife, Sarah, who tempered all such enthusiasm with the drudging reality of six small children, made a vow that one way or the other he was going to get to a point high enough above the earth so that, at least once in his life, he would have an unobstructed view of celestial splendor.

NASA saw in his presence the opportunity to gain much from his experience and, discarding the reports of scientific heresy that followed on Pollard's heels, invited him inside the NASA fold as a consultant on deep-space radio tracking of unmanned and manned spacecraft. Pollard seized the opportunity. Within a short time he found himself in great demand, and served as a consultant to the British and Canadian governments whose satellites were being launched from Vandenberg Air Force Base in California atop NASA boosters. But Pollard's most heartfelt enthusiasm was reserved for his work with those scientists who sent telescopes and other instruments in giant, swaying balloons to the upper reaches of the atmosphere. In a vicarious fashion Pollard was getting his unobstructed peek at the universe. It wasn't enough, and it redoubled his determination to sustain the vow made to Sarah.

With his ear to the doors of the aerospace industry, Pollard was in close touch with the thinking that would result in the *Epsilon* space station. It was like the sound of the bell to an old fire horse. Tim Pollard knew the British government would be invited to submit a scientist-astronaut for the forthcoming station, and he lost no time in flying home to England to pound on official doors. He succeeded admirably in making an intolerable nuisance of himself so that belabored officials only wished they *could* dispatch him into space, just to be rid of him. An overjoyed Pollard received the word—he was "in."

The RAF whisked him off to a test center and put the lanky scientist through an intensive flight training course mixed with liberal doses of severe physical training that Pollard looked upon as refined torture. He breezed through the scientific aspects of his training with an offhand, mild contempt that did much to restore an ego battered at the hands of those who felt he should be trained to Olympic stature.

Six months after being drawn within the folds of the Royal Air Force, Pollard flew jet trainers with a better-than-even chance of surviving his flights, and was packed off to Houston. NASA scientists, astronauts, and engineers hammered him with the technical details of boosters, spacecraft, and their systems. The reasoning was sound. In the event of disaster, NASA wanted the added insurance of its scientists being able to perform as astronauts.

In late 1970, Timothy Pollard became the first British subject to become an astronaut as a crew member aboard an Apollo Applications Program mission in Earth orbit, during which he was the primary scientist testing the systems of a massive optical telescope. He had realized the dream that had remained constant all these years. But it was *Epsilon* that fired his imagination. Six months in orbit! Extensive equipment with which to work; equipment that he would help to design and build. The opportunity to break down a domino-row of astronomical barriers had finally arrived.

And now the primary mission was history; the final glowing tendrils of the plasma cloud were swallowed up in vacuum. Pollard had intended to spend his last week in space strictly on his own projects, taking advantage of the leisure time to study the planet spinning below, to experiment with his own fears in weightlessness within the S-IVB tank. But now this new experiment posed a rare opportunity, indeed! The chance to snatch from space the original debris of the solar system would be a heady finale to his long months in orbit.

When he first read the message that Earth would be moving through an area of dust, he felt that the chance to obtain this material would be impossible. Even a "heavy concentration" of dust in space was close to vacuum. Still, there was the opportunity, and the others believed the problems much less severe than did Pollard. If only they were right.

They could be on the brink of significant breakthroughs in understanding not only the formation of the solar system, but of the origins of life within the system. From that dust, which would undergo meticulous examinations by the world's leading scientists, mysteries could be unlocked that for centuries had confounded all who had sought the truths of the worlds they saw about them. The potential of those studies thrilled him much as unexpected findings must have exalted archeologists uncovering bones from the dust of centuries.

Pollard spent hours discussing the matter with Earthbound scientists. The dust, it appeared, was not simply a cloud of tenuous matter orbiting the earth. It had been discovered through its interference on astronomical plates; long exposure had revealed what ordinarily would have gone unnoticed. If the preliminary calculations were correct, then this vaporous swirl of material was moving in a high orbit through the solar system—a tenuous mass, barely detectable, that swung far beyond the reaches of the outermost planet. This thought alone excited Pollard.

He brought to mind the theory put forth many years before by the distinguished Swedish scientist, Svante Arrhenius, who had propounded the panspermia concept, that all life forms had a common origin in a single creation, and that the ultramicroscopic "seeds" of this proto-life were distributed, at random, through the vastness of space. The proto-life continued to be distributed by gravitational tides that locked galaxies in their grip, and were flung immeasurable distances by pressures no greater than the light of stars.

Perhaps this dust they sought had originated within, and was confined to their own solar system. Well, now they might be able to ascertain some of the answers. They could obtain specimens before it vanished for centuries along its path far beyond Pluto. Even if the material were meteoroid, the opportunity would be no less unique; they could examine such matter before its contamination through exposure to water vapor, the debris floating in the planetary atmosphere, and terrestrial microorganisms.

Material indigenous to the solar system could still reveal answers sought for hundreds of years by scientists of many disciplines. It might be possible to discover within this dust microorganisms alien to the forms known on Earth. Such a find, confirmed and unquestioned, could rock several of the sciences down to their foundations. The presence of such organisms would lend solid proof to the theory of Arrhenius, and others, that life-forms existed in space long before life began to stir on Earth itself. Could it be true that life came to the worlds around stars through the inter-galactic seeding of proto-life?

These were the questions, Pollard knew, to stir the souls of men. He said a small prayer of thanks that he might have some role in seeking out the answers.

Chapter IX

"Watch that cable!" Mike Harder shouted the angry warning to Page Alison and Tim Pollard.

The two scientists looked up in surprise to see a cable snaking dangerously close.

"Tim, you and Page get the hell out from under," Harder ordered. "If that cable catches you right, it'll bust an arm." He switched off suddenly and went back to directing the efforts of Jordan and Parsons.

Pollard and Page Alison thrusted upward to safety and watched.

"Bill—she all played out?" Harder called to Jordan for a status check on the first cable.

"Stand by one," Jordan grunted. He was braced within the airlock servicing room, playing out the last of a hundred-yard length of lightweight steel cable. He checked off the marker and tightened the friction locks. "All set, Mike," he replied. "Full length and locked. How does it look from there?"

Harder examined the cable. Drifting well above

the station, he had a perfect view of the way the cable extended. "She's trailing a bit," he said. "Got some snaking in the line I don't like."

"Resonance? We shouldn't have that much." Jordan was puzzled by the quivering motions Harder reported to him. "Mike, what do you think about some extra mass on the end?"

"Should do it, I think. Clip a couple more weights to the next one, and let's see what happens."

"Okay. Hang loose," Jordan said. He wired several wrenches to the end of a coiled cable, checked the security, and began playing out the cable through an open hatch. "Here she comes," he warned.

"Got it," Harder confirmed. "Nice and tight so far."

"I'll let it out a bit slower this time," Jordan said. "It should damp out the motions."

For several minutes Harder was silent. Then he called in again to Jordan. "Bill, it looks good. No twisting this time."

"Roger. I'll keep it coming this way."

Several hundred feet above the station, Page Alison and Tim Pollard drifted together, eager observers of the cables extending outward from the airlock hatch. "By God," Pollard exulted, "it's working. You see it, Page? It's working!"

She laughed at his excitement. "Not all of it yet," she corrected. "See the first cable? They're pulling it in."

"A mere detail," he said. "Apparently Jordan wants to get some more weight at the end." Several minutes later he pointed to the airlock. "See? They'll be all set in a few minutes." He strained to see the collection bottles. "I can't see the blasted things," he complained. "Can you make them out?"

Page caught the reflection of light from a shiny

surface. "There they are," she said quickly. "You've got to catch them just right, when the light shines on them."

"I'm going down for a closer look," he said.

Page grabbed his arm. "No you're not," she said firmly. "Mike will brain you. Leave the details to them."

Pollard grumbled into his microphone. "I suppose so," he muttered.

Harder heard their remarks. "You can relax now, Tim," he called to them. "They're all out, and they'll stay."

"Aren't you going to inspect them?" Pollard asked.

"What for?" Harder sounded indignant that Pollard should miss the obvious. "You'd have to chase them around. Besides, if you grab that cable the wrong way you'll mess up the balance."

"Oh." Page smiled to herself. Pollard sounded like a small boy denied the chance to play with his newest toy.

"You can see everything you need to with binoculars," Harder continued. "Okay?"

Pollard hadn't thought of that. "Of course, Mike," he replied. "That should do it nicely."

"Anything else? A guided tour? A dedication of the Pollard-Alison Space Bug Collecting Society?"

"No, thank you," Pollard said acidly. "Your barbaric sarcasm has glutted me for the moment."

Harder laughed. "Okay, let's go inside."

They thrusted carefully to the long tank of *Epsilon*, maneuvered to match speed with the rotating cylinder, and grabbed at the guide cables. They worked their way to the open airlock and clambered inside. Several minutes later Bill Jordan signified full pressure and they opened their helmets. Now all they had to do was wait.

*   *   *

The centrifugal force of rotation assured the cables' extending outward for a hundred yards from the "down" end of the S-II cylinder. Along each of the three cables were six plastiglass containers with snapseal lids open. The eighteen jars swung in a giant circle. When *Epsilon* passed through the cloud, particles of dust would be trapped in the jars, rotational movement keeping them there until the seals could be closed.

Two days later, they had visible proof of the enigmatic cloud. *Epsilon* orbited nightside when the atmosphere beneath them flickered with needle-thin streaks of flame that were produced by minute particles of rock. With velocities anywhere up to a hundred thousand miles per hour, even a pinpoint creates a dazzling display. At the peak intensity of the cloud, the earth seemed covered with a canopy of darting fireflies.

One "night" the summons from general quarters brought them tumbling out of their beds. The Geophysics Compartment on Level 9 had taken a meteoroid strike from a chunk about the size of a pea. The meteoroid punched into the outer bumper, pulverized metal, and gave up most of its energy. There was enough remaining to blast several holes in the compartment wall. Instantly the temperature shot up, followed by a steady drop in compartment air pressure. This set off the alarm.

Swiftly they slipped into emergency suits and checked the boards. Harder called for voice verification; everyone checked in immediately. Parsons notified Harder of the puncture in Level 9. He reported also that the automatic systems had closed off the level and were replacing the air lost through the breaks.

Harder and Parsons moved quickly to the scene where they released a brightly-colored spray. Within seconds they located the punctures by the flow of the spray where air whistled out into space. They applied an emergency sealing patch to the breaks, and increased the compartment pressure from its normal six-to-fifteen pounds per square inch. One hole, invisible to the naked eye, revealed itself by the slow movement of the spray. They brought the pressure back down to station normal and cancelled emergency status. An hour later, Jordan and Guy-Michel were outside the station to repair the outer meteor bumper and the exterior station wall. End of emergency.

The next day they retrieved the plastiglass containers, the lids sealed tightly. Ten jars were stored in the upper airlock room, to be returned to Earth for examination by scientists in the United States, England, France, Norway, and West Germany, as they had requested. Page Alison and Tim Pollard carried the other eight jars to the Life Sciences compartment on Level 12. There, under the light gravity of the station, they would begin a meticulous study of the dust. Page could hardly wait to place specimens in various solutions to see, as Pollard put the matter laughingly, "what crawls out to say hello."

Life within *Epsilon* entered a subtle but noticeable change. The time was now close to the period earmarked for going "home," and the sense of identification with the station and their group became almost a live force among them. There were the inevitable mixed emotions of regret at leaving what they had created, and the eagerness to pick up where they had left off "down there." As scientists, they were busy assembling the bits and pieces of their long months of work.

Dr. Koelbe, ever observant, and dutifully making notes in his records, smiled at the unavoidable tendency of them all to act as if there weren't sufficient time to get everything in order before the spacecraft boosted up from Cape Kennedy. There was also a fumbling about their action which they failed to understand but he could comprehend.

In the sharing of dangers and successes they had made of *Epsilon* more than a scientific project and more than a collective victory in an environment of constant danger. It had become a part of them. It had taken their best, and they understood, consciously or otherwise, that what they had created could never again be achieved in the same manner. Most of the results of their experiments and tests had long since been transmitted to Earth. Radio and television transmission, and the firing of equipment cassettes, had guaranteed that there would be no loss of the vital information derived from their mission far above the planet, even if some unexpected disaster in space should obliterate them all. There had been constant checking, monitoring, reporting—a Niagara-like flow to receivers waiting on Earth.

At the same time, Koelbe and the others realized, there was so much more to be returned in the form of their own persons. The impressions upon minds, recollections, crosschecking, conclusions, observations, visualizations, and, above all, their individual and collective interpretations. For years to come, what they had accomplished would stoke the fires of new planning, would create the material from which a vast new base of knowledge would be built. Man had determined to make space an environment of which, one day, he would be knowledgeable, within which he would be secure, and over which he would be master. Just as he was on Earth.

For Werner Koelbe, it had not been easy. There had been a cross to bear. Koelbe was still mildly surprised that he had been accepted as a member of *Epsilon*. For a while it seemed that he had come as a social leper into their midst.

"Please sit down."

Koelbe took his chair carefully, his eyes never leaving those of the man across the desk from him. Colonel Harder extended a cigar box but Koelbe smiled thinly and shook his head. Harder withdrew a cigar, clipped off the end, and lit up.

I wonder if he is like the others, thought Koelbe. *He is confident, this man. Completely certain of himself. The reports must be true that with him rests the final decision. But if he is like all the rest of them. . . .*

Suddenly he felt a taste of nausea. It all seemed so futile. One could not run forever from ghosts. Koelbe had been surrounded by phantoms as long as he could remember—phantoms that materialized in human form to point accusing fingers at him. It didn't matter that there was no guilt. Some people believed inheritance to be as much a factor as a commission of deeds.

The colonel tapped his finger on a thick file before him. Koelbe knew it was his complete record. Idly he wondered if they contained—

"I see you've completed your flight training."

Koelbe nodded. Why did the colonel have to engage in idle conversation? He knew full well that Koelbe had completed his jet training. He knew what time Koelbe woke up in the morning, when and how he brushed his teeth, how long after breakfast he went to the bathroom. He knew everything, and, Koelbe thought bitterly, he knew nothing. Statistical reports paint meaningless pictures, and Harder must be aware of that.

"How did you like the flying?" The question came softly and Koelbe knew it was loaded.

The doctor shook his head. "I did not," he said ruefully. "There is so much else I have to do, and those machines demand all your attention. They are terrible masters."

Harder gestured at the file on Koelbe. "Johnson says you're good."

His instructor had said that? "I'm afraid Johnson is only happy when his feet are off the ground," Koelbe said. "He would be kind to anyone who went along for the ride."

"Well, he's given you a good report," Harder said. "For the record, you're all through with flight training."

"Ah. That is good to hear." Koelbe eyed Harder warily. There was no use in delaying things. "Is there anything special you wished to bring up, Colonel?"

Harder opened the file and brushed through its contents. Koelbe tried not to lean forward to see the papers. There was an air of finality about Harder that dismayed him, as if his worst fears about this man were to be realized. When the colonel spoke, his words were like a thunderclap.

"We may as well get this out in the open, Doctor. I want to talk about your father."

Koelbe said goodbye to his chances for *Epsilon*.

If Pollard came into *Epsilon* with an air of quiet competence, and Guy-Michel with the reputation of a satyr, then Dr. Werner Koelbe brought with him a storm of controversy and condemnation. The good doctor represented Germany which, to a voluble press in Communist lands, was still a nation where the dreams of the Third Reich had not been fully expunged.

Germany, claimed the Communist press from Moscow to Havana, should not be brought into a position of authority in space any more than the German army should be provided with nuclear weapons. That one lone doctor, thirty-four years old, had been a mere child when the Nazis flourished, and was not even remotely a source of danger to anyone, appeared to have been overlooked—as was the fact that the space station would have an international crew and would not be armed with so much as a slingshot. Nevertheless, hysteria was created deliberately, and, to the surprise of NASA, quite effectively. The decision to provide Dr. Werner Koelbe—on leave of absence from the Berlin Institute for Advanced Technology—with advanced training as a possible member of *Epsilon* raised a storm that caught the space agency off balance. What should have been a tempest in a teapot boiled over.

Incited by the bellicose condemnation from Moscow, Latin and South American nations, in particular, took the position that the candidacy of Koelbe, without representation from the Americas, was nothing less than a calculated affront. The Japanese, providentially ignoring their own role in recent martial history, seized upon the opportunity to echo South American sentiments, and announced their intention to join in space ventures with the Soviets.

Through all this, Dr. Werner Koelbe maintained an air of indifference, surprising in a man of his age who was being subjected to such widespread castigation. Few people realized the falsity of the indifference, that Koelbe had withdrawn behind a hard shell cultivated long before this moment. He appraised with keen insight the official American position which, rather than being a defense of Koelbe, was a cold rejection of outside interference, stating that NASA alone knew what was best for NASA.

In Germany there was an unprecedented sense of alliance with the Americans. German pride in the selection of Koelbe as a possible astronaut soared. The surviving veterans of the early rocket experiments in Germany saw in Koelbe a German taking his rightful place in the march to the stars. He was an outstanding scientist, had participated in experiments with the American biosatellites that sent plants, insects, and animals into orbit to examine their reactions to prolonged weightlessness. German magazines and newspapers feted the Koelbe family, and made much of his wife, Renata, and their three fair-haired children. He was idolized as the "new German," dedicated by fate to join with scientists of other nations in the great adventures that would see man walking the surfaces of other worlds. Certainly Koelbe was the personification of such national idolatry. He stood five-feet-eleven-inches tall, and was a quiet, obviously rugged individual. Light blond hair, and blue eyes set deep in a strong face, inevitably brought to mind the uncomfortable description—"Aryan."

There were other outcries. Those who wished to go themselves, or who saw unquestionable reasons for others than Koelbe to join the *Epsilon* crew, claimed favoritism on the part of the old-line Germans such as Doctors Wernher von Braun and Kurt Debus. No matter that all such bedevilments of Koelbe were unfounded, or that West Germany had accepted a major share of the financial burden, or even that Koelbe was among the elite who had qualified, he was still soundly damned in much of the world press.

But the worst had never happened. Koelbe lived every day with the gnawing fear that someone would rip away the veneer covering his past and, in that single calamitous move, vaporize his hopes for *Epsilon*. It had not happened. But he knew the records were being sifted; the reporters were searching, digging. There were ugly rumors. Koelbe adopted an air of resignation. He would continue to work. He would not denounce his own hopes, but neither would he be blind to what the future might contain for him.

Now the worst was at hand. Somehow, Harder and the others had found out. Koelbe *knew* the terrible secret lay in the papers on the colonel's desk. What had he said?

"I want to talk about your father."

All right, damn you, then talk. Werner Koelbe was suddenly very tired of running from the past.

"What do you wish to know, Colonel Harder?" Koelbe couldn't control his voice. He heard his almost shrill tone and cursed himself for the lack of self-control he wanted desperately at this moment.

"Look, Werner," Harder said suddenly, "I'm aware that this isn't pleasant for you. I'm not grilling you, man. And I'm not pointing fingers. But if you make this team, we're all going to be living in each other's hip pocket. It's better all the way around if we get this—" he rapped his knuckles against the file—"out in the open."

Koelbe clenched his teeth. "You Americans have a favorite expression," he said bitterly. "Let sleeping dogs lie."

Harder studied the other man. "Yes, we can do that," he said, his voice deceptively soft. Koelbe was startled by the abrupt shift in tone. "You can tell me to go to hell and you can get up and walk out of this room, and I give you my word of honor that this file will never be opened."

The silence was ugly. Koelbe very nearly did just what Harder proposed. The other man was right. He didn't have to be subjected to anything from Harder or anyone else. But . . . it was the colonel, and not himself, who had said that.

"Maybe you don't understand, Doctor," Harder said finally. "I have no interest in the contents of this file. I don't give a damn about what happened twenty or thirty years ago."

The startled expression on Koelbe's face spoke more than words. "But, why then are you—"

"Let me finish, please. I don't care about the past, but I have the greatest interest in what happens in that station we're going to send up. If it so happens that you're selected, and you already know you're running out in front, I don't want problems cropping up on me. Not," he said emphatically, "when I can get rid of them now."

He looked carefully at the German doctor, who sat slumped in his chair. "If you feel I'm prying, say so. That door you came in works both ways." Harder took time deliberately to bring a match to his cigar, and thought: *He doesn't know he's made the team, and I can't tell him yet. Not until he beats this. The last thing I want in that station is a man with ghosts trailing after him.* Harder leaned forward. "Your name isn't Koelbe."

Deep within him Koelbe sighed. The relief that rushed through his body was overwhelming. Now it would be out in the open. No more shadows. Thank God! To get it over with, not to hide from himself! He returned Harder's gaze and shook his head.

"Bayerlein. Hans Bayerlein." His voice was hoarse.

Harder nodded slowly. "Your wife doesn't know, does she?"

"No, of course not. I could never tell Renata."

"That's a matter of opinion."

Koelbe looked up, startled. "What do you mean?"

"Hell, you've passed sentence on yourself, Doctor," Harder said. "Judge, jury, and executioner. Maybe you've been wrong all this time."

Koelbe looked at him, eyes narrowed to slits. "That is easy for you to say."

Harder laughed harshly. "Do you hate my father?"

"What?"

"The question is simple enough. I asked you if you hated my father."

Koelbe looked at Harder as if he had gone crazy. "*Your* father? Of course not. I don't know him. Why should I hate him?"

"You're a German."

Koelbe didn't answer. This whole thing was insane.

"Bremen, Kiel, Berlin, Dresden, Stuttgart, Schweinfurt, Hamburg. That'll do for a starter," Harder said.

"I don't understand you, Colonel."

"No, I daresay you don't. You know those cities, of course."

"Of course."

"My father bombed them. Steve Harder. He flew a B-17. He bombed those cities, and many more, I suppose. All told, he dropped about four hundred tons of bombs on those cities." Harder's face was inscrutable. "Now I'll ask you again. Do you hate my father?"

When there was no answer, he said, "Let me change the question, Doctor. Do you hate *me?*"

Koelbe gripped the chair. "If I did not know better," he said tightly, "I would say you are going mad."

Harder chuckled. "I'm not. But I wondered if you hated me because my father bombed German cities. For almost certainly he killed women and children, destroyed homes and factories, maimed and crippled people for life. German women, German children, German homes. *Your* people."

Koelbe gaped at him.

"All right, then," Harder said, his voice flat. "Let's get it over with. Your father was Otto Bayerlein. He was a major in the SS. He was responsible for the torture and the killing of several thousand helpless people. He was a hangman. Otto Bayerlein. Killer. Torturer. Murderer. No official proof of his death."

Koelbe wanted to shout at Harder to stop, never again to say. . . .

The colonel's voiced pierced his agony. *"Don't you think we've always known this?"*

"You—all this time, you *knew?*"

Harder closed the file with a gesture of finality. "Of course. I had these papers before I ever met you. Maybe you find this difficult to believe, but I don't give a damn about your father or what he did. No more," he said slowly, "than you would have it in for me because of a man named Steve Harder."

"But not everyone else will have your attitude, will they?" Koelbe forced a smile.

"Perhaps not," Harder acknowledged. "However, they don't make the decisions around here."

"Ah, and you do. But not completely."

"No, not completely. Six other people know the contents of this file and they don't give a damn either."

"Who—who are they?"

"That's none of your affair, Doctor."

Koelbe couldn't believe it. All the time they had known! He had worried himself sick about. . . . The smile that came to his face this time was genuine. He had a great deal to say but it came out in only two words. "Thank you," he whispered.

Harder crossed the room to a safe and placed the file inside. The heavy steel door closed with a muffled thud. He returned to his desk and looked at Koelbe.

"We need a medical scientist and a doctor in *Epsilon*. A man named Koelbe has qualified for that position. Time's running out, and I need his answer now."

Koelbe didn't trust himself to speak. But there was no doubt about his hand gripping Harder's.

Bill Jordan stretched out on his bed, hands clasped behind his head. He wriggled his toes and belched. "You know, it's crazy," he said.

Luke Parsons looked up from his desk where he was busy assembling his meager personal belongings. He would leave almost everything behind when they deorbited and started home.

"What's crazy?" he asked.

"For nearly six months I've been dying for a cigarette," Jordan said. "I went off smoking three months before we came up here. Getting ready, I suppose." He grinned. "I've been out of my mind for a smoke. Now we're going home in a week, and I couldn't care less."

"You know the old line," Parsons said. "The grass is always greener, and that sort of jazz."

"I suppose so. Luke, what do you think we'll be doing after we get back?"

"Evaluations, I suppose. Then they'll stick us in training. All those new space cadets are going to need older and wiser leaders."

Jordan laughed. "And that's us?"

"Yep, that's us."

"Well, I'll tell you something," Jordan said. "The first starry-eyed kid that comes up to me and says 'sir' and asks for my autograph—I'm gonna kick him right in the slats. I don't feel so much older and wiser." He swung off the bunk to place his feet on the deck. "And I sure don't want to be stuck in training."

"Oh?" Parsons said. "You got ideas?"

Jordan looked wistfully through the viewport where a thin curving moon was visible. He nodded at the scene. "Yeah, that."

Parsons looked at the moon. "Not a chance," he said.

"Why not?"

"Fifty guys are standing in line for their shot at the moon. You know that."

Jordan scowled. "Maybe so. But I don't intend to stay Earthside any longer than I have to."

"There'll be another station, Bill," Parsons said. "I don't mean *Epsilon*. The big one—twenty thousand miles out, and always having the same half of Earth looking up at you."

"They won't cut that job easy," Jordan said. "Take a lot more than it did to put up this tin can."

"They'll do it," Parsons said with assurance. "Two or three years from now."

"I wonder," Jordan said. "It would be fun, I suppose. Think you'd be interested?"

"Ask Henri if he'd like to get laid," Parsons shot back. "What about you?"

Jordan smiled at him. "Wouldn't be right to break up this team, would it?"

Parson's face was sober when he replied. "No, I don't think I'd like that."

*   *   *

Bill Jordan and Luke Parsons had been selected for *Epsilon* more for their skills as a team than for their singular qualifications. Both men were veterans of Apollo flights, and their engineering experience with space systems made them particularly desirable for the critical tasks of station maintenance and operation for the long six-month stay in orbit.

A rapport of mechanical and engineering systems had brought a mild sort of fame to the team of Jordan and Parsons. Early in the planning stages of *Epsilon* their skilled double-teaming had assured their selection for the station. In short order they had become known as the space twins.

As far back as he could remember, Bill Jordan's vision had been enhanced by the stardust he had seen everywhere in his future. Vacuum beckoned to him as had the high reaches of clouds to the preceding generation. Square-jawed, hair cropped short, Jordan was, to the public, the satisfying image of an astronaut; his face had the craggy proportions most people like to associate with explorers and adventurers. But, more important than appearance—among his peers, Bill Jordan remained the tireless idealist of what was to come. He never missed an opportunity to expound his philosophy that they, the astronauts and cosmonauts, were certain to break across to the planets of the solar system.

He spoke with unbridled enthusiasm of microwave-transmitted power for launching monster spacecraft, and he accepted nuclear power as just around the corner. To him the Saturn V was a clumsy ark imposed upon the astronauts by the technological inadequacies of their age. His was a clarion call to space, but he tempered idealism with the reality of firsthand knowledge of the problems to be overcome.

Prior to October of 1966, Jordan, like many of the

other astronauts, was an engineering and experimental test pilot in the Air Force at the flight test center in the California desert. He was unique, yet similar to his peers, for all of them had met the severe requirements for entry into test flying. Jordan was a graduate of Ohio State University, and M.I.T., where he received his master's in electrical engineering; he was also a graduate of the Air Force Experimental Test Pilot Course and the Aerospace Research Pilot School. And, like many of his fellow pilots, he was a happily married man, with a daughter nine years old and a son, eleven, who was (to Jordan's secret delight) the unholy terror of the neighborhood.

Jordan's space twin, Luke Parsons, had graduated from North Georgia Military Academy before enlisting in the Marines. The thirty-five-year-old astronaut held his BA in mechanical engineering, was a graduate of the Navy Test Pilot School at Patuxtent River, Maryland, and as an exchange pilot had gone through the Air Force's Aerospace Research Pilot School. Parsons entered NASA one year later than did Jordan, but by 1969 the two men already had become recognized as a team, and were together for a sixteen-day orbital flight in an Apollo module. Luke considered his own position as "absolutely ordinary" among his select, professional associates. He and his wife Charlotte had twin boys, Gary and Gordon.

Yet the two men, Parsons and Jordan, were far from similar in their attitudes. Where Jordan was the enthusiast, Luke Parsons existed as a stark counterpart. Parsons never waxed eloquent on their roles as spacefaring men. What intrigued Parsons was the machinery within which they cocooned themselves and to which they entrusted their lives. His near and far horizons were filled, as far as the eye might sweep, with the mechanical implements of their pi-

oneering trade. He enjoyed an affinity with machines
that comes to few men; he understood them. His
off-duty hours at Houston were spent in rebuilding
old cars, and in building an airplane he and Jordan
had designed themselves. Parsons' idea of relaxation
was to be buried up to his armpits in gadgets and
machinery; if a motor were to grind with some inner
fault, Parsons would rush to its side, armed with
tools and understanding. He conducted his studies of
Epsilon with an almost religious fervor.

He was never satisfied with the performance of
any station device. He had to know its every cog, be
aware of every movement. To him, the machinery of
Epsilon had to be regarded as a living, functional
entity. There was no one to step forward to fault his
judgment—for *Epsilon*, through all its six months of
exposure to searing heat and bitter cold, to penetrating radiation and scouring meteoric dust, to internal
stresses, and a ceaseless demand for operation every
second of the day, had yet to fail the eight humans
who lived within the cylindrical cocoon.

It was late that "night," during their sleep shift,
that Luke Parsons awoke, a suspicion of alarm just
beyond the edge of consciousness. Normally he was
a sound sleeper, untroubled by dreams or apprehen-
sions. Now he came awake with his sheets matted
with perspiration. In the gloom of the compartment
he sat upright and was surprised to feel his heart
pounding. He threw aside the covers, got up and
walked to the viewport, undogging the shield and
staring out.

The dream, shadowy now and with fading substance, disturbed him.

"What's wrong?"

He turned, startled. Jordan rested on an elbow, looking at him.

Parsons forced a smile. "Nothing, Bill. Just a bad dream, I suppose."

"That's strange. You're the guy who never has funny pictures in his head."

Parsons laughed weakly. "That's me." He didn't want to tell Jordan what he had dreamt: an image of *Epsilon*, clear, sharply defined. Nothing wrong, at first. And then a gray fog had swept over the station, a fog that penetrated the metal seams, shadowed its way through airlocks, and spread everywhere. The station had faded from view, and when the fog disappeared, Parsons in his dream was seeing a gaunt, corroded, ribbed, metal skeleton.

He turned back to the viewport. Still facing away from his friend, he felt the words forming by themselves. "Bill, do you believe in premonitions?"

Jordan thought that one over. "Yeah. Or I *did*, that is." He laughed at himself. "Until I followed a real strong hunch one day, and it blew up in my face."

"What happened?"

Jordan shrugged. "I had the feeling real strong. I just knew something was going to happen."

"And it did?"

"Sure did," Jordan said with a grimace. "I put two hundred on the nose of the filly. The horse fell and broke its leg coming out of the gate."

Parsons didn't laugh. "That isn't what I mean."

Jordan sensed the grave tone. "You sound like something's bugging you, that's for sure."

"Maybe."

"Wanna tell poppa?"

"Oh, it's nothing, really. I suppose, what with our getting ready to clear out of here—" He looked wistfully around the compartment, letting the sentence hang. "Just nerves," he said finally, and without humor. "I just have the feeling that maybe all of us aren't going to get home."

"So that's it! All you airplane drivers are alike," Jordan chuckled. "You're never comfortable when someone else is at the wheel."

"No, nothing like that," Parsons broke in. "That's why it's strange. I just have the feeling that some of us aren't going to get home."

"You mean—stay here?"

Parsons nodded. "Crazy, isn't it?"

Jordan joined him at the viewport and slapped him vigorously on the shoulder. "You're just space-happy," he said. "In another week you'll be home between the sheets with Jeanne, making babies. Then you'll remember this conversation, and realize just how many loose nuts you had rattling around inside that mechanical skull of yours."

"Sure," Parsons said. But he didn't go back to sleep that night.

Chapter X

Bill Jordan stretched, and made a feeble attempt to climb from his bed, then dropped his head back to the pillow. He thought that getting up under one-tenth gravity really wasn't any easier than it was Earthside. He didn't like leaping from his sheets. Balls to that nonsense. But Luke did just that. Every morning he came out of the sack prepared to do battle with the world, alert and sensitive. Jordan met the day with a ponderous yawn. And lecherous thoughts. Another week and he'd wake up in the morning with Charlotte by his side. He thought of his wife and sat up abruptly. The first thing I need *now*—he laughed—is a cold shower. Have to watch that sort of thing.

He sat with his feet on the deck and shivered. Damn Luke and his cold air at night. Jordan yawned again, scratched his side and shuffled across the compartment to the thermostat. He dialed in another ten degrees and headed for the bathroom. Luke was already gone. He probably already had his ear to a pump. He could listen to the damn thing and tell which bearing had a scratch on its side. Machines purred to Luke and told him things. Having Luke Parsons around was a rabbit's foot that worked.

They had plastered the bathroom with signs. *Remember—Good Aim Is Everything at 1/10 G!* Wasn't it, though? A little bit went a long way up here. Jordan stood before the toilet and grinned. *Stand Close And Aim Carefully—The Next Space Cadet May Be Barefoot.* Some day, Jordan grunted, I'm going to hit that damn sign dead-center.

He rubbed his chin and felt the stubble. His beard grew faster under this light gravity. If he went two days without a shave it itched like hell. He opened the wall cabinet and plugged in the electric razor. Hold it! Forgot the lotion. He unscrewed the before-shaving lotion, rubbed it into the palms of his hands, and looked into the mirror.

In the first moment he didn't believe it. The thought came that somehow Luke had rigged up a joke. But it wasn't that. He jerked back from the sight, and the face in the mirror responded. Jordan took a deep breath. Across the left side of his face was a mottled rash. He brought up his hand but stopped his fingers just before they touched the angry skin. The discoloration, red and in places a dark purple, extended from the side of his temple down his entire cheek. He leaned forward to get better light and saw that the skin had raised slightly in welts.

"Jesus Christ," he swore softly. He turned to examine the right side of his face. Nothing there. Carefully he examined his body, turning from side to side, raising his arms. The rash, or whatever the hell

it was, was also under his left arm. He brought his
fingers to the angry skin and winced. It hurt.

Jordan quelled his sudden alarm with a shaky laugh.
You're acting like a scared schoolgirl, he reprimanded
himself. Getting a sudden rash, or other skin problems wasn't so strange in a station. He knew that. It
wasn't the first time he'd seen an outbreak of this
sort on someone cooped up in the artificial world of a
space cabin. *But nothing like this*, he said to himself.
And his own voice answered immediately. "So what?
Are you an expert? There's a doctor here. Remember? Stop playing guessing games with yourself."

He walked slowly across to the intercom, forcing
himself to keep from making a hurried dash across
the room. He knew skin problems weren't rare. He
reminded himself again of that. All sorts of strange
things happened in a spaceship atmosphere. One
time an Apollo mission had been brought back to
Earth after only six days out of a planned thirty. One
of the astronauts had broken out from head to foot in
bumps that swelled up so badly he could hardly get
back into his suit.

It had taken the medics a week to find the cause.
One of the new fire-retardant chemicals had reacted
on his skin. It hadn't showed up in the ground tests.
It took the peculiarities of zero-g, and time, to mix
the stuff with his skin. And then it was a dilly. When
they'd taken him out of the command module he'd
looked as if a thousand wasps had worked him over.
In a couple days it had gone away. Now, by the time
he reached the intercom, Jordan figured that this
was pretty much the same thing. But it was strange,
he reflected, that it would show up at this point, instead of at any time during the preceding six months.
Well, let Koelbe figure it out. He punched the numbers for Koelbe's quarters. The doctor was still asleep

but he came awake in a hurry. He told Jordan to come to Level 11 immediately.

All doctors are the same, Jordan thought wearily. Koelbe had poked and prodded and tested and examined and asked questions for an hour. Then he leaned back in his chair, chewed the end of his pen, and admitted that he had no idea what was causing the outbreak on Jordan's skin.

"I'm puzzled," he said.

"That makes two of us," Jordan added wryly.

"Yes, I'm sure of that," Koelbe laughed. "But I don't think there's any cause for alarm. You know even better than I do how these things happen in this sort of environment."

Jordan nodded. "Did you read the report on McIntyre?" he asked, referring to the astronaut who'd been stricken in the Apollo.

"Yes. That's precisely what I mean," Koelbe said. "It could be anything."

"What about the specimens you took?"

Koelbe shrugged. "Nothing. The skin is irritated, of course. The swelling is from a concentration of blood along the surface. That isn't unusual. Do not be alarmed if there is some bleeding. That, too, is common."

Jordan looked sharply at the doctor. He didn't know that. He'd never heard of open sores or bleeding aboard a ship. He said as much to Koelbe.

"The concentration of blood would cause that," the doctor said. "If you brush against something, for example. The skin is under pressure. It would be easy to have bleeding then."

"All right," Jordan said. "What's next?"

"Rest," Koelbe said quickly. "There's no use irritating what's there. I want to examine the skin specimens and blood samples a little more thoroughly. In the meantime I suggest you take it easy. No work," he said firmly. He was lost in his own thoughts for several moments. "I think we will give you some antibiotics as a precaution. There's no evidence of infection, but we may as well play it on the safe side."

Jordan rolled up his sleeve and smiled bleakly. "Okay by me. Shoot."

"That's not the question," Koelbe said. "It's not a happenstance matter of being alarmed at something strange. I'm disturbed, have no doubt of that. I don't like a situation where I have no idea of what is happening to my patient. And I have never seen anything quite like this."

Mike Harder always looked for hidden meanings. Koelbe was giving him plenty. Harder didn't miss the reference to Jordan as "my patient." That was a long way from a minor skin irritation. Whatever Jordan had picked up was bothering Koelbe even more than he indicated.

"Have you checked with Houston?" Harder asked.

"Of course. I spoke with Zystra."

That surprised Harder. Dick Zystra was the medical director for *Epsilon*. He didn't think a rash, or a skin irritation, was cause for going that high up the ladder, and he said so to Koelbe.

"If I knew what Bill had," Koelbe explained, "I'd never have bothered. But I don't know. And I don't know where it will go. I can't play guessing games, Mike. This may be a big fuss over nothing, but I can't be sure, and certainly I can't take chances. In this closed environment"—he waved his arm to encompass the station—"there's no getting away from something that may break loose."

"You think that's possible?" Harder's face was blank.

"I don't *know*," Koelbe said with a sense of exasperation. "And what I don't know makes me uneasy."

"Then you did exactly what you were supposed to do," Harder said quickly. He reviewed what Koelbe had told him so far. "What about Bill? How does he feel about this?"

Koelbe smiled. "I spoke with him just before I came here. He was propped up on a dozen pillows like a king, and watching some terrible cowboy movie."

Harder chuckled. "Cheering for the Indians, no doubt." He looked up at Koelbe. "Do you have any leads?"

Koelbe appeared upset. "No. That's what bothers me so much. Usually there's some indication. I mean, you can trace it down to the source. I've tried to think of everything, but there's so much here. No one has ever lived this long under the oxygen-argon atmosphere. Maybe there are long-term effects we don't know about. That's a guess. But when you mix it with water vapor and dust, and the metallic impurities . . ."

And chemicals from life-support cycling systems; from mechanical and hydraulic and electric equipment and motors; from the forced-air systems; from water purification of waste water and urine; from reactions to oxygen after six months of plastics, chemicals, neon, velcro, metal, and all manner of synthetics, thought Harder, *anything* could happen. What effect, for example, might there be on everything else from the hard radiations of space?

Cosmic particles swept through *Epsilon* as if it were so much fog. Solar storms lashed the station with floods of electrons, with furious gales of penetrating protons, with all manner of atomic nuclei. At times the station passed through the fringes of the

Van Allen radiation belts. But the real problem wasn't
trying to discover what had produced such a reaction
in Jordan. Reactions were easy. It was the inter-
reaction of a dozen steps that produced the final
result. It could take days or weeks, or even months,
to narrow it down. And if Koelbe was showing this
kind of concern, they wouldn't have that much time
in which to play detective.

The problem didn't promise a swift solution. There
was always the chance that Jordan was suffering from
a hit-or-miss proposition, that he'd been exposed
briefly to some short-lived condition that had already
dissipated. There was that chance—but also the grim
possibility that things could get worse. Koelbe, Harder
knew, was boxed in. Despite the best diagnoses from
past experience, they still existed in an environment
with many unknowns. It wasn't as bad as a ship
under zero-g; then you had complications born of
other complications. With even a tenth of a g, liq-
uids, vapors, dust, and impurities all went through a
settling effect. The centrifugal force of rotation protected them from mixtures that gave engineers night-
mares under zero-g. Yet there remained the inescap-
able fact that theirs was wholly a mechanical, artificial environment.

There was another matter to consider. After six
months in orbit, inevitable changes had taken place
in the body chemistry of every one of them. Jordan's
body had changed. Metabolism had undergone shifts
they didn't yet understand fully. *Epsilon* was expected to provide the answers to these very questions. But in the accumulation of data there was the
hard reality that any one of a hundred factors could
be regarded as the possible source of their trouble.

"*Ach,* it is frustrating, no?" Koelbe kneaded his
brow. "I think maybe I am making an elephant out of

a mouse. Perhaps I'm leaping to conclusions." He smiled at Harder. "Certainly Bill does not look unhappy, and he doesn't seem to be suffering any discomfort."

Harder nodded.

"We will watch him carefully," Koelbe said, consulting his notes. "He has a slight fever, which is of little account. There's also an increased rate of respiration and pulse. All this—" and he waved the papers—"can be psychological as much as physiological. Jordan did not see a pretty sight when he looked in the mirror. It would unnerve anyone." Koelbe rose to his feet. "I'm sorry if I've made too much of this, Mike," he said. "It's just that I don't want to take any unnecessary chances."

"No sweat," Harder said. "Let me know how things go. I'll drop in on Bill, but I'd like to hear from you if anything changes."

"Of course."

"And if things get out of hand we can always get the ship up here a few days ahead of schedule," Harder added.

Koelbe frowned. "I wouldn't like to see that happen, Mike. We're so close to a perfect mission, and—"

"Not if this thing breaks loose," Harder interjected. He knew anything might happen but didn't want to voice that opinion. "Like you said, let's not make any elephants out of mice."

Luke Parsons paused outside the airlock hatch to Level 5. Koelbe had said Jordan was sleeping, and he moved carefully so as not to awaken his friend. He turned the hatch handle, swung in the door and stopped. The compartment was silent, shrouded in semidarkness. Quietly Parsons closed the hatch behind him and peered through the gloom. He couldn't see whether or not Bill was in his bed.

There was just enough time to see the shadowy form loom before him, only an instant to hear the maddened cry before a terrible blow smashed against his ear. Parsons felt himself hurled to the side. Through the pain he cried out. There was no time to think. A fist bounced off his cheekbone and he felt his body falling, his legs rubbery.

"Bill! For God's sake, what are you doing?"

Frantically he rolled to the side as his assailant hurled himself bodily after him. This time the blow caught Parsons on the chest and slammed the wind out of him. He scrambled desperately to his feet, trying to avoid the continuing rush. In the shadowy light he caught the dim reflection of a contorted face rushing after him. Instinct took over. Parsons side-stepped the clumsy blow thrown at him and drove his fist into the midsection of his opponent. He heard a gasp of pain. Then fingers raked his face.

Again Parsons stepped to the side. The other man clawed wildly after him, arms flailing senselessly. There was no coordination in his actions. For a moment he saw Jordan's silhouette against the dim night light. Parsons pivoted, and put all his strength behind his right arm. His fist cracked against the side of Jordan's jaw. In the light gravity Jordan's head snapped back against a cabinet and he tumbled unconcious to the deck.

Parsons sagged against the wall, gasping for air. His ear throbbed with pain. He brought his hand to his face and it came away wet. He'd been clawed. . . . Quickly Parsons hit the light switch. He winced from the glare and turned.

"*Mother of God. . . .*"

For a moment he couldn't move. Horror rooted

him to the spot. Lurching to the desk, he banged his hand against the intercom switch. "Werner! Do you hear me? Koelbe! Damn it, man, *answer* me!"

Koelbe wasn't in his compartment. Parsons forced himself to think, and flipped the cover switch from general emergency. He stabbed the button to broadcast his voice to every part of the station.

"This is Parsons," he gasped, sucking in air. "Level 5, Level 5. Emergency for Koelbe. Do you read me, Koelbe? Acknowledge!"

Throughout the station they froze at the sound of Parsons' voice. In the time it took for Koelbe to respond, Parsons looked again at the crumpled form of Bill Jordan. He shuddered, swung angrily back to the intercom to shout for Koelbe.

The doctor's voice burst from the speaker. "Parsons? Koelbe here."

Parsons leaned close to the mike. "Get down to Level 5, Werner. Don't waste a second."

"I'll be there right away," Koelbe snapped, and switched off.

In his quarters Harder went to emergency transmit. "That goes for Koelbe only," he said. "I repeat, for Koelbe only. The rest of you continue what you're doing. I'll be back to you in a few minutes."

Harder headed for the airlock hatch at a dead run. He spun the handle and let himself fall into the tube. As he drove downward, his hand pumping for speed, he realized he had left the airlock door open, an unforgivable sin. He dismissed it from his mind, watching Koelbe enter Level 5.

"Leave the hatch open!" Harder shouted.

A moment later he gripped the teflon pipe and felt pain in his hand. He'd forgotten the thermal mitt. To hell with it. He applied the insteps of his feet to the pipe, squealed to a stop, and scrambled through the hatch where he saw Koelbe and Parsons bending over the prostrate form of Jordan. He saw blood streaming down Parsons' face. He ignored it—Luke was on his feet, and a little bleeding wouldn't hurt him. It was the sight of Bill Parsons that stopped Harder.

He sucked in air noisily. The last time he'd seen Jordan, only a few hours ago, the rash on the side of his face had spread toward the neck. It wasn't pretty but he'd seen worse. Now . . . Harder took a grip on himself. The rash covered most of Jordan's face. His eyes were almost closed from the welts across his cheeks and brows. He lay prostrate, like a creature dragged from the sea. The flesh of his nostrils was swollen almost shut, and he breathed hoarsely through his open mouth. The discoloration and swelling extended down his sides and over most of his ribcage. The soft flesh, especially, was swollen. Worse were the open sores, exuding a thick yellow substance that reflected the overhead light. Harder clamped his lips together.

Koelbe looked up. "He's burning up with fever. His pulse is weak. His breathing is irregular." The German doctor turned to Parsons. "What happened?"

"It—it's hard to say," Parsons said in a muted voice. "When I came in here, it was dark. The next thing I knew Bill was all over me. Like a madman. He was trying to kill me." He looked at his friend. "He didn't know what he was doing. I'm sure of—"

"Of course not." Koelbe turned to Harder. "He's going to need oxygen," the doctor said. "We can't keep him here." He rose to his feet, looking around. "We've got to get him to the dispensary. But he's liable to go . . . to go berserk again." Koelbe started for the hatch. "You'd better restrain him. I need my things. I'll be right back." He disappeared into the tube.

"What in the name of God happened to him?" Parsons stared wide-eyed at Harder.

"I don't know, Luke. We'll find out soon enough." He gestured toward the bathroom. "You'd better get some cold water on your face."

"It can wait." Parsons watched Jordan's arm twitch. "He's coming around. We'd better be ready for him."

Koelbe heard the screaming even before he started back for Level 5. He cursed his slow fall as he drifted downtube. The voices of Harder and Parsons could be heard over the shrieking sounds. Koelbe saw the two men gripping Jordan's arms and legs, struggling to hold him from tearing loose.

"Hurry, for God's sake!" Parsons shouted at the doctor.

Koelbe took a hypodermic from his bag. The needle went neatly into Jordan's arm. Koelbe looked down, his face impassive. "It will take effect in a few moments," he said.

Chapter XI

He looks like something out of a science fiction movie. Jesus, what's happening to him?

Anguish swept through Luke Parsons. He wanted desperately to help Jordan. The wild exertion in their compartment had worsened the condition of his friend. Jordan lay helpless in the oxygen tent rigged up by Koelbe. Some horrible force had gone berserk inside his body and was fighting its way to the surface. Parsons thought of McIntyre's trouble with the welts. This was infinitely worse. Every so often Jordan's face twitched. Through the plastic shroud they heard his hoarse gasps for air, the subconscious struggle to breathe.

Koelbe had distended the nostrils with plastic tubing to keep the flesh from swelling shut. Several times he had treated the open sores. It didn't seem to do much good. They exuded the thick yellow liquid as fast as they were wiped clean.

It was still spreading. They'd cut away Jordan's shorts, and now the angry welts showed along his groin and thighs. His scrotum was swollen. Thank God he couldn't feel the pain.

Behind him Parsons heard the hatch from the central corridor swing open. He turned to see June Strond.

"I said I'd notify you as to what happened," Harder said, his voice reprimanding.

June ignored him and walked quickly to the bed, staring down at Jordan. Her face went pale and she closed her eyes. When she opened them again her voice was steady.

"I know what you said, Mike," she replied. "But we could hear Bill all through the station." Abruptly she turned to Koelbe. "I was a nurse on the Arctic expeditions," she told him. "There was no doctor. How can I help?"

"Thank you," Koelbe said. It was as if the others weren't in the room. "He will need sponging off with alcohol. Everything is right here on this table. Do you know how to use these things?" he asked, gesturing to the blood pressure and other instruments.

She nodded.

"His readings are on this chart." Koelbe handed her a clipboard. "His temperature is one hundred and four. It must be taken again in one hour. If there is a sudden rise, call me at once." Koelbe went on in clipped sentences with instructions to June. "He is strapped down. Under no conditions will you release these restraints. Meanwhile, I must talk with Zystra immediately." He started to leave, then turned to Harder.

"One more thing," he said. "The moment this condition—or anything like it—appears with anyone, I must be notified."

Harder nodded. "I'll pass the word."

Koelbe gestured suddenly. "No, that is not enough. I am not thinking properly. I wish to examine everyone. We should not wait for that." He beckoned to

Harder. "We start with you. Then send the others to me."

As he undressed in the examination room, Harder remained silent. Koelbe's words had shaken him. The doctor hadn't said he was to be notified *if* the rash appeared. He had said *the moment it appears,* as if he were almost certain that Jordan was only the first.

Harder flipped the switch for open line to StatCom in Houston. Stubby Dolan was on shift. That was fine! Stubby wasn't the kind to ask questions if Harder called for a security patch to the line. Dolan responded immediately to the signal.

"How goes it, Mike?"

"We've got problems," Harder said. That was enough to alert Dolan not to play guessing games. "I need a secure line to Garavito. *Now.*"

Dolan's brows went up. "Not available, Mike."

"This is priority. Can you raise him?"

"Negative. He's en route to Washington. Commercial. We can get a message to him, but there's no way to hook up for direct contact."

Harder chewed his lip. "All right. Set up a line direct to Dave Heath."

Dolan was good. Not even the request for a line direct to the NASA administrator shook him. He had plenty of questions but he was saving them for later. "It'll take a few minutes," he said. "I'll have to track him down."

"Stay with it, Stub. No matter where he is or what he's doing, I've got to reach him."

He saw Dolan nod on the video. "Will do. Keep the line open and I'll signal the moment I have him."

"Okay." Harder leaned back in his chair. Fatigue dragged heavily at his limbs. *I wish I had a cigar,* he thought. I wish I was somewhere getting laid. Or drunk. Or anything. *Epsilon* had become a time bomb. He knew it. Animal instinct and experience told him this. Jordan might not make it. He tried to look at the situation coldly and without emotion in the light of his position as station commander. He could and would do exactly that, yet he couldn't avoid the sadness that spilled through him. His whole world might come apart at any moment.

"*Epsilon* from Houston."

Harder leaned forward to the video-phone. "Harder here."

"Mike, I have Heath for you," Dolan said. "He's at the Cape and I have a secure line into KSC."

"Thanks, Stub."

"Stand by, please." A pause. "Mr. Heath? Colonel Harder, sir, direct from *Epsilon*." Then the warning: "This is a requested security line."

That was enough for Heath. He'd play it accordingly. Heath didn't waste time with banal nonsense. He knew if Harder had set up the call in this manner there wasn't time for word games.

"Mike? Heath here."

"Good. How do you read me, Dave?"

"Five by. What's the flap?"

"Hang onto your hat, Dave. . . ." He told Heath the full story, keeping it pertinent but leaving out nothing.

Heath asked a few questions but for the most part let Harder spill everything to him. "Have you told Manny?" Heath asked.

"No. Stubby said he was on a commercial flight to Washington and couldn't be raised."

"All right. I'll take care of that," Heath said. "I imagine you have some ideas?"

"I don't know," Harder said. "Of course I've already thought of raising the return ship without delay. The more I think about it the better it sounds. Get everybody the hell out of here before this thing runs loose and it's too late. What's the status?"

"That's why I'm here at KSC, Mike. There's trouble with the booster. We couldn't get this ship off the pad in less than ten days."

"What about Air Force?"

"Uh-uh. Take too long to shift. Adapter problems would hold us up. We've got to go with the bird on thirty-seven. That's the first pad that will be ready to lift."

Harder chewed his lip. "I think maybe you'd better crack the whip, Dave. This thing is liable to blow. I don't want to overdo it but I've got an awful feeling we may be in for it up here."

Heath was silent for several moments. "If things come unglued we can get a lifting body to you. But it's only a three-man ship. At least it could take back anyone who's got this—who's affected."

"Well, it may be better than nothing. But the big ship is the answer in case we've got to move out of here on short notice."

"I'll do what I can, Mike. I think we'd better keep this a security matter for now."

"Sure. I'm not anxious to shout it to the world."

Dave Heath smiled grimly. "Neither am I. I'll have the word out for Garavito as soon as he lands. On second thought, I'll have a car pick him up."

"Good. I think Koelbe is setting up a direct TV line. He wants to beam Jordan direct to Zystra. You'd better get to him, also. I'm sure there'll be a mob of medical people on this, and you're going to have to throw a blanket over the works."

"I'll take care of it. I'll also clue in Ed Thayer. He's here with me now."

Thayer was director of the Manned Spacecraft Center in Houston. Stop worrying about details, Harder told himself. Heath will handle it.

"Anything else, Mike?"

"No. That covers it."

"How are your people holding up?"

"They're good people, Dave."

"I know. We'll stay on top of this."

"So long."

They sat around the long table in the dining area of Level 4. Koelbe hunched forward in his seat, hands clasping a coffee mug. It was his third cup, and actually he needed sleep more than coffee. With the doctor was Mike Harder, June Strond, Page Alison, and Henri Guy-Michel. Luke Parsons was asleep, aided in his vitally needed rest by a sedative from Koelbe. Tim Pollard watched over Bill Jordan, taking his shift in the constant care of the stricken astronaut.

"If I only knew *what* we were facing," Koelbe sighed. "But I don't. I haven't encountered anything like it." He was tied up in a mystery that defied his experience and skill as a doctor. Being helpless was cutting him up inside.

"What did Zystra say?" Page asked.

"Nothing, really," Koelbe said. "We have sensors on Bill, and they're receiving everything on his condition. That, and video color. Nothing has been omitted. They know more than I do right here by his side." Koelbe took a long sip of the steaming coffee. "Zystra has called in the leading dermatologists of the country. They've even contacted Fuchida in Tokyo, and what he doesn't know about the skin isn't worth knowing."

Guy-Michel made a rude sound. "Except what has hit Bill."

"I'm afraid so," Koelbe said. "So far, neither Fuchida nor anyone else has been of any real help."

Harder looked at Guy-Michel. "What about the Russians, Henri? You've been closer to them than anyone else."

The Frenchman shook his head slowly. "They have had problems, of course. But nothing different from ours. Eruptions on the skin. Things like boils, for example. But always related to something they could identify. Chemicals, ionization, whatever it was. Always they found the source."

"Fever?"

"No. I never heard of a fever," Guy-Michel said.

"He's slightly over one hundred and five now," June advised them.

Guy-Michel's eyes widened. "He can't stand too much of that—no?"

Koelbe shrugged. "There's a slow but steady rise. We've rubbed him down with alcohol. It doesn't seem to help," he added unnecessarily. "But what puzzles me most is the vertigo."

"Vertigo? No one said—"

"The fever doesn't account for it," Koelbe went on. "Oh, there would be some dizziness, of course. But in this case, there seems to be complete spatial disorientation. I've never seen it so pronounced. And what complicates matters is that he suffers this loss of balance even when he's lying down."

No one spoke. They waited for Koelbe to continue. The doctor placed the coffee mug on the table, pushed it away from him with an exaggerated motion. "When the sedative wore off and he regained consciousness," Koelbe said, "for a while it seemed the worst was over. I mean, he was coherent. He spoke normally. He felt pain, and told us about it. Then"—Koelbe shrugged—"he tried to reach out with his arms. He began to scream."

"He acted as if he were falling," June said. "He was trying to reach out with his hands to grasp something, to hang on."

Complete, total vertigo. Spatial disorientation. No up, no down—nothing. Everything goes to hell in a man's mind when that happens. Even if he's lying flat, lying on a solid surface, even if he's strapped down and hanging on with his fingers like claws, he remains disoriented. Things are scrambled inside the brain and sickness plucks at the stomach.

Nausea had drenched the hapless Jordan with sudden ferocity. He had vomited, spraying the inside of the oxygen tent. He had gagged. June had gotten to him just in time, her finger in his mouth, cleaning him out. She hadn't told the others in detail what had happened. All she'd said was, "He became quite ill." But Koelbe knew she had saved Jordan's life.

The doctor buried his face in his hands. Exhaustion hammered at him. He didn't dare sleep. He had to know more. He must continue the conferences with Zystra and the others at Houston.

"There must be a staph infection," he said aloud. "The leucocytes . . ."

Guy-Michel looked at him. "The what?"

"White blood cells," June said. "The pus. He's fighting infection of some sort, apparently. But we don't know what kind. There shouldn't be anything in this station to cause that. The white cells are evolvers. They develop from processes within the body. But with Bill . . ." She shook her head. "It's almost as if his own body defenses were confused, and trying everything. There is so much liquid. More than there should be, I mean, even if there were an infection."

She was thinking aloud, reviewing in her mind the confusion not only of Koelbe, but the NASA doctors who had struggled with the problem. "Yet there's no solid indication, even, because of the pus."

"What do you mean?" someone asked.

"The infection doesn't necessarily have to come from a staph, from what most people think of as infectious bacteria. Certain types of infections are not staph, and they've been around for thousands of years. Like gonorrhea, from diplococci. They're not staph," she emphasized, "but they do result in pus. We tried to—"

"Could it be a virus?" Harder broke in.

June glanced with sympathy at Koelbe who was almost asleep in his chair. "It could be *anything,*" she replied. "If he were reacting to a virus—well, some of the signs are there. Like toxicity. There may be engorgement of some organs." She smiled bleakly. "But we really can't tell right now. Bill needs to have a thorough examination, tests, and . . ." Her voice trailed off in frustration.

Koelbe raised his head slowly; he was not asleep after all. "There may be brain damage," he said after a long pause.

Stunned silence met his words.

"I am not certain," Koelbe cautioned them. "But the signs are disturbing."

"What signs?" Harder snapped. Koelbe hadn't said a word about this.

"The vertigo, delirium, his inability to recognize us at different times. His urge to attack his best friend. As I said before, the fever does not account for this."

No one spoke for a while. Harder's face remained blank. They all appeared numb with the enormity of the sudden disaster.

"Have you thought of quarantine?" Harder asked suddenly.

Koelbe nodded. "I have thought of it." He looked up. "It would serve no purpose. Whatever is loose here with us is everywhere. I'm certain of that. We can't isolate Bill. He needs attention. It would take too long to set up a separate area for air circulation, for heating, for everything else. And I don't think it would do an ounce of good. If something is mixed in with the air, then it's been circulated a hundred times already."

He was right, and they all knew it.

"Werner? This is Page."

"Yes, yes. What is it?"

"I'm—I'm afraid I have some bad news."

"Please be brief."

"I'm sorry." She took a deep breath. "Several of my test animals have died."

"Died?" His voice sounded hollow.

"Four of them. Their skins are—well, mottled is the best description. They seemed to go . . . to go mad first. They tore at one another and tried to destroy their—"

"I will be there immediately."

Koelbe wanted to talk with Harder. He had come to detest the intercom and its flat, lifeless tone. He needed to speak with the man, face to face. Sometimes that helped. You brought everything out in the open and—well, sometimes when you listened to yourself talk you saw things differently, things that had been buried. It offered a fresh perspective.

The animals and the manner in which they had died upset him. He and Page had dissected the creatures. Their bloodstream, their organs, their whole systems, were aswarm with organisms he didn't comprehend or recognize. He was frightened. He wanted the help he could gct only on the ground. They should leave the station—at once. It was the only way. He glanced at the chart on his desk. He had just sent Pollard to his quarters to get some sleep; the man had stood watch for twelve hours with Jordan. June had taken over. Koelbe made the call to Harder.

"Come on down," the colonel said quickly.

Koelbe entered Harder's compartment to hear the intercom ring. Harder motioned for Koelbe to come in while he acknowledged the call.

"Harder. Go ahead."

"Colonel—Pollard here." Harder started at Pollard's use of the military. The scientist's voice was strained.

"What is it, Tim?"

"Colonel, whatever it is . . . this malady. . . . I mean, what Jordan has. . . ." Pollard's voice died out and there was a long silence. Harder glanced at Koelbe.

"Mike?"

"I'm listening. Go ahead."

"I've got it."

Chapter XII

Video-phone signals leaped with the speed of light between the planet's surface and satellites twenty-two thousand miles out in space. For most of the hour-long emergency conference, *Epsilon* whirled around the other side of the planet from Houston. No one gave even a passing thought to the electronic miracle that made it all possible. There were more pressing matters at hand. What had been a medical problem now loomed ominously as a question of survival.

Mike Harder and Luke Parsons sat together in the station, trouble-shooting with the experts in Houston— Dave Heath, Emanuel Garavito, Ed Thayer, and Dr. Richard Zystra. Several others listened to the exchange: Stan Tyson, NASA's public affairs director from Washington headquarters; Ben Blanchard, his counterpart in Houston; Raymond Lafferty, the Coordinator of International Programs for *Epsilon;* Charles Lynch, presidential aide from the White House. Several astronauts were silent listeners to the meeting. There were two other men whose presence was being kept secret—Dr. Lodovici DeRosa, Medical Director of the United Nations' World Health Organization, and a man who had flown directly to Houston from the Soviet Union—Dr. Anton Kustodiev of the U.S.S.R. Academy of Sciences, chief medical scientist for the Soviet manned space program. The Russians had kept three men and two women in a ship for three months. They might have learned something that could be of help.

Kustodiev, however, proved to be as helpless as the Americans. Nothing had ever taken place in a Soviet craft to compare with the menace stalking the astronauts inside the American station.

"Goddamnit! Fat lot of help that was." Mike Harder glared angrily at the video screen a moment before he cut the connection to Houston. "We chewed the fat with each other and ran around in circles, and didn't come up with a single goddamn thing that would help." He swung around in his chair to Parsons. "Luke, there's got to be a hole in all this somewhere. We're not seeing it, that's for sure. And if there's one thing I hate," he growled, "it's sitting on our asses and waiting for things to happen."

Parsons didn't answer. He was still turning over in his mind the key points of the conference. But Harder was right. They'd been taking it, instead of doing something on their own.

Harder stabbed his finger at Parsons. "You know this station better than anyone else," he said. "You know it better than the people who designed it or built it. Somewhere there's got to be an answer." He paused, thinking. "We've got to do *something*."

Parsons nodded. "We should have thought of this sooner," he said slowly.

"What?" Harder was almost snarling.

"It stands to reason something's mixing with the station environment," Parsons said. "We don't know where it came from or what it is, only that it's here."

"Go on," Harder urged.

"It looks like we'd better empty the station."

Harder looked carefully at his engineer. "You mean dump the air?"

"Uh-huh."

Harder thought about it. "Get everyone in suits and let down to vacuum?"

"It's a starter, Mike. It would give us the chance to test out the support systems to see if anything's gone haywire. If something is wrong, it should show up now. It hasn't so far, obviously. But we could be missing it, and we might spot it if we shut down and start up again."

"It won't be easy getting Bill and Tim in suits, the way they are."

"Better than this," Parsons said. "By the way, how is Tim?"

"Not good." Harder showed his frustration. "Koelbe is up against the wall. The disease is not following the same pattern with Tim. He's got some sort of a skin eruption, but nothing like Bill. No open eruptions, I mean."

"What else?"

Harder rubbed his chin. "He doesn't recognize anyone."

"Jesus!"

"High fever. He won't take any water. He's burning up, on the edge of delirium."

"Doesn't *anything* show? I mean, in his bloodstream?"

Harder stared blankly at Parsons. "Yeah. That's what has Werner ready to bang his head on the table. Bill is loaded with white blood cells—you know, fighting the infection. Tim's body shows a *decrease* in white cells. I sure as hell don't understand it."

Parsons weighed Harder's words. "Mike, what about getting them home? Maybe they could do a lot more for them down there."

"Don't you think I've already gone through that? I spoke with Heath yesterday at KSC. They've got problems with the booster. He said it would take ten days to raise ship. They can do better if they have to, but it will still take some time. They can get a smaller ship to us. I don't know, Luke. We may have to go that route." Harder leaned forward, his hand poised over the intercom. "We can talk all we want to later. Right now, let's get this place flushed out." Harder switched to open-line to send his voice throughout the station.

"This is Harder. I've decided we're going to evacuate the atmosphere. We have about one hour to get ready. Since we don't know how long we'll be in vacuum, you will don your main suits." He paused, trying to think ahead. "Werner, we'll need sedatives for Bill and Tim before we get them suited up. We'll be down to give you a hand as quickly as the suits are ready. Any questions?"

Several seconds went by, then: "Mike, Page here."

"Go ahead."

"I'll lose the test animals that are still alive."

"Can't be helped. For all we know they may be carriers."

"What about moving them to the S-IVB? We can save them that way."

"No dice," Harder said harshly. "The animals, plants—everything in this station goes under vacuum."

Harder turned to Parsons. "Anything you need? Henri can give you a hand."

Parsons rose to his feet. "I can use him. You, too. I'll want to go through the ship from top to bottom."

"Good enough. As soon as we get Bill and Tim squared away I'll be available. Anything else?"

Parsons shook his head.

"Okay. Let's get with it."

Three hours later they admitted defeat. Harder, Parsons and Guy-Michel stood together in the Level 13 airlock. The only thing above them was the tubular corridor leading to the S-IVB tank. Beyond that was the second S-II stage with the powerful nuclear reactor. They had even worked their way into the emergency reactor control room to confirm proper functioning. Everything checked out. They hadn't missed a thing. Parsons was repeating the message for the third time to Houston. In the airlock he plugged his suit umbilical into the master line connecting him through the station transceivers to the Manned Spacecraft Center. Ed Vogel, chief designer for *Epsilon*, was on the other end of the line.

"Like I said," Parsons repeated, weary in every bone, "we've gone through the ship with a fine-toothed comb. Batteries are all on low charge, and there isn't any leakage. The fuel cells are right on the money. Regenerative systems for air are perfect. The same for liquid waste recovery and the dump systems. We ran toxicity tests with anything that might be producing chemicals. All radiation levels are where they belong. Hell, we even checked for ionization."

Vogel was persistent—he had to be. "What about water supplies you've been using the last couple of days?"

"Yeah—that, too," Parsons confirmed. "Koelbe ran tests on samples of everything. It all checks out."

"How about food? Any problems with—"

Parsons cut him short. "We pulled all the drawers. Refrigeration is okay. Nothing open. All seals as they should be."

"What about main power systems, Luke?"

"You know better than that!" Parsons exploded. "We draw power from the nuclear system. There's nothing here, no exhaust to get into the life support setup."

Vogel didn't push it. The men near him nodded with understanding. Parsons was walking the fine edge, and he was as tight as a bowstring. Vogel would have been the same way, he knew, searching for the proverbial needle that might not be there. There was *something*. But from the examination they had given the station it wasn't in the mechanical, hydraulic, electrical, or nuclear systems.

"All right, Luke," Vogel said carefully. "There's no question, then. The station gets a clean bill of health. We suggest you return to normal status."

"*Hold it!*" Parsons' voice knifed through the radio line.

They heard it on the radio intercom—strange sounds, a man gasping, followed by a thud and snarling curses. A moment later Page cried out in a mixture of fear and pain.

"What is it?" Harder barked.

"It—it's Jordan," they heard Page gasp. "He's loose . . . he—he's gone mad."

Harder threw himself toward the open airlock to the long tunnel running through the station. Parsons and Guy-Michel were only seconds behind him. As he tumbled into the corridor, Parsons called for Page to tell them what was happening.

It was another voice they heard: Koelbe straining to talk. "The sedative," he said with obvious effort. "Worn off. He's going for the down airlock. Trying to get out."

Harder pumped his body furiously through the tube. "Stop him, damn it!" he shouted. "He's liable to do anything!"

"Tried. We tried." Koelbe's voice was indistinct. "Couldn't stop . . . him. I—I think he broke my arm." Then, realizing they must know, he added, "Pollard . . . Tim is all right. He's still out."

"Page!" Guy-Michel shouted her name. "Are you and June all right?"

"Hurry!" Page cried. "He's trying to get out of the ship!"

Harder caught a glimpse of a pressure-suited figure sliding through the airlock at the end of the corridor. He cursed his clumsiness in his own suit. If Bill ever got through the outer airlock, he'd be in serious trouble, particularly since he wouldn't know what he was doing. The rotation would swing him away, curving out from the station. He'd be helpless.

The ninety feet seemed endless as they pushed their bodies downward. Harder hit bottom, turning even as his boots touched metal, driving himself through the corridor hatch into the lower airlock. Both hatches were open. There was no sign of Jordan. Harder threw himself at the outer airlock.

Jordan's body tumbled slowly. Already he was thirty feet away, drifting outward—helpless. A wild laugh rang through their helmets.

Harder felt Parsons and Guy-Michel push against him, staring out through the open hatch. Jordan's figure was diminishing in size, falling away at a curving angle.

"Give me a thruster!" Parsons screamed. "We've got to get him!"

Harder pushed him back roughly. "Hold it," he snapped. "There's no use going after him like that." Parsons stared at him through his visor, his mouth working. "You won't do anyone a damn bit of good going off half-cocked," Harder pointed out. "He can't go anywhere. He'll drift into an orbit around the station." Harder thought of the air tanks. "How much oxygen has he got left?"

Parsons took a deep breath. "Two hours left."

"Okay. What about his suit light?"

"Automatic."

Harder knew the answer but wanted Parsons to be thinking, instead of throwing himself out of the ship after Jordan. Every suit had a bright flasher beacon that went into action automatically when ambient pressure dropped below three pounds. They'd pick him up visually without any trouble.

"Henri, get me a backpack and a safety line. Give him a hand, Luke."

The others moved quickly to the equipment racks, returned with a backpack thruster unit that would give Harder thirty minutes of continuous firing time. He hooked the safety line to a ring on his equipment belt.

"Leave the tanks on," he ordered. "There's more than enough in the right tank. Just get that thing on me." He extended his arms for the pack. "Page? You reading me?"

"Yes, Mike."

"You know what's happened?"

Her voice trembled. "Is Bill outside the station?"

"He's out, all right," Harder said grimly. "He won't drift too far. I'm going after him in a moment. How's Werner?"

"He'll be all right. He may have a broken arm but he's holding up fine. We'll take care of him."

"Tim?"

"Still asleep," she replied.

"Good. You or June hook up Houston. Tell them what's happened and what we're doing. They're probably having fits down there." He shifted his body for Parsons to cinch the straps. "June, you'd better get something ready to calm Bill down when I bring him in."

"I'll take care of it," June said. Werner wouldn't be able to get a hypo into Bill and she would have to do it.

Parsons rapped him on the helmet. "All set."

Harder turned, clumsy in the backpack. It rode his shoulders like a massive harness. He rested his elbows in the braces, fitting his fingers into the control slots. The backpack gave him a powerful thrusting force in any direction and enough fuel to propel himself more than a mile from the station, with ample reserves for maneuvers and returning. He'd use the safety line to secure Jordan, tie his arms and legs if necessary, and tow him back to the station.

Guy-Michel was hanging halfway through the hatch, searching.

"See him?" Harder asked.

"No. We're still coming around the turn."

The great swing of the station had taken them out of sight of Jordan. As the long tank swung around again they should pick up a view of the helpless astronaut.

Harder shuffled to the edge of the hatch, waiting to push out. "We're all right," he said to the others. "Let me know as soon as you see him so I can intercept his curve. He just foundered out there instead of kicking off, or we'd never get him."

Harder's plan was simple. With Jordan's body swinging into a wide curve around the station, a line would be thrust out to intercept him. Jordan couldn't control himself, no matter how much he twisted or turned within the suit. Without a thruster, or something for him to grasp, he was completely helpless. Harder knew he must immobilize Jordan's arms to keep the other man from grabbing him or his equipment. In his present condition Jordan was liable to do anything.

They heard Jordan's voice just before Guy-Michel caught sight of the blinking light. Harder didn't waste a second. The others lifted him bodily through the hatch and pushed him away from the station. Immediately Harder's body began a slow tumble. He worked the thrusters to steady himself and swung around to get a sighting on Jordan.

The astronaut babbled through his suit radio, a mixture of words and unintelligible sounds.

"Jordan! This is Harder. Can you hear me?" As he spoke, Harder squeezed the controls. The thrusters spat briefly to send him forward in a long curve. He aimed well ahead of Jordan's path, thrusting again. He seemed to float beneath the canopy of stars. Everything moved in eerie slow motion. He kept his eyes on the flashing beacon, saw the station lights reflect off Jordan's helmet. The astronaut was still in a slow cartwheeling tumble. "Bill! Do you hear me? Answer me, man!"

"*See? We're all out here . . . can't hide. . . . I'm here. See me, God? Right here with you . . . 'sallright- Mike God says everythings just fine . . . where are you God, I can't see you . . . Jesus that's funny . . . funny, funny, funny! . . . where the hell are you . . . you can see me, God . . . you know we're here, right? All here . . . all of us . . . we live here, God, right next to you. . . . Everything's fine . . . gonna be fine . . . hear me? I'm here . . . here . . . I'm coming to you . . . where are you . . . ?*"

A cold wave of fear rippled through Harder. Jordan was still fifty yards away and they were on a converging path. Another few minutes—that was all. An anguished cry burst through his earphones.

"*God! I can't see you! Can't see you. . . .*" The voice ebbed away in a dying sigh. Jordan sobbed. The sound tore through Harder. He thought of what it must be doing to Luke Parsons.

"Visor . . . wrong . . . that's what's wrong . . . can't see you because of visor . . . gotta take off . . . visor. . . ." A burst of shrill laughter.

"Right, huh? Visor's in the way . . . damn visor . . . gotta see God . . . take off stinking visor. . . . Hey God! Don't go way. . . . Be right there . . . then see fine . . . hahahahaha . . . all the time right next door, but never see you, God . . . get stinking visor . . . can't reach. . . . There. . . . Wait for me, God . . .coming . . . right there. . . ."

"Bill—don't!"

Harder was only twenty yards away when he screamed at Jordan. He squeezed the thrusters savagely, shouting. He wasn't in time. Jordan's gloved hands unscrewed the helmet locking ring, grasped the helmet, and twisted.

They all heard it. The sound lasted only a moment, but it would live with them forever. It was a sudden explosive hiss, a burbling sigh. They heard a last gasping cry of *"God . . ."* as the air screamed out of Jordan's suit.

The fabric seemed to wrinkle, to deflate slightly. Harder never knew whether he had really heard the bubbly sound. He didn't want to know. He'd seen explosive decompression before.

He stared at the pink spray floating around the lifeless form. The lights from the station sparkled off the thin mist of frozen blood.

Chapter XIII

Mike Harder found June in the dining area. She sat stiffly, unseeing. The coffee before her had been cold for a long time. He stood to the side, watching her for several minutes. June gave no indication that she was aware of his presence.

He took a seat directly in front of her but said nothing. Words right now were useless. Harder turned to take her hands and held them in his own. Slowly her eyes regained focus, as though for the first time she recognized him. Her hands squeezed his until she seemed to feel pain. Still he remained silent. He saw the first tears and waited for the storm to break.

It came quietly. She leaned forward until her head rested on his arm. She wept silently, only her shoulders showing the convulsive sobs.

He looked at her in quiet wonder. He knew what she had been through. Koelbe's left arm was broken, now angled stiffly in a splint. There really hadn't been any choice. Koelbe had had to perform an autopsy. And he had a broken arm and could use only his right hand.

June had done the rest, handling the instruments, helping the doctor to cut and to slice, to open and dissect, to probe and to examine, to snip free, and to puncture. That was a hell of a thing to have to do on the body of a man with whom she had lived so closely. June had been a nurse, had tended men with bloody wounds, with broken bones, abrasions and burns, but she had never had to cut open the body of one of her best friends.

Harder sighed. It was more than that. Koelbe had told him about it. Peering into a human body that had been opened by steel instruments, no matter how precisely, was a task unnerving even to the strongest of wills.

Bill Jordan was a horror. June had become violently ill. Koelbe told him she had left the dispensary for several minutes. He had become concerned and had gone after her.

"She was leaning against the wall in the bathroom," Koelbe said. "She wasn't making a sound. Just leaning there with the side of her face against the wall." Koelbe shook his head slowly. "I didn't say anything. What had to be done with Jordan could wait. When she came back, she just asked me what she had to do. And she did it. My God, that is a wonderful woman!"

When they were finished, Koelbe ordered her into a disinfectant chamber with water that was almost scalding. Ultraviolet exposure followed, and was repeated several times. While she tried to cleanse herself of something which never really would go away, Koelbe called the others. Harder ordered Parsons to remain with Tim Pollard. He didn't want

Luke around for a while. Harder and Guy-Michel helped Koelbe spray a hardening plastic over the corpse. Then they got Jordan's remains into an emergency pressure suit, sealing all but one outlet. They donned their own suits and towed the corpse to the upper airlock. There they vented the pressure from the suit and, while they were still in vacuum, sealed the one remaining outlet.

Jordan's body rested in the storage room of the S-II nuclear reactor. It would remain there until they could come to some decision about burial. Harder knew Luke wanted his friend to be given the spaceman's burial. The body would be placed in a thin shell and a retrorocket fired to break orbit. At eighteen-thousand-miles-an-hour, re-entry would cremate the corpse. The last spark of life would appear as a shooting star across the heavens. But Jordan would have to wait. They still weren't certain what had killed him.

So Mike Harder sat holding June close to him while her head rested on his arm, and she wept. And all the while, he was suffused with a deep sense of love for her.

Hank Marrows untied his shoes and kicked them free. For several minutes he rubbed his feet, kneading the skin. He wasn't thinking about his feet. His mind raced with the information he had acquired during the preceding hours as he'd sought to separate one facet from the other. This thing was bigger than a Chinese hydrogen bomb. Hank Marrows had been in news communications for a long time and after a while, he knew, people became saturated with bombs and horrific visions of another war. "Screw it," they said, and turned back to the more immediate things in life like shiny new cars, and steaks, and a night on the town, and color television, or pot parties, and getting laid. Everything revolved around getting laid. Call it making babies, or saving the world, or just getting laid for plain goddam fun—it was always the same.

Getting laid was the number one kingpin of news no matter what shape it came in—whether it was a neighborhood party or a rape or a hooker or a gang bang. Produce a good story in which someone's getting it, and the story is better. You could circle warily about this, and get some hot stories on murder or larceny, but if you wanted to stay spotlight-center, you managed to titillate your audience with the oldest sporting game known to man. That was the key. You didn't have to mark it with screaming red paint, just so long as the connotation was there. People had a habit of thinking. No matter how stupid they were, or seemed to be, you had only to jog them and start a sort of dribbling chain reaction. Their own minds would take over and they would go through their own sort of smutty vicarious rendition.

Hank Marrows sighed. The strangest thing about this business was that he didn't like his news this way. It smacked of hedging his bets for getting across to his audience. But that's the way the ball bounced. When his editor once raised hell about his pointed remarks becoming too much of a finger, Marrows told the editor to quit his belly-sucking complaints.

"A phonograph record is just a lousy lump of wax unless someone listens to the damned thing," he had retorted. "And eloquence on my part ain't worth a shit if no one reads what I say. I make sure they pay attention."

When his peers wrote detailed copy about the first Chinese hydrogen bomb, Marrows wrote about the coed dormitories in which the technicians lived—with

no distinction between male and female. The bomb
story left the front pages after twenty-four hours, but
Marrows' description of life among the devotees of
Mao kept people grinning and talking for weeks
afterward.

Hank Marrows had moved into the space business
by accident. The reporter assigned to what was then
Cape Canaveral crapped out—flu or something—and
Marrows was the only name reporter available. Would
he cover the launching of John Glenn?

"Sure," Marrows had agreed affably. "Why not?
It's big news."

For a while it had threatened to be run off the
front pages by any crime of passion. Glenn's anticipated blast-off from the Cape had turned into a wea-
risome repetition of delays that went from the end of
1961 into mid-February of 1962, and still that damned
Atlas sat on the ground. Marrows was stubborn; he
didn't want to quit. Editors screamed for copy from
the Cape, and Marrows thanked his personal deities
when an estranged husband walked into a motel bar
on Highway A1A, where, in full view of the astonished patrons, he pumped seven bullets into the
shapely body of his ex-wife.

Marrows was the only newsman there and wasn't
more than eight feet away from the murder. While
the bar patrons still screamed, or stared in shock,
Marrows was in a telephone booth hammering out
the story to New York. Screw the Atlas. Marrows'
newsbeat became the bulletin, and his column
splashed across the front pages of more than three
hundred papers.

And now this monkey business with the space
station. Marrows rubbed his feet and sifted the reports in his mind. Ever since the first hint that there
would be two women in the station, Marrows had

been given the story to cover. He had that instinct for coming up with what people wanted—not simply to read, but to talk about after they listened to his voice or read his column. Marrows' sarcasm about that orbiting satyr from Paris had enraged NASA, and delighted millions. His pointed references to the possibilities of *outercourse* produced a thousand cabaret jokes and snickering comments by television comedians.

Hank Marrows believed in hunches. Sometimes an alarm bell clamored in the back of his mind and warned him to lay off his banter. He sensed a story that had to be handled straight. Then he was at his best: he wrote news the way he really wanted to write—with power and feeling. He had the ability, the intuitive sense that smelled out drama and pathos that dug right into the hearts of people.

He had that feeling now. It disturbed him. At least a dozen times he'd started his lead on *Epsilon*. The six men and two women were scheduled to return to Earth in less than a week, and Marrows was ready with backroom speculation about what their behavior might have been among themselves. It was the kind of copy that couldn't lose.

But he couldn't write it. Every time he started, his fingers became clumsy and the words wouldn't follow one another with their accustomed ease. The floor became littered with crumpled pieces of paper, and Marrows began to hate his typewriter. He sifted through his thoughts and suddenly cried out—"Of course!" This afternoon he had driven to a restaurant a couple of miles from the NASA news center near Houston. For once he had wanted a decent lunch and remembered a steak joint. He was seated at his table when he recognized a group of women across the room. Jeanne Parsons—that was it. Her husband was in the space station. While he was looking at her, someone rushed over to her table. The man— Marrows recognized him as a minor official of the space agency—whispered in her ear. Jeanne Parsons turned white and dropped her fork to her plate. For a moment she buried her face in her hands. Then she left. *With* the NASA official, Marrows reminded himself.

Marrows padded across his room to the telephone. An hour later he was sure of his hunch. No one in the Parsons family had been hurt or killed. He rummaged through his files and checked out other names. Nothing unusual. Yet something had happened to shake the Parsons woman. A NASA flunky had carried news to her and she had left with the man. Marrows had a list of private telephone numbers. He dialed the Parsons' home number. A woman answered. No, Mrs. Parsons was not at home—probably at Mrs. Jordan's. He dialed the Jordans' number. A man answered—Mrs. Jordan was not available; no, he didn't know *when* she'd be available. He had hung up abruptly. Then Marrows stared at the receiver in his hand. He'd recognized the voice.

It was NASA's chief flack at Houston—Ben Blanchard. Marrows began to add it up—the scene in the restaurant and the phone calls. It didn't mean much by itself. But then—mix in Blanchard being at the Jordans', his gruff manner and the way he had hung up—it added up to something.

Marrows made a direct-dial call to Cocoa Beach, Florida, the news center just south of Cape Kennedy: "Les? Marrows here. Yeah, fine—just great. Look, I'm onto something. It's strictly off the record for the moment. I need some answers."

He talked for ten minutes. Another piece dropped into place. There was a flap at the Cape. Trouble with the S-IB booster at Pad 37. This was ordinary enough, but to have crews working around the clock was something different. Even more out of the ordinary was the Air Force working around the clock at the launch pads for the Titan IIIC. They didn't have anything scheduled for two months. But they were rushing a booster to the pad. Why? No one knew. NASA claimed it had no idea what the Air Force was doing, and the Air Force gave out a polite "classified." Crap. They'd never slapped the security label on a IIIC from the Cape before.

Slowly but surely the finger pointed to the space station. Marrows followed his sixth sense, the sense that was warning him to play this one straight. Marrows smelled a disaster in the making. You didn't joke about the assassination of a President; you didn't joke about casualties in Vietnam; and you didn't crack funnies about a catastrophe on or off the Earth. The time, back in 1967, when those three astronauts fried in their capsule on the Cape, had proved that. People didn't care a rat's ass about space. But let there be some human crisis and you had yourself a story.

Two hours later, Marrows returned to the telephone. It was a gamble but he'd done that before. He had just enough information with which to speculate, and to make enough points for the story to see print. He'd called NASA in Houston and inquired about the launch pad flap at the Cape. The flack in public information denied it outright. He was lying and Marrows knew it. His own contact at the Cape had never been wrong.

That's when the paper began to flow steadily through his typewriter. When he finished, Marrows phoned his editor in New York.

"It's taking a chance, Hank," the editor said.

"Sure. So did the Wright Brothers."

"But you're sticking your neck way out."

Marrows was scornful. "So what? It's my neck."

"Yeah, but it's *my* ass!"

"Listen, goddamnit, I *know* I'm right."

There was a long pause. "Well, you haven't missed yet," the editor sighed.

"Jesus Christ, Sam, we're wasting time."

"Okay. We'll go with it. But God help you if you're wrong."

"Save that for the bleeding hearts." Marrows smiled grimly. "I want a full head with this. We don't have enough for the exclamation at the end but we won't need it. Just run 'em big and bold at the top. Okay? Good. You ready to copy . . . ?"

In his mind he saw the black headlines:

DISASTER IN SPACE

Page Alison had just enough strength left to brush her hand over the emergency alarm. The bells clamored shrilly through the station as her hand went limp. She collapsed to the deck, unconscious.

Later in the dispensary, Werner Koelbe looked down at her motionless form with a sense of helpless rage. "It is the same pattern," he said heavily. Henri Guy-Michel and Mike Harder looked inquiringly at him. "The rash," Koelbe pointed, "along the side of the face. The fever. It is already at one hundred and four."

A stricken look appeared on Guy-Michel's face. He kept a steely grip on himself. "What can I do to help?"

Koelbe met his eyes. "Do you believe in God?"

Dr. Emanuel Garavito trembled. He gritted his teeth and called on every saint he knew to keep from losing his temper completely. The saints must have been looking the other way. Garavito felt something snap inside him and suddenly hurled the newspaper into the face of Ben Blanchard.

"Don't give me that shit!" he roared. "How did this son of a bitch *get* the story in the first place? Damn you, Ben, someone in your office has been shooting his mouth off to Marrows!" Garavito dropped heavily into a chair and glared at his public affairs officer. He stabbed a finger at Blanchard who sat pale and stiff in his chair, his own anger barely in check. "You know what this has done to us?" Garavito said, his voice steely. "Ever since this project got started we've leveled with every one of them. We've played ball. Now—" the words hung in the air—"we're a bunch of ivory-tower bastards. Too big for our britches. Holding out on the public. Goddamnit!" he swore. "Someone opened up to Marrows. I can't fault him even if I have no use for his muck-raking. He's a reporter and he's doing his job." The finger stabbed again at Banchard. "But *someone* slipped him the word. I want to know *who*, and I want the mother crucified."

Abruptly Garavito ended his tirade. Blanchard watched him carefully, struggling not to hurl his own rage at the *Epsilon* director. He couldn't blame Manny. The thing had blown sky-high, and Garavito, one of the most highly respected scientists and administrators in the country, was already being tarred and feathered in the press, besides catching hell from the White House. Blanchard picked the newspaper from his lap and folded it carefully, using the time to rein in his own emotions. Garavito would never have spoken like this unless he was convinced someone within his own organization had finked out on them.

"Manny, you've known me for a long time."

Blanchard said the words quietly, knowing they would have the desired effect. "No one in this outfit has told Marrows a thing."

Garavito glared at him, the scorn and disbelief naked in his eyes.

"I'm giving you my word on it," Blanchard said. Suddenly he was tired of all this. One by one, he'd called the entire staff into his office and personally had questioned them. Blanchard's business was to know people. He did. He knew when someone was lying to him. Ben Blanchard's get-tough attitude with the press had earned him few laurels among the fourth estate, but they took him at his word. Blanchard would rather be known as an honest son of a bitch than a smooth-talking flack who scurried behind the safety of "official lies" for the good of the administration. Shove that nonsense, was his attitude. Blanchard considered himself a necessary watchdog to protect NASA scientists, astronauts, and officials from ill-behaved newsmen.

"How do you know?" Garavito snapped at him.

Thank God for little favors, Blanchard breathed. Manny didn't say he didn't believe him. He wanted to know *how* he could be so certain. Garavito was on the carpet, and he had to come up with answers in a situation that right now was rotten, and promised to get worse.

"Among other things," Blanchard sighed, "I had Hank Marrows come to my office. I asked him. He told me. He told me no one in this office—or anyone else for that matter—had spilled to him."

"You believe that . . . that bastard?" Garavito jeered.

"Yes, Manny, I believe that bastard."

"How the hell can you take Marrows' word? You must be out of your mind!"

Blanchard shook his head, a strange smile on his face. "Maybe, just maybe," he answered. "But not about Marrows."

"*Why*, damn it?"

"I'll keep it pertinent, Manny. You know I was in Vietnam?" Garavito nodded, still sullen. "All right," Blanchard continued. "One of the newsmen I got to know pretty well when things were hot over there was a reporter. The son of a bitch got under my skin."

"Marrows?"

"One and the same," Blanchard laughed harshly. "He'd written a series on how the GIs spent their leisure time. Saigon, rest camps, Japan—the whole bit. The way he told it, they all took dope, and screwed everything that walked or crawled, and the Army was responsible for mass debauchery."

"That's Marrows," Garavito muttered.

"Yeah, I know. A lot of what he said was true."

Garavito looked up in surprise.

"He doesn't make up his stuff," Blanchard went on. "He digs, and he knows how to needle, and he leans heavily on his stuff but it always stands up." Blanchard waved his hand to change his tone. "I'm getting away from what I started to tell you. I drove to Saigon, mad as hell, and found Marrows in the bar at his hotel. I made a scene of it, I guess. I threatened to punch him in the mouth, and then thought of something else. I invited him out in the field with us. We were going on a fire sweep, and it looked like a bad time. I told him to come along and get his ass shot at, and write about the side of the war that counted."

Despite himself, Garavito paid close attention. "What happened?"

"Hank looked me in the eyes, told me to wait a

minute, and left. I thought I'd never see him again.
A few minutes later he showed up with a portable
typewriter and a pocket tape recorder and said, 'Let's
go!' " Blanchard fished for a cigarette as he let the
memories run through his mind. "We were in the
field for three weeks," he said, his voice strangely
hushed. "We took a beating. We took sixty percent
casualties in dead and wounded. They chewed us up,
Manny. They ambushed us a dozen times."

"What about Marrows?" Garavito demanded.

"I figured he'd run. Any sensible man who didn't
have to be there would have gotten the hell out. We
had a bad fight and I offered to send him out on a
chopper. He'd already lasted longer than I figured."

"So he—"

Blanchard shook his head. "He was a strange sight.
Overweight, face puffy, eyes gleaming behind those
thick glasses of his. He wouldn't even answer me
when I offered him a way home. He just walked out
of my tent. I didn't see him again for three or four
days." Deliberately Blanchard waited, knowing that
Garavito must listen.

"Well, what happened? Did he go back?"

"Nope. That fat, half-blind son of a bitch threw
away his typewriter and his tape recorder. He went
to the outfit right behind ours. Brazen as hell. He
walked into their headquarters section and he lied
through his teeth. Said he was on special assignment, verbal orders from me—*me!* We had guns up
the ass lying around with all the people who'd been
killed. He got himself an automatic rifle and stuffed
grenades into his shirt, and no one knew he wasn't
just another poor bastard who had to be there. I said
I didn't see him for three or four days. Next time I
saw him, he showed up in my tent and asked for that
ride home. Said he had a column to write and did I

have a seat on a chopper. He looked like hell. He didn't say anything else, but fell asleep outside. He woke up when the chopper came in. Then he left."

"And that's all?"

"I didn't find out the rest of it until later, when one of my officers came around looking for the fat guy with the round face and the glasses. They were looking for him pretty bad."

Garavito leaned forward in his chair, intent.

"They had put the fat guy in for a citation and no one could find him."

"A citation! Marrows?"

"Uh-huh. Seems like some of the boys were pinned down, and the 'fat guy with the round face and the glasses' had crawled through the grass. The way they told it, he threw all his grenades and used his rifle like a pro. Knocked out a machine gun nest and then dragged a dead man he thought was wounded two hundred yards back through the swamp. He never told me a thing about it. Just showed up and asked for a ride home. I was glad to get rid of him at the time. Figured he'd learned his lesson."

Garavito seemed more calm, and was silent for several minutes. "I never heard that story," he said.

Blanchard snorted. "He never wrote it. So far as I know, he's never even *told* anyone about it." He paused. "No matter what you think of him, Manny, or what you've heard—Hank Marrows is honest. Like I said, I asked him face-to-face. He told me to relax, that my office was 'clean.'"

"Did you ask him how he latched onto the story?"

"I asked him, and he laughed in my face."

"Then how the hell did he grab it?"

"There are ways. He's better than a good reporter. He's a great newsman, even if I'd never let him know I knew it."

Garavito sighed. "All right, Ben, we'll let it go." He straightened suddenly in his chair. "But we've still got a can of worms to deal with."

"I know," Blanchard said soberly. "What do we do about DeRosa?"

"That guinea son of a bitch," Garavito muttered.

Blanchard smiled to himself. For someone who should have been sensitive about his Mexican background, Garavito never hesitated to call the cards as he saw them.

"I was going to ask you the same thing," Garavito said. "The way he shot off his mouth . . ."

That had really blown the lid. Not Marrows' story, which Blanchard knew was shrewd deduction and a gamble. But DeRosa. The medical director of the U.N. knew the whole story. He'd been in on the conference between the space station and NASA officials here on the ground. Even Kustodiev had kept his word of honor and refused comment to anyone. But Lodovici DeRosa had been badgered in his office by newsmen waving copies of Marrows' story, and he'd panicked. He said the *Epsilon* crew was in deadly peril and that they were diseased. He thought long-term exposure to radiation was the answer—the blundering idiot.

Radiation had nothing to do with it, and every scientist who thought he was an authority made statements to the press. That was the capper. The public was confused, which was bad enough. But the White House was confused. And the people on top, also angry, wanted the mess cleaned up. It was easier said than done.

"What are you going to do?" Garavito asked.

"Interesting you should ask me that," Blanchard replied. "Until now you didn't want anything said about this."

Garavito gestured impatiently. "Don't play games with me, Ben."

"I'm not." Blanchard was unruffled. He knew what had to be done but he didn't want to jam it down Garavito's throat. Let it come out by itself. "In fact, I was going to ask you the same question."

Garavito's tone showed acid. "You're the chief honcho for this outfit when it comes to news. I'm asking you about your plans."

Blanchard stubbed out his cigarettte and leaned forward. "Manny, when all else fails there's always one thing on which to fall back."

Garavito couldn't help the smile that appeared. "I suppose you're right." He repeated Blanchard's words. "When all else fails—" He paused, and they said the final words in unison: "—tell the truth."

"Werner can't leave Page and Tim right now," Harder said. "But I've had a talk with him about the situation and we've both come up with the same answer."

Harder pressed his knuckles against his temples. If only he could get rid of this damned headache. Nothing helped. Nothing would, he knew, except a long drunk and a week's sleep. But neither of these were available. He looked at the others. Luke was withdrawn, still hating himself for Jordan's death. He felt they could have gotten to Jordan sooner. They could have saved his life. It really wouldn't have mattered. Koelbe said Jordan would have died in forty-eight hours. In fact, the way he had died was almost a blessing in disguise. But you couldn't tell that to Luke Parsons.

He hardly knew Guy-Michel. The man contained a towering anger with himself. Frustration and helplessness nagged at him with a searing kind of misery because he was unable to relieve Page of her pain. Several times she had emerged from her coma, her eyes intense, the pupils narrowed and gleaming hard. Each time Henri was there. He slept on the floor near her bed where they had strapped her down. He took care of her with a tenderness Harder never would have believed possible. Semiconscious at times, in mute agony when she came fully alert, Page had no control of her body. Henri kept her brow cool, hovering like a stricken angel by her side. He was tearing himself to pieces.

Harder looked at June. Her eyes met his and in their shared glance was a whole story. She had become all-important to him. At the same time, she had made herself indispensable to all of them. They had always taken turns in the kitchen, observing the amenities of dining. Now, on top of everything else, June had accepted this task. During the day June managed to show up, no matter where the men were, bringing hot meals to them. She was nurse, cook and saint—all in one.

"As you know," Harder went on grimly, sensing that time was passing quickly and relentlessly. "We've been batting this thing back and forth with the people below. We've all got theories, but nothing else. You have your own ideas. Somewhere along the line it's been necessary to make a decision. You all know that." He looked at each of them. "I want no doubts as to the way that decision goes." Suddenly he wanted to get it over with, to say what had to be said.

"There are two problems that need immediate attention. We don't know what's hit us. We're doing everything we can. You know that as well as I do." He heard his own voice becoming flat, with an official tone—he couldn't help it.

"Whatever it is that's loose among us is unknown.

Call it an X-factor. We've never run into it before, and the Russians are just as mystified." He glanced at Guy-Michel. "Kustodiev has been in Houston for the past several days. The Russians have offered all the help they can give. But they don't know what to do." He paused. "I think I know the score. I don't like it. Nobody does."

They kept their silence.

"But that can't push aside something we *can* do." He knew his voice was harsh, impersonal. Again he looked at them, one by one.

"I've cancelled the ship."

They were prisoners, four hundred and sixty miles above the earth.

Chapter XIV

He didn't expect the explosion. Every one of them knew the score. You didn't take whatever was running amuck within the station and carry it back to Earth because you were frightened, or because your friends were dying. Or because all of you might die.

But everyone didn't see it that way. Because, as Harder knew he should have anticipated, they weren't thinking with their usual logic. Not now. Now they were simply reacting, and the pressures and frustrations building up to this moment blew the lid right off.

Their conclusions were inevitable. The science of man had put them here. It had performed miracles. Men were walking the dusty surface of the moon, living at the bottom of the sea, taming the atom, transplanting hearts and other organs, thinking directly with great computers. Now were they simply to accept that this same science was stricken helpless, that they were the untouchables beyond medical or scientific ken? It didn't hold water—not when the woman Guy-Michel loved lay strapped to a table, only an injection away from pain stabbing through her system. The lovely skin he knew so well now yielded inexorably to discoloration and swelling and hard-ridged welts. The thought that what had gouged its way through Jordan was now ravaging Page's system filled Guy-Michel with a towering rage and a terrible, soul-shaking sadness. But the flat pronouncement of doom from Harder was something even more unbearable.

Henri rose slowly to his feet, disbelief mirrored in his features. "Just like that, eh?"

Mike Harder studied Guy-Michel. *Oh-oh, Henri's bought the farm.* Harder recognized the signs. He also knew it wasn't going to do any good trying to placate the Frenchman. Harder's own gaze was unflinching as he nodded. "Yes, Henri. Just like that."

"So. We are to be abandoned?" Henri's voice was hard and brittle, his eyes carrying a dangerous sheen. Harder knew his friend might still come straight across the table at him. There was nothing else against which Henri might strike, no other way to vent his helpless anger, the terrible conscience that gnawed at the man who is powerless to help the woman he loves—when that help is no farther away than a wrong decision.

"It's not a matter of abandoning anyone. You know that as well as I do."

Henri smiled coldly. "You officious son of a bitch." June gasped and Luke Parsons started from his seat. Harder's hand held him back. "It is easy for you to say that. It is easy for those frightened rabbits in Houston to say it! They are down *there,* and up here people are dying. Now, like that!" He threw his arms out. "Page suddenly is a leper! She is untouchable! And Tim? He also, eh? We shall all sit here and we shall watch them die—is that it?"

Harder groaned to himself. Everything Henri was saying was true, if you looked at it closely, if you kept it personal.

"If it turns out that we sit up here and die," Harder said, "then that's the way it will turn out. I've asked for help."

"That was big of you." The acid in Guy-Michel's tone was almost visible.

Harder struggled with himself. "Henri, you aren't helping matters by this kind of attitude."

"Never mind what *I* am doing!" Guy-Michel snarled. "It is *she* who needs help!" He gestured in the direction of the dispensary. "It is Tim Pollard who needs help! And you are a rabbit like the rest of them, sitting up here while they are dying!"

"Do you think for one moment I don't want to get the hell out of here? Don't you realize I want the best available medical help for Page and for Tim? God *damn* you—do you think I wanted Bill to die?"

"To hell with what you think or I think. *Do* something! That is what matters. Tell Houston to send up a ship to take them home, to get them into a hospital." Guy-Michel's fingers curled into claws as he gesticulated wildly. "I do not care what you think!"

"You had damned well better care." The words came out as a growl, startling even to Harder. Suddenly his patience evaporated. Screw Henri and his emotions. Screw the whole goddamned thing.

He didn't realize that he had gotten to his feet and was leaning forward with his hands flat on the table. He experienced a tight sensation in his throat, the feeling that always came just before he lost his temper completely. He struggled to hold it back.

"Get something straight," he snapped. "All of you. Before your lives come up for consideration, before any of you have a goddamned thing to talk about, there's a *greater* responsibility. There's a whole planet full of people down there and *they* come before everything else." He straightened slowly, looking down on them. "I've told you the way it is and the way it will be unless something happens to change the situation. That's it. It wouldn't be any different if . . . It wouldn't matter *who* was up here with us. The decision isn't even mine alone, but if it were, it wouldn't change."

He took a deep breath, then went on. "We know what's happening to us."

The suppressed outburst from Guy-Michel was no more than a low, strangling sound.

"We're carriers. All of us." He looked directly at Guy-Michel. "You said that suddenly Page was a leper, didn't you? You're right, Henri. Only it's worse than that." Guy-Michel stared open-mouthed at Harder.

Mike Harder heard his own voice as if from a long way off. Fatigue squeezed every fiber of his body. "Everything started when we brought the containers into the station. The dust. You know the theories— that microorganisms drift in space. You also know we were looking for just that in the dust. The kind of things that may have lain dormant for millions of years. Maybe billions—I don't know. It doesn't matter. Not now, anyway." He knew his words were a death sentence. "What does matter is that they aren't dormant any longer."

No one broke the silence. In the background they heard the pulsing, mechanical sounds of the station. Then Harder said what they all knew by now.

"They've come alive. They have warmth and pressure. They have gases, water vapor, oxygen. They have living creatures on which to feed and grow."

He saw in their eyes the admission of what they had suspected, but had feared to acknowledge.

"That's right," Mike Harder said. "Living creatures—*us!*"

Chapter XV

Luke Parsons secured the last bolts and stepped back to survey his work. The small television scanner pointed to where Page Alison and Tim Pollard were strapped to their beds. A second scanner also surveyed the beds to provide a cross-view of the dispensary. The receiver sets could be switched from one transmitter to the other, encompassing most of the medical area. Mike Harder had ordered the installation.

"No one knows how this is all going to end up," he told Parsons. "We may all get this . . . this thing. Maybe only one or two of us will still be on our feet. Even if one of us is left, someone's got to look after station systems. He can't be two places at one time. Rig up a cross-scanner system and open audio with it."

Parsons looked around the dispensary. Red lighting cast its blood-color in every area. The sounds of machinery whispered in the background, carrying vibration through the deck beneath his feet. The dispensary crawled with its own acoustics—the hiss of oxygen, the coughing murmur of the refrigeration units, the rasping sounds of two people on the verge of dying. Parsons shook his head, flooded with a wave of sadness. He looked at Page and Tim for a long time.

In the red glow, the terrible skin affliction faded as if, by light, they could be cleansed of the horror that was consuming their bodies. Neither man nor woman moved; each lay heavily drugged, beyond the reach of the pain that spilled through their systems. Parsons looked at Pollard and was sickened. There lay one of the finest minds that had brought meaning to the human race. Now it was beyond their reach. The brilliant brain cells with their finely-tuned reasoning power and sweeping imagination were being eaten away by something they did not understand, and against which they had no defense.

How strange it all was, Parsons mused. The same microscopic forms that once gave life to the world beneath us have returned to destroy that life. Untold billions of years ago, this same proto-life had drifted through radiation-lashed space, floated through a murky atmosphere. It encountered water and pressure and gases. It floated into a world lashed with violent storms, burned by the terrible radiation that spilled through a thin and still-forming atmosphere. On anything that would support its voracious appetite, it fed, rushed outward, inward, downward, in every direction. No enemy then, it had come to a world and produced life. Now, after billions of years, it was returning. But this time it was different. Now the end result of that evolution had thrust outward and upward from the planet—and was encountering the beginning of its own existence.

Parsons moved slowly to the TV scanner and locked the plugs. Immediately a small red light winked on. The astronaut reached out to switch on microphones suspended from the ceiling. Every whisper, every sound was picked up by the mikes and would carry with the TV picture to the receivers placed on every level of the space station. Parsons stood in the center of the room. "Mike?" He said the name softly.

The answer came immediately. "You came in clear, Luke."

Parsons walked in front of one of the scanners. "How's the picture?"

"Perfect. Stand back so I can check the beds."

Parsons waited.

"Luke—shift number two about ten degrees left, will you?"

Parsons loosened the bolt and swung the camera to the side.

"That's it," Harder confirmed.

Meanwhile, Werner Koelbe slept, exhausted, every fiber in his body aching. He had had no rest for thirty-six hours, and Harder had finally ordered him from the dispensary. The doctor acquiesced only when he realized he was of little use to any of them in his condition. He attached sensors to the patients. These recorded physiological processes on tapes within the station, and broadcast them simultaneously to receivers on the planet. Even as they lay quieted by drugs, the vital life processes of Page Alison and Tim Pollard were being studied by the finest doctors and scientists on Earth. It was this knowledge that finally closed his eyes and brought sleep to Koelbe.

Parsons took the next medical watch and completed his installation of the audio-video scanners. He glanced at the wall clock and punched in the numbers for the bedside intercom of Guy-Michel. The minute the bell chimed, Henri was awake and answering.

In moments the Frenchman appeared through the airlock hatch. He moved quickly to the side of the woman, staring down at her, his own face a mask. Parsons watched him for a while. "No change, Henri," he said quietly.

Guy-Michel did not turn around. Parsons could scarcely hear his whispered "Thank you, my friend."

June Strond paused before the airlock hatch to Mike's quarters. The locking systems were all left open now. He had ordered them to leave every compartment free to access from the outside. No one knew when they might collapse behind a secured hatch. She turned the handle and swung the door away from her. Mike heard the dull sounds, looking up from his desk. Through the open viewport June saw the disc of the full moon. Ghostly light filled the compartment. She closed the hatch, and in the half-light studied his face, the gaunt expression in his eyes.

"Hello, Mike."

For a long moment he didn't answer. When he spoke his voice was deep, strained. "I'm glad you're here."

"Close the ports, please." She didn't want to see the moon or look out on the unblinking stars. Not any more. No warmth came from those gleaming messengers of infinity. She forced everything from her mind but this moment. Mike rose and dropped the heavy metal shields over the ports. The moon became shadows.

When he turned again, she stood waiting for him, her clothes in a pile by her feet.

Werner Koelbe tossed fitfully, cursing, his head throbbing with pain. Inside the cast his skin tormented him. Finally he threw off the covers and padded to the bathroom. The light stabbed into his eyes. He groped for a vial of pills and washed two down with water. Gasping, he returned to his bed and stretched out. It took the pills fifteen minutes to dull the agony to an ache he could endure. He tried to lie quietly and let the drugs numb the pain centers. He turned his head to the side. For several minutes he tried to understand what was happening to him. He focused on the doorway to the bathroom. The straight lines of the door, silhouetted in light, wavered slowly in a sluggish undulation from top to bottom. Koelbe rubbed his knuckles fiercely against his eyes, forcing them to tear. Still the doorway throbbed in a series of liquid pulsations.

Koelbe climbed shakily to his feet, then stood, weaving from side to side. He had to think, to *think* . . . . He wiped his arm across his face, smearing perspiration in his eyes. Wet . . . how did he get so wet? Why was he perspiring like this? It must be the drugs. Clumsily, he scrambled into his jumper, struggled to get the cast of his broken arm into the sleeve, and fumbled the zippers closed. He had to get to the dispensary. Who was there now? June. Thank God for June. Without her he would . . . what? The thought dissolved as he reached the hatch and swung it open.

For what seemed an eternity he clung with his good arm to the pipe in the corridor. He couldn't remember whether he had to descend, or move upward through the long tube. He was at Level 8.

Medical was a higher number. Eleven—that was it. He pulled his body upward, feeling the sweat drenching his ribs as he ascended. My God, how far is it? He seemed to be losing track of time. He forced himself to count. *Ach, better! One thousand at a time. Now it is two thousand, three thousand, four hundred, six thousand, three hundred.*

He gasped as nausea assailed him, and fought it down. Blinking his eyes rapidly, he tried to focus the wavering image before him. Clinging to the pipe, he leaned forward. There it was—number eleven. His level. Medical. Dispensary. He wrapped his legs around the pipe and reached out for the handle. For a moment he looked down. The bile ripped upward and burst through his mouth, a violent forcible vomiting that wracked his body. Instinct, habit, practice saved him, and he clutched the pipe. Again he started up, and reached the hatch. He stopped. Who was laughing? Where was that sound coming from?

"Who is laughing at me!" he screamed. His voice echoed through the corridor, bounced off the curving walls, welled up, and sprang back at him. He roared at the sound. "Shut up! Enough, I tell you! Laughing, are you? Stop! Stop!"

Through the hatch he slipped. All sense of balance had vanished. He flung out his arms and screamed with the sudden pain. The deck came up to meet his face in a crazy, slow-motion, slanting movement. His head struck metal. He climbed to his feet, his skull knotted with pain, his eyes twisting in their sockets. He stared into the dispensary. A corridor stretched forever before him, its edges indistinct. He looked through a tunnel, its rim fuzzy. What were those faces? Who were they? He stumbled forward, reaching out with his good arm, fingers clawing at the faces. "Who are you? Tell me who you are!"

We know.

"What? What did you say?" He gasped for air.

We have always known.

"Tell me who you are! Let me see you!"

You could not hide forever.

One faced emerged from the swarm, hovered, swaying from side to side. The features began to coalesce, to shape and form—

"No!" he shrieked.

Did you think you could hide forever from your own father?

He saw the face in instant clarity. Face? It was a picture, a photograph. He could not remember his father's face. He remembered only the pictures. The face changed into a photograph. Instantly it was again a face, swaying, dancing, glowing from within.

You are your father's son.

The swastika gleamed at the throat. Pulsating light stabbed at him, a thousand jewels glowing and slicing into his brain.

"Go away, go away!"

Never. I am with you forever. The face expanded, rushed at him, the eyes burning into his.

"I'LL KILL YOU!" He struck out blindly, madly. Animal sounds came from his throat.

The others heard the sound through the station. There was a loud crash, and another. Voices mixed with the sounds, then the vibration of severe blows was heard. Harder leaped from his bed to the TV monitor. Something blurred on the screen and it went dark. He spun the audio knob to full volume and a terrified scream ripped from the speaker.

Harder punched the intercom to all stations. "Luke! Henri! Get to medical right away!"

His voice was still echoing in the compartment when he raced into the corridor and started for the dispensary. The airlock hatch to the medical section yawned wide. Harder could hear inarticulate cries mixed with screams. Only one woman could be there—June!

Harder scrambled through the hatchway. His hand sought the light switch, brushed it on. At the instant light flooded the scene, Harder was already moving. June lay crumpled on the deck, blood streaming from long slashes down one arm and across her breast where Koelbe had torn the clothes from her. Blood seeped from her mouth and nose. Koelbe's arm was raised to deliver another blow.

"Koelbe!"

The doctor turned a contorted face to him. Harder didn't reason or think. There was no time. Koelbe stopped his arm as it started down, staring blank-eyed at the man who shouted his name. In the light gravity Harder came off the floor like a human torpedo. Tensed muscle and bone pounded with battering-ram force into Koelbe's ribs. The impact hurled the doctor wildly through the air.

Harder glimpsed June's upturned white face, blood smearing her mouth, before Koelbe crashed against a wall, Harder's weight punishing the air from his lungs. Harder rolled from Koelbe's body and his fist whistled through the air even before he consciously commanded the blow. The sharp crack of bone meeting flesh rang through the compartment. Harder hit Koelbe again. His hand pistoned through the air. It didn't reach Koelbe. A body hurled Harder to one side, smothered his arms. Snarling, Harder twisted around.

"Mike, for the love of God, stop it!" Harder stared into Parsons' face. "Mike, he's out. He can't hurt anyone. You'll kill him."

Harder's eyes slowly came into focus. He nodded at Parsons. "I'm okay, Luke. Let me get to June."

Guy-Michel was already lifting her carefully to a bed.

"I'll—I'll be all right," she said quickly as she caught sight of Harder. "You must strap him down right away, Mike," she said with a note of desperation.

Guy-Michel pushed her gently down, covering her with a sheet. "Luke, get a wet towel from the wash-room," the Frenchman said.

Harder turned to the unconscious form of Koelbe. "Take care of her, Henri. I'll get Werner strapped down."

He carried the doctor to another bunk, tightened the wide straps, careful of the broken arm in its cast. Though he was unconscious, his features were still distorted, his mouth working soundlessly.

Parsons soaked a towel and called from the wash-room. "What happened to him?"

"He didn't know what he was doing. He wasn't after me," June said. "He thought I was his—his father."

"His father!" The words burst from Guy-Michel. "But for what reason? What can his father possibly have to do with you? With us?"

Parsons returned with the towel. "What's this about Werner's father?"

June shook her head. "I don't know." She winced as Guy-Michel began to clean the blood from her face.

"Luke—in the next room. Compresses, gauze, some spray disinfectant. It is in the cabinet," Guy-Michel said. "Would you, please?"

"Of course." They heard the cabinet door opening.

Mike Harder hadn't said a word. He alone knew. He glanced at Koelbe. *The poor son of a bitch. He*

couldn't get away from the past, after all. He didn't
explain what he knew about the medical man. It didn't
matter now. There wasn't any question but that the
microorganisms were flooding through Koelbe's system,
that they had lodged in his brain. Werner Koelbe
was insane. Now they were without a doctor.

Parsons hurried into the room with the medical
supplies. "I couldn't hear you in there," he said.
"What was this about Werner and his—" His voice
halted, and a sliver of fear knifed into him. "What's
wrong?" His hand started up toward his face. "You're
all staring at me as if I have—"

"Yeah, Luke."

Parsons turned to a mirror. Along the side of his
face the rash leaped out at him.

The conference hall seated twelve hundred, and
more than two thousand newsmen and women jammed
in for the confrontation with the big guns of NASA,
Project *Epsilon*, the White House, the United Nations, and God knew who else. The press didn't care
about "God knew who else." They wanted Dave
Heath and Ed Thayer from NASA, and they got
them. Charles Lynch was down from the White House
but was scorned as a poor substitute for the Vice
President, who also held the chair as Director of the
National Space Council. Emanuel Garavito and Dr.
Richard Zystra would answer for the space station
itself, as Project Director and Medical Programs Director. Ray Lafferty, who handled international liaison for *Epsilon*, could be grabbed after the conference
for what might be some good sidebars to the story.

An aide leaned close to the ear of John Towers
from CBS. He had to shout to be heard over the din
that filled the hall. "What about DeRosa?" he asked.

Towers glanced at the tall figure of the United

Nations medical authority. "What about him?" He
didn't conceal the scorn in his voice. DeRosa was a
pompous ass who had won his appointment through
political chicanery. That crap about radiation. . . .

The aide was shouting again. "We can get some
good material from the guy, John! He's liable to say
anything now, the way everyone went after his ass
about that radiation stuff!"

Towers fixed his assistant with a frosty glare. "What
the hell's the matter with you? You don't need to
hoke up this story, for Christ's sake! This is the end
of the world as far as news is concerned!"

Ben Blanchard stepped to the microphone at the
side of the stage. As if the uproar were controlled by
a thrown switch, the hall fell silent. Blanchard waited
for the final coughs and shuffling of feet. He wanted
to get right into the thick of it, quit sparring, and
slug it out with the newsmen. He hated protocol,
but there was no way out of it. Not when the television giants were in here loaded for bear, when
microphones would relay every whisper out into the
world. It was a world, he thought sourly, with
newspapers, magazines, editorial pages, front pages,
and flickering screens and rasping speakers—opening its maw, waiting to engorge what would be said
from this platform.

Did they really want news, he wondered, or did
they come for something new with which to titillate
the billions of eager listeners, after using up their
ration of jungle war, hydrogen bombs, LSD, murder, rape, carnage, natural atrocities—the latter, of
course, the ungovernable actions of murderers, rap-
ists, and sadists on whose psychological shoulders
there rode some fierce-countenanced, white-haired
mother who had once beaten her son for jazzing
himself in the back seat of the car. Blanchard was no

fool. Today he recognized something different. This crowd out there had a smell to it.

It was an animal smell—the mob. Out there were the many hundreds who were simply the front wedge of the howling pack that waited at television screens and radio speakers and newspaper stands. Get a crowd together and give them something into which they could sink their collective teeth and, *wham*, just like that, the crowd became a mob. He was standing before a mob.

They were frightened. *And I don't blame them,* thought Blanchard. *If I had any sense in my head I'd be scared, too. Maybe I'm just too tired.*

The cameras were live and the microphones ultra-sensitive. And the reporters were poised—about to become a shouting mass, so Blanchard played it by the book. *I'll give them protocol so far up their asses, it'll be coming out of their ears.* He did his best, but it didn't take. They were too keen.

"Let's get with it, Blanchard!" The shout came from somewhere out in the sea of faces, and Blanchard knew it didn't matter who it was. The cry was taken up, and the uproar filled the hall. Garavito, who knew the respect in which the thundering hundreds held him, rose to his feet. Blanchard's pride crawled down around his ankles like trousers without a belt, but he stepped aside with a nod to the project director of *Epsilon.*

"We will review the entire set-up," said Emanuel Garavito.

Television cameramen tightened their focus, microphones were adjusted, and pencils made ready to capture high points.

He laid it right on the line. "The situation is critical. Before you ask your questions—and this panel is ready to answer them to the best of our ability—I will bring you up to the present."

He cut it straight. " . . . the pathogen, the microorganism that has brought with it effects unknown to us has created a critical situation. But it is *not* fatal." He gave the word *not* its proper emphasis and caught the murmur that swept through the hall. "The symptoms include high fever, skin eruptions, a condition of vertigo, difficulties with vision."

Garavito paused, then resumed, in a dogged, determined fashion. "The disease, so far, has produced unknown effects upon the brain, upon the senses. The pattern, however, is not consistent. It is impossible to predict its course with any one individual. Actually, we are speaking from ignorance rather than from knowledge. To draw definite conclusions at this time would be premature and possibly disastrous to our hopes for effecting a cure. As you already know, Astronaut William Jordan is dead. But it was *not* the unknown malady that brought his death. I wish you all to understand that most clearly. This condition, this disease—whatever it is you wish to call it—*has not yet produced the death of any human being.* Whatever it was that struck down Astronaut Jordan did not kill him. His loss was the result of irrationality—and hallucinations. This led him to violate the most basic precepts of survival in space. What Jordan did brought on his own death. He is, you might say, an indirect casualty. As for Miss Alison—she has a high fever. She is in a coma but has no pain.

Garavito decided not to say anything at this moment about the massive injection of drugs to keep her from the insane screaming—there would be time enough for that later. The first impression was critical. "Professor Pollard's condition remains unchanged. His fever has not increased. He remains semiconscious or in a coma. We have hopes there will be an improvement soon in his condition."

Play down Koelbe, Garavito's instinct warned. So he told them only that Dr. Werner Koelbe had suffered a serious attack of vertigo and had had to be restrained for his own safety. He didn't tell them Koelbe had gone mad and had tried to kill June Strond or that Harder had nearly killed the doctor in going to her defense.

Garavito kept the case of Luke Parsons until the finale of his review. In truth, this case did offer hope. He was the fifth to contract the enigmatic malady, indicating some greater resistance to its onset. The reactions were mild. "The rash is prominent. But it is encouraging, you may well agree, to note that Astronaut Parsons remains in full possession of his faculties. There has been no impairment of balance, no loss of physical coordination, no diminution of his capability to function as a full member of the space station crew."

Garavito knew the switch was vital to his words and that it was now imperative to continue along a positive vein. "We are maintaining constant monitoring through telemetry. Three crew members—Colonel Harder, Dr. Guy-Michel, and Dr. Strond—remain absolutely free of any effects."

He realized the questions would soon be pouring in. This was all preliminary to the big show. He knew what they would shout from their sweating midst, what they clamored to know, what the whole world wanted to know.

Is there a danger to the people on Earth? Is some inconceivable terror to be loosed among us? *What are you doing to protect every mother's son of us?* Well, let them wait, make them bide their time, dull them just a bit with facts. Speak to them calmly, and maybe it won't all blow up in our faces. Garavito was a spellbinder, cloaked in the dignity of the scientist, leaning as heavily as he dared on their respect for him.

He almost made it.

A side door to the stage opened and a white-faced official from StatCom walked around at the rear of the group, as unobtrusive as he could make himself. He might just as well have carried a flaming torch and entered to the clash of cymbals. The newsmen smelled him out without a moment's delay. He reeked of *story*.

Even Garavito sensed the change in mood. He cut himself off and studied the mob, noticing the eyes looking elsewhere, to the side. Garavito turned slowly and saw Ben Blanchard with a note in his hand.

"Dr. Garavito?" The project director knew Blanchard well. Garavito nodded to his public affairs man. It was the signal to the executioner. Blanchard faced the crowd squarely.

"Dr. Timothy Pollard is dead."

Chapter XVI

Hank Marrows flipped a cigarette stub through the open window of the trailer and reached for another. He blew smoke through his nostrils and gazed at his typewriter. He held a great affection for the battered old machine. It was his thinking cap. He wrote most of his copy on a portable electric, but when the cobwebs wouldn't go away he got out the old typewriter and pecked away like a mechanical crow. Leaning forward, he rested his hands on the keys. A sudden roar burst over the trailer and Marrows smiled. His fingers began to move.

"Today," wrote the newsman, "homo sapiens showed his true colors. Today the dominant race on this planet tucked its tail between its legs, shivered through its rump, and howled fearfully at the moon. Today the shit hit the fan."

He read the words with pleasure. "Too bad I can't write that for print," he muttered to himself. He had no desire to answer to a howling mob—and the mobs were in full cry. Yet his jest was in earnest. Humanity was scared stiff and howling at the moon. He kept the radio on low. The reports poured in from various sections of the country. All hell was breaking loose at the different launch sites and space centers across the United States. It began with picketing and demonstrations, but the quiet stuff didn't last long. You can't beat honest fear for whipping a crowd into a savage, unruly mob.

The roar from outside surged again through the trailer. Marrows went to the window and watched a bearded young man gesticulating wildly as he harangued a crowd of thousands, his voice wind-whipped from crackling loudspeakers.

". . . don't care about us! They don't care about our children or our mothers or our loved ones! The *plague*—that's what they want to let loose among us! It's a warning from God! He doesn't want us out in space. He wants us right where He put us. Here on Earth! Are we going to let them get away with it?" The voice screeched through the loudspeakers and fanned like little flames through the massed crowd.

"I can't hear you!" the speaker shouted as the thousands of people responded with a low, swelling murmur. "Let me hear you!" he cried, his arms wide. "Are we going to let them get away with poisoning the Earth?" The murmur rushed like a breaking wave across the causeway, boomed in volume to become a tearing, ragged *"NO!"* that shook the guard gates where heavily armed men fingered their weapons nervously.

Jesus Christ. They're whipping themselves into a frenzy. If they ever bust loose. . . . There must have been a hundred thousand people camped on the roads around the complex that made up the Kennedy Space Center. Only the fact that Cape Kennedy and the moonport itself—Complex 39, the "breeding grounds" for the giant Saturn V boosters—were well isolated physically had saved them from the mobs that threatened to inundate the launch sites and tear down the rockets.

The space center sprawled along the edge of the Atlantic, separated from the Florida mainland by two rivers and by desolate swampland, swarming with poisonous snakes. Causeways ran from the west and the south into Cape Kennedy and Merritt Island, and this natural protection had until now averted devastation. But it would be impossible to hold them much longer. The mobs were being restrained by barricades at the South Gate to Cape Kennedy, and the Bennet Causeway that led to the Cape from the west. The NASA parkway running from U.S. 1 on the mainland was wide and spacious, and the troops flown in from Fort Bragg were having their hands full.

It was more than venting spleen or responding to fright. The space center hypnotized the crowds because the road to space was still open. On the Cape a Saturn IB was at launch status on Pad 37. Directly across the Banana River, a Titan IIIC loomed from its man-made island on Pad 41. And, still farther to the northwest, a Saturn V had been moved to Pad 39A, and was being readied for any launch contingency. Those great boosters connected the fear of what was happening in the space station to people on Earth.

Nothing moved on the roads in or out of Cape Kennedy or the Merritt Island Launch Area. Helicopters buzzed through the air like angry hornets.

There were also gunships, the *Huey Cobras*, armed with cannon, machine guns, and rockets. No one had ever expected it to come to that.

Hank Marrows glanced at the bearded prophet who ranted about God's will, and he wasn't so sure. Marrows knew the signs. People outside were doing more than to look over the water north of the causeway where the great towers and buildings loomed above the horizon. Passive gazing had become pointing fingers and brandished fists.

For a while the mob made a sort of collective picnic out of their presence. This, too, was inevitable. They built fires and roasted hot dogs, drained beer cans, and uncorked stronger stuff. A mob like this, penned into the restrictive confines of the causeway, brought its own filth with it, Marrows knew. There weren't any mobile privies, and sooner or later nature made its demands. People held back as long as they could, but soon the sight of little boys spraying automobile tires and little girls squatting protectively behind their mothers loosened adult zippers and panties. There wasn't anything else to do. They couldn't get back to the mainland if they wanted to. They were wedged tight by the confines of the causeway and the shuffling humanity on foot, in stalled cars, and on trailers. They had nowhere to go unless they thundered right over the barracks to the Cape, and Marrows was convinced this was only a matter of time.

For the moment they listened to the harangue, played car and transistor radios loudly for the latest bulletins, ate what they'd brought along and drank themselves silly, then sure as hell began to line up along the edge of the causeway, the men voiding with self-conscious laughter and the women squatting miserably wherever they thought they wouldn't be on center stage. Before too long, embarrassment would turn to anger and frustration. Gradually, too, impatience, hunger, discomfort, the annoyance of mosquitos, the sense of entrapment would build to an explosive point. And this crowd couldn't go back. Ergo, it would surge toward the launch sites.

The Big Scare was on. Not even in his wildest dreams did Marrows anticipate the overwhelming impact of the *Epsilon* disaster. But then, he mused, people had never before been faced with the reality of invasion from space. There had been other frights and scares, but in the morning everyone had woken up and laughed at their fears of the night before.

Not now. This time they came awake in the cold morning and found that the nightmare was real. The aliens *were* here, just outside the fringe of atmosphere. *We should have remembered Orson Welles better. How could we forget so easily? Didn't anyone, including me, remember the riots, the wild, unreasoning fear that took hold of people all over the country, in their frenzy to avoid the horrors of what they believed to be an attack on Earth from outer space?*

But that was in 1938, and people weren't surfeited with world wars and thermonuclear bombs that could poison a world. We didn't have astronauts on the moon, and laser beams, and huge electronic brains, and television. People were a lot simpler, and so was the world, in 1938. And when Orson Welles went on the air with his hoked-up invasion from Mars, the public swallowed the whole thing as real and the panic started. Ever since then they had snickered about what happened, but now the snickering gagged in their throats and they looked up at the stars and their bowels turned weak.

The prophets of doom came bounding from their caves with the fire of vindicated zealots burning in their eyes. The placards appeared like wheat springing from the ground. The end of the world had come, as prophesied. It was in the stars, the crystal balls, the holy books. God has given us a warning. Mend our ways! Is it not clear?

The malignancy is not yet here on Earth. It was hurled against those who trespassed the domain of God.

"Heretics in a space station," sighed Marrows. "That's better than anything I ever came up with. . . ."

With explosive speed the world made *Epsilon* its dominant theme. The refrain was simple enough. If ever the astronauts came back to Earth they would bring with them the alien organisms that would, in turn, decimate all mankind. Man must stay on Earth as God intended. If God had wanted man to fly, He would have given him wings.

When in doubt—riot.

When bored or looking for kicks—join the squares, and tear up everything in sight.

They came like locusts, with a throaty roar, beating the air with invisible wings. Wherever the tools, the implements, the engines, the vessels of space were built, the mobs assembled.

By dusk the fun was over. Even the kids had stopped laughing, sensing with animal instinct the mood that gripped the adults about them. The last few hours had passed with slavish attention to radios. One after the other the bulletins had come in until the radio stations abandoned all pretense at any other programming. The hundred thousand frightened, cold, tired, hungry, dirty, impatient human beings, wedged onto causeways and standing on shorelines around the periphery of the space center, felt themselves joining with their equally frightened citizens across the country.

Word spread that the plague was rampant in the space station. Close on the heels of that news came the rumor that the astronauts were being returned to Earth. Fear mushroomed that all the peoples of Earth would be exposed to a scourge unknown even in the musty pages of the Bible. Surely the people must take things into their own hands.

The little-known NASA launch center for sounding rockets and small satellites at Wallops Island, Virginia, sank beneath a screaming mob of ten thousand frightened people. Some scientists were killed, but most were allowed to escape. The invading throngs went to work with crowbars, hammers, axes, pieces of pipe, and wrecking bars. Then they brought in cans of gasoline and sticks of dynamite. The smoke was visible for a hundred miles.

Japan's satellite launch center was isolated from the main islands, safe enough from the shrieking mobs on the streets. More than a thousand boats, large and small, plied the waters to bring the frenzied mobs on to the scientific island outpost. Years of frustration, hatred, and fear spilled over in an orgy of wanton devastation. Hiroshima and Nagasaki became identified with the present. American atomic bombs, America in space, the American space station . . . and anyone who worked with the Americans or worked on such terrible things must be punished.

There is no peopled mass quite so savage as the Japanese when they cast away their civilized fetters. The scientists, engineers, technicians, janitors, truck drivers, cooks, wives, children—one and all—were hacked to death. Fire was the answer. A plague threatened. Fire could destroy the plague. From one end to the other the island ran with gasoline and oil, and belched flame as would a newborn volcano.

Throughout the United States dozens of test centers and laboratories came in for their share of grief. If the plague was in space then it must be on the moon. In laboratories were samples of rock and dust brought back from the moon. The mobs stormed these labs and offices. They smashed, burned, pillaged, fired, wrecked. No one could tell lunar soil from any other kind. So they burned anything and everything that came within their reach.

They were not willingly destructive. They were frightened. There are only so many who riot for the fun of it—a small percentage. Most of those who roared through the streets were normal human beings. Good citizens. Good parents. Upright people. But terrified.

Acting under orders from the President and the Governor, National Guard units rushed to the Manned Spacecraft Center outside Houston. Helicopters airlifted astronauts' families from the housing areas only minutes before the homes went up in flames. MSC went under a state of siege. The mobs held back because of the frightened actions of a young lieutenant. Without orders from above, and prompted by adrenalin pouring through his frightened body, he screamed out an order to fire. In the flare-lit darkness several machine guns cut a savage, bloody swath through thousands of people jammed together at the barricades. More than two hundred died from the scythe of bullets. Six hundred more died in the panic that followed. But it held them at bay. Word went out that the mobs were not to be tolerated. A closer fear held them off.

At Huntsville, Alabama, the people demonstrated that they could wrench old hatreds from their memories. The Marshall Space Flight Center—the old Redstone Arsenal—was famed as "little Germany." Here was the office and the home of Dr. Wernher von Braun and of other scientists, who, decades before, had worked for the Third Reich when the swastika was in ascendancy. Sullen, fearful crowds began to gather in the streets. Scientists, whose families had been born in this country and had never lived elsewhere, found their garage doors and the sides of their homes smeared with crudely-painted emblems of the crooked cross. Mobs gathered in cars and trucks and buses, attracting a huge crowd of hoodlums on motorcycles. The roar of engines and exhaust sounded for miles as they converged on the great research center. The main gate went down under the battering-ram-force of a truck driven full speed through the gate, scattering guards like tenpins. The mob poured in behind, led by the black-jacketed heroes on motorcycles who roared through the center, hurling Molotov cocktails at any likely target. Within an hour most of the laboratories and workshops were engulfed in flames.

The crowds gathered outside the great aerospace factories. Boeing, North American-Rockwell, McDonnell-Douglas, Aerojet General, Bendix, General Electric, Beech. All the plants shut down. The workers were sent home for their own safety. National Guard units rolled in with tanks and armored vehicles and thousands of troops with bayonets to stand guard.

Waiting in his trailer, Hank Marrows knew the time had come at Cape Kennedy and at the Merritt Island area to the north. The tension was ready to burst. On the NASA Parkway leading from U.S. 1 to the Complex 39 launch area the troops that had been rushed in would best handle the job. The Titan IIIC complex also was well defended and physically isolated. Cape Kennedy was another matter.

The breaking point came with a one-two blow. But no one man set it off. A news bulletin shocked the crowd into new panic. Marrows heard it, and felt all the nerves in his spine quake with cold. He couldn't believe the official stupidity that permitted the information to be flashed to the nation at such a critical moment.

. . . interrupt this program to bring you a special news bulletin. The federal space agency has just announced that Dr. Werner Koelbe of the Epsilon *space station has died. There are reports that all the astronauts of . . .*

Moments later, almost as if the two events had been coordinated, a roar came from the sky. From the first moments of public unrest the government had issued sweeping restrictions of flying anywhere near the environs of the Kennedy Space Center. It didn't hold water with everyone. Zealots especially made immediate plans to circumvent the emergency restrictions and to avoid the helicopter gunships hovering along the periphery of the sprawling launch area.

Marrows heard the roar of engines in the air and rushed to the window. Two gunships were pounding after a twin-engine airplane diving toward Cape Kennedy. Fire streamed from one engine, but there was no stopping the misguided fanatic at the controls of the diving plane. The machine plunged into a tall orange launch tower on the Cape. Marrows watched with binoculars as a dazzling ball of flame ripped into the air, followed by thick smoke.

Nice touch, thought Marrows. The creep wipes himself out by crashing into Pad 19. Talk about your ironic justice. Pad 19 hadn't been used for years. It was a national memorial, the launch site for the old Gemini program.

It was also the final straw. The long hours of fear and frustration, the shock of the news bulletin announcing Koelbe's death, and now this demonstration of sacrifice all combined to light the fuse of mob violence.

The door to the trailer crashed open. Marrows and the men with him looked into wild-eyed faces. Their leader shook his fist. "What side are you on?" he roared at Marrows.

Hank Marrows had been a few places in his life. He knew this moment was inevitable. He knew also that if the mob felt you weren't actively with them, then you were against them, in which case your life wasn't worth a plugged nickel. Marrows had anticipated the moment. He pointed to a stack of placards leaning against the wall of the trailer. "WE BELONG ON EARTH!" "DOWN WITH NASA!" "GET OUT OF THE MOON!" He liked the touch of that last one. Certainly he had no desire to go to the moon. As far as he was concerned, the Vietnamese jungle had been his first and last visit to another planet.

Marrows pointed to the signs. "Our side!" he shouted back, trying to make his eyes bulge. "Just tell us when you're ready to get them bastards!"

His visitor bared yellow teeth and smiled hugely. "That's the way, brother. Amen!"

"Amen!" Marrows cried.

But the delegation didn't go away. They expected Marrows and his news crew to pile out of the trailer and join them. There was no choice. The crowd was yelling now, waving torches, brandishing Molotov cocktails.

They took the South Gate easily. A souped-up Ford thundered along the edge of the highway, people scattering before it. At eighty-miles-an-hour, it ripped into the wire mesh fence twenty yards from the gates. Three more cars roared through the gap and the mob streamed behind them like water pouring through a funnel. In a matter of minutes the guards had been overpowered and their weapons torn from their hands. Thousands of people broke off to the right, rushing over the roadway to Port Canaveral where the nuclear submarines received their loads of Polaris missiles. That helped somewhat—it diverted some of the energy.

Marrows knew the decision to defend the Cape had anticipated the loss of the guard gates and the south fence. The people thundered onto Cape Kennedy, forced to remain on the roads. The moment you moved off a paved strip or the road shoulder, you were deep in palmetto scrub and thick underbrush. Tearing thorns, spiked plants, and swampy soil combined to slow down the crowd, as had been planned.

Other hordes, meanwhile, surged around a sharp corner in the road, hurling their blazing Molotov cocktails into a power substation. Instantly flames roared upward to light the scene in a garish, ruddy glow. The people swept on, maddened, screaming in their frenzy. A massive barricade fell as the Molotov cocktails forced the guards back. Marrows climbed a pole for a better view as citizens fired rifles at the retreating guards. Some of them crumpled to the ground. They never knew the roadblock had been for their own protection, and the barricade set up to keep them out of the cryogenic production area. Cryogenic fuels! "Good God," Marrows whispered to himself. *"The fools!"*

He estimated roughly that three thousand men and women had poured into the area where tanks of liquid oxygen and hydrogen were stored. Super-explosive fuel. Once that started to burn . . . Marrows stared in fascinated horror as the first Molotov cocktails hissed through the air. The rest happened so fast he never remembered the details.

A gigantic spear of flame sped across the ground, following fuel pipes, in a tremendous explosion that covered nearly a thousand feet in a fraction of a second. In staccato fashion the tanks went up. Flame ripped hundreds of feet into the sky. The only sound that penetrated the cracking thunder of the blasts was that of human voices, screaming as the blaze slashed through their massed ranks. Marrows felt heat sear his face, saw a crazy slow-motion scene of debris hurtling and tumbling through the air. Something wet smacked against his face and clung to his skin. Frantically he tore it from him. It was a piece of a human body. Marrows dropped to the ground and vomited violently.

More than two thousand people died that night at Cape Kennedy. Not one had been shot.

Terror transformed the surging mob into mindless creatures. Surrounded on all sides by dense and impenetrable underbrush, forced to remain along the roads, and ditches, they were not difficult to control. The method of defense was the same along the Cape and the Merritt Island Launch Area: let them get through to the critical turnoff points and then shunt them into open areas where they can rave all they want to.

Crowd control was effected by the simple expedient of digging huge ditches, filling them with oil and setting them aflame to create blazing walls through which the crowd could not pass. They veered from their intended path, spilling along side roads until they reached the beaches and the canals. Many leaped into the entrance to Port Canaveral, trying to swim south. Many drowned. Helicopter gunships cruised along the beaches to attend to any raiding parties that came by boat. Those who refused to turn back received a warning burst of fire. Those who shot back at the helicopters were blown out of the water.

On the NASA parkway to the north, the flaming barricade held back the crowd until dawn. The flames ebbed, died finally from lack of fuel. Someone had fouled up. By the time more gasoline could be brought, the mob, pressed by sheer weight of numbers from behind, surged across the smoking barrier. Many were burned; others fell and were trampled. There was no stopping them. Mass and inertia carried them forward. They were permitted to run more than two miles, to waste their energies and thin their ranks before staggering to a halt.

Across the parkway, extending out over the water, six powerful helicopter gunships hovered thirty feet above the ground. Engines howling, dazzling lights pointing at the onrushing mobs, they presented a terrifying sight, weaving and bobbing in the air like monstrous dragonflies. The lead gunship moved to the side and fired a canister of rockets. The shrieking projectiles tore over the heads of the mob, sounding like the end of the world. Several hundred yards away, in open water, the rockets exploded with an ear-smashing roar. Then the gunship slid back into formation. The crowds came to a halt. Within minutes the situation was completely under control. Helicopters cruised low overhead, giving orders through loudspeakers. The people had finally been cowed. Their energies were spent, their hatred sapped.

Meanwhile, the crews at Pad 40 never stopped work on the giant booster pointing away from the planet.

Chapter XVII

"Are you certain you understand what's involved?"

Astronaut Ken Sanborne's gaze was steady as he looked at Dave Heath. The NASA administrator had flown in from Washington to speak personally with them both. Sanborne nodded slowly. "I understand." There was no hesitation in his voice.

Heath turned to Hal Gunner. "Hal?"

The second astronaut slouched low in his chair, chin resting against his chest. For all the concern he showed, Gunner might be getting ready to go fishing. "No questions, Dave."

Heath snapped his lighter and inhaled deeply. "I already knew that," he said.

Gunner raised his brows. "Then why the flap, Dave?"

"Because we've got to be certain we cover every aspect of this thing," the administrator said with nervous movements of his hands. "You see," he

233

smiled, "you're the known commodities in this affair. But there are other factors. The Congress and the public."

"Somebody biting you in the ankle, Dave?" Sanborne asked with a knowing look.

"Uh-huh. Big dog, big teeth."

"Who lives in a great big white house?" Gunner threw in.

"And when he barks I jump," Heath said.

"And he never forgets the public, either," Sanborne laughed.

Heath looked at them carefully. "Don't sell the public short, boys. At least two hundred doctors—all of them qualified—have volunteered to take your places."

Gunner whistled. "Hey, surprises will never cease. You leveling?"

Heath nodded. "I'm not counting those who aren't qualified to go. Headquarters and MSC have received more than a thousand telegrams, phone calls, and personal visits. All volunteers clamoring to go."

Gunner looked at his partner. "Never thought we still had so many Paul Reveres around."

"More Reveres than horses, though," Sanborne said.

"You two act as if you're going on a picnic." Heath showed a trace of irritation.

"Can't complain about the price of the ticket," Sanborne said with a shrug. "Even if the food is lousy."

"And the service—" Gunner rolled his eyes.

The phrase *into the jaws of death* flashed through Heath's mind. These two would make the trip with a last drink and a casual nod.

"I haven't finished what I came here to do," Heath

said. Again he appraised these two young men—skilled doctors, skilled pilots, skilled astronauts.

"You understand that if things don't work out you may never be able to—to come home?"

"You're coming in five by five," Gunner answered. He didn't make a joke of it.

Heath sighed. "I—"

"Make it easier on yourself, Dave," Gunner went on. "We know the bit." A smile appeared. "We understand what you're trying to do and we appreciate it. Hell, if the situation were reversed, there isn't a guy up there who wouldn't do the same for us."

"I guess they would."

"You know damn well they would."

The administrator felt the tightness leaving him. "Would you two characters believe I would like to be in that ship with you?"

"We believe it."

"Jesus, but I—"

"Yeah, Dave, but somebody's got to mind the store. And I wouldn't take *your* job for a million."

Damn it, maybe there's hope yet. There's *got* to be, Heath insisted to himself. He stood up and extended his hand. "Have a good trip," he said. "That's a rather inane remark, isn't it?"

"It's better than 'don't forget your rubbers.'"

The sight of their faces and their laughter remained with him all the way back to Washington. He wanted to stay for the launch, but couldn't—not with the White House on top of this thing. The bird would get off the pad whether he was there or not. The lifting body was ready, medical supplies and equipment secured within the arrow-shaped spacecraft. Jack Dexter would fly as command pilot, and rendezvous with the space station. He was under strict orders not to dock with *Epsilon* but to hold position above the S-IVB tank, into which they would transfer the medical gear.

"Dump everything out of the ship, disembark Sanborne and Gunner, and back off to a thousand yards for station-keeping." Those were Dexter's orders: no contact with the station. No one from the station was even to approach the spacecraft. That way, Heath thought, we can have the balm of at least one human being who will return alive.

The odds were—and he insisted on being brutally honest with himself—that the others would never make it. Bill Jordan, Tim Pollard, Werner Koelbe . . . dead. Page was still critical and under drugs. And Luke was getting worse. Damn, damn! He had known Luke Parsons since he was a kid.

Christ, I wish it was me in that ship instead of them. . . .

Mike Harder slipped into the dispensary. His intention had been to jolly it up a bit with Luke, but a glance at the astronaut held him quiet. June stood by him, her finger and thumb holding his wrist. She made a notation on the chart and took a thermometer from his mouth. If Harder hadn't been watching carefully, he wouldn't have noticed the momentary sag in her shoulders. He reached for the instrument— nearly 103. With a small motion meant only for him, June shook her head. Harder studied his friend. Luke lay on his back, his features a mask, his eyes open but unseeing.

"They're sending a ship," Harder said. "Ken Sanborne and Hal Gunner. They're sure they can whip this thing. They're bringing new medicines and . . ." His voice trailed away. Luke hadn't so much as flickered an eyelash. "Luke?" He watched the astronaut turn his head slightly and saw that the eyes didn't move. Parsons responded to his name but couldn't, or wouldn't, make the effort to see who was speaking to him. Harder clenched his teeth.

June led him to the adjoining room. "He's been that way for a while. It started out with a general withdrawal, almost as if he were intensely preoccupied. He reacts less and less to outside stimuli. He's not in a coma. He's fully awake, but it's as if his mind were elsewhere."

"God damn" was all he could say.

"He's not in any pain, Mike."

"That's something, anyway."

"I could stick a pin in him and he wouldn't feel it. It's as if sensations were cut off before the brain registers them." When he didn't respond, she went on: "The fever is rising slowly. What I don't like is that the postules are appearing. It's following, in a certain way, the pattern we saw with Bill. Much slower, but the pattern is repeating itself."

"You've strapped him down," Harder said.

She glanced toward the other room and nodded. "He asked me to." She saw the startled look on his face. "We would have had to, of course. There's no way to tell when he might react like the others and lose control." He nodded. "Luke felt the same way. It was before he began to lose touch with things around him. It's more than if he just didn't care. Anyway, he told me I'd better strap him down in case he. . . ." She faltered. "He said, in case he suffered any brain damage."

Harder closed his eyes for a long moment. That was the worst of it—watching them coming apart before your eyes.

"You mentioned a ship," she said.

"Uh-huh. Got the word just before I came here. Dexter is flying, but he won't come in the station.

He'll bring Sanborne and Gunner as close as he can and unload the supplies. He's under orders to back off and wait."

She thought over his words. "It's surprising—and comforting—that someone would come. Willingly, I mean—into all this."

"They're good people, June. Any one of the team would do it. They all volunteered."

"When will they be here?"

He glanced at his watch. "Launch window opens just about four hours from now. They should lift off on schedule."

"I thought the booster was—"

He anticipated her question. "Not the Saturn," he said. "We're using blue-suit hardware. Titan IIIC. Good reasoning. They can count that thing to minus-one-minute, and hold until launch time."

She thought about the two doctors. Thank God they were coming. She couldn't keep going much longer. She was far more tired than she would admit to Harder or the others. Sometimes the headaches worried her, but she forced her thoughts away from her own problems. Leaning forward, she kissed Harder on the lips. He watched her leave, then went back to his command quarters. There was work to do. Running the station systems was a backbreaker for only two men. But that's all they had—Henri and himself. And they were taking turns to relieve June with Luke and Page.

He thought again about the ship waiting to lift from the Cape. *Hurry up, you guys. There may not be anyone left by the time you get here.*

It took them thirty-two hours. In that time, Sanborne and Gunner found what they were looking for. Sanborne went to Harder's office and sank gratefully into a chair, his face lined with fatigue. Counting the time it had taken for boost into orbit, and their work here, Sanborne and Gunner had been working steadily for nearly forty-eight hours. Harder reached for the cabinet latch. "Brandy?" Sanborne nodded. Harder filled a plastiglas for himself and the doctor. They drank in silence. Sanborne and Gunner were members of the new breed—doctors, medical scientists, and then astronauts.

"We're ready to file the report, Mike."

Harder nodded.

"But I wanted to go over it with you before we spoke with Houston."

Harder refilled the glasses. "Let's have it."

"Zystra has been right, of course."

"The dust is responsible?"

Sanborne nodded slowly. "The organisms are in the dust. We've run a whole battery of tests. There's no question."

"And when we opened the dust traps—that did it." Harder shrugged.

"Uh-huh. Whatever mixed with the air was carried through the ventilation system," Sanborne confirmed.

"There's something I don't understand," Harder said. "Some of the dust would adhere to a surface. Cloth, velcro, a surface with a film on it. Dust collects in corners, behind equipment—that sort of thing. You have to consider even static electricity."

"Go on," Sanborne prompted.

"It doesn't fit, Ken," Harder insisted, a frown reflecting his confusion. "The only place in this station where we opened the containers with the dust was in Life Sciences. That's top deck in this tin can. The containers weren't opened anywhere else. You follow me so far?"

Sanborne nodded.

"Okay. Luke Parsons never went into Life Sciences after the dust came aboard. Yet he's down with it. Except for Page, who worked pretty closely with the dust, there wasn't that much exposure to the crew. Yet they came down with it. In fact, Jordan and Pollard were hit *before* Page." Harder toyed with the brandy glass. "The only conclusion left is that exposure to the dust and the microorganisms it contains was caused by the forced-air draft and ventilation systems."

Sanborne motioned with his hand. "That's how we feel. I don't see it happening any other way."

"All right, then. All the air in this station moves constantly. The flow always goes on. Forced-draft of fresh air and a constant pickup of air. What's used is cleansed. The air goes through one hell of a cleansing process. It's dehumidified, scrubbed with chemicals, heated, cooled, exposed to ultraviolet. It goes through sampler screens and is checked automatically before it's sent back into the station system." Harder's hand smacked with a loud report on his desk. "Then how the hell could those organisms survive to do their damage?" He shouted the question. "The systems are designed to clean out anything that could be harmful. *Including* dust or anything that's mixed in with it. So how the hell—" He waved his hand in apology. "Christ, I'm repeating myself. But I *don't* understand it. You got any answers in those black boxes of yours?"

Sanborne stood up. He had to move. If he sat in one place too long he knew he'd fall asleep. He bounded awkwardly above the deck, stumbling as he threw his arms out wildly for balance, then caught himself on the edge of Harder's desk, looking with astonishment at the colonel.

Harder returned his gaze. "Takes a while, doesn't it?"

"Jesus! Sitting there I forgot all about this low g. Just came up from the seat, and when I thought I'd stopped I found myself still going." He moved gingerly back to the chair. "But to answer your question, Mike," he said quickly. "Normally everything you say is correct. I emphasize the word 'normally.'"

"Yeah. And what we have here isn't normal," Harder said bitterly.

"Obviously. It's the nature of the microorganisms," Sanborne continued. "In recent years we've learned a lot about the basic forms of life. The theory of proto-life—of spores drifting through space—has a great deal more meat to it than we once believed."

"Spare me the lecture, Ken. I'm too damned tired."

The doctor smiled quickly. "Sorry. The gist of it is that this type of microorganism—and we've identified them in meteorites, by the way—has a survival factor that's way out of reason. It shouldn't be able to withstand the things to which it's exposed, but it does. It can take any degree of cold to be found in space, and that includes getting down as close as you can to absolute zero. There's a theory that it could even take that and come up spitting. Heat? It's been exposed to the sun at distances much closer than we are. It survives it all. It takes tremendous shock, and acceleration doesn't seem to bother it. We brought a small centrifuge with us, spun dust particles to a thousand gravities, put the dust into nutrient solutions, and the growth was fantastic."

Harder drummed his fingers on the desk. "What about radiation? That should affect it."

Sanborne shook his head. "Not even radiation. Mike, that stuff can take a radiation dose a million times greater than what's necessary to kill you or me.

I know the figure I'm using. It can take a million times the lethal rad dose for a human being—and it doesn't faze it." Sanborne threw up his hands. "Heat, cold, radiation, acceleration, ultraviolet—the works. It swallows it all and comes back for more."

Harder knew a sense of desperation when he saw it. "What about fire?"

"It *should* eliminate it. But right now I wouldn't even bet on a blast furnace."

"That's not very encouraging, is it?"

"No. I'm hardly the bearer of good tidings, am I?"

Harder smiled—no humor in it. "Not exactly." After a pause, he added, "What's been the pattern with our people here?"

Sanborne gave a slight shrug. "Nothing mysterious, Mike. The organisms were brought into the body by inhalation—ingestion. That's common enough. But once there, reproduction has been—well, fantastic is the only word for it. Think of it as a pathogenic organism, a disease-bearing organism, although that's not strictly true. You'd have to equate 'alien' with 'disease,' and that's assuming—well, that's also neither here nor there. Multiplication of the organisms was overwhelming. We still don't know the process of cell-splitting, or even if this is the case. The effects were unmistakable but," he hedged his own conclusions, "we're not certain we understand that many ramifications of spread and dispersal through the body.

"The more obvious effects have been a massive blockage of the arterial system, degeneration of brain cells, a growth—almost cancerous in its appearance and effect—within the vital organs. The postules, of course, are the result of the body's own defenses. Sometimes this defense, which is blind, so to speak, can get out of hand in the frenzy to repel what the body considers to be an invader."

Mike Harder listened in silence. Sanborne paused, found no verbal reaction, and went on. He talked for several minutes, falling more and more into the detailed physiological aspects of those who had died and the others who were ill. The turn of the conversation was predictable.

"Do you have any ideas why three of us so far have been immune?" Harder asked.

Sanborne didn't miss the reference to "so far." He smiled self-consciously. "You can change that three to five, Mike."

Harder's expression was sour. "Yeah. For the moment I forgot. Welcome to bug country."

Sanborne returned to the question. "No, I don't. That's the only honest answer I can give you. Just as we have no idea why the course of the attacks and their effects have differed in manner, and in rate of progress, from one person to another. We don't know."

Harder pressed the point. "Is there an immunity involved?"

Sanborne shook his head slowly. "Again the answer is *I don't know.* But I can give you an expert opinion, for whatever it may be worth, based on hardly more than one full day's work."

"Let's have it."

"I don't believe there's an immunity involved. There is some factor, obviously, that retards the onset of the disease from one person to another. I don't know what triggers it off, or what might be the mechanism for its spread. To be blunt about it, I'm convinced that every one of us in this station is a carrier."

"Including you and Hal?"

"I said there were five of us yet unaffected, Mike."

"Yeah, you did."

Harder chewed his lip. He wanted desperately to think the problem out, to consider all aspects. Something hovered on the edge of his conscious mind, tantalizing him, but always just beyond his grasp. He needed a rest. There hadn't been time to think— there was so damned much to do! Now, with Sanborne and Gunner here, at least they were off the medical watch. June could relax. Harder was amazed that the woman was still on her feet. She hadn't deceived him; he knew only too well the crushing burden she had accepted without hesitation.

"Anything else?" The question brought Harder out of his reflective mood with a start. Sanborne was standing by the desk. "No, no," Harder said. "Sorry, Ken, I was wool-gathering. Thanks for coming by. You'd better get your report in."

Sanborne hesitated. "You need sleep, Mike."

Harder grinned, but it wasn't easy. "Who doesn't?"

"I'll let you know if we have any new developments."

Harder nodded. He didn't have anything else to say.

Harder poured his fourth cup of coffee. A black mood diffused his thoughts. No matter where he turned, he felt anger. For the first time in his life he faced the need for a decision that left him no room for maneuvering. In every direction he failed to find help or guidance.

He'd faced the need for decisions before—critical moments when the lives of men depended solely upon which way he moved. Every man in combat had faced precisely the same situation. He didn't stand alone in that respect.

Until now.

If Michael S. Harder played it safe, his decision lay before him, clear as a white flame. Above all else, he must consider the safety of the people on Earth.

There it was, unquestionable in logic. He must sacrifice the human beings in *Epsilon*. He must not bring to Earth a plague that could decimate the world. Those in the space station were condemned to exile—provided the wisdom was unassailable and the logic sound. But was this really so? Was the sacrifice—if this were to be the decision—applicable? Harder wasn't convinced. Somehow the logic seemed faulty.

To accept exile and almost certain death in the space station was to accept far-reaching and profound conclusions. Would this be the end of man's outward thrust from his planet? Did this signal the end of manned space flight, of expeditions to the moon and, in the near future, to Mars? If man's excursions in space threatened to bring to Earth a plague of unimaginable proportions, then a frightened populace would see to it that man imposed a wall around the planet.

Harder couldn't accept it. It smacked of a finality that ran against everything he believed. A race doesn't impose chains upon itself, upon its explorations. Not unless it wishes to condemn itself to a course that contains the seeds of its own destruction. Everything Harder knew of history and of man presupposed a constant curiosity, an outward push to remove existing boundaries, and find new worlds.

Somewhere a link was missing in all this. But it remained beyond his grasp. Hours later, he fell asleep in his chair.

He slept badly. His mind refused rest and continued its searching. For the first time in as long as he could remember he had a nightmare. He was going through reentry, the heat building up to thousands of degrees. In the dream, something went wrong with attitude control, and the shock waves began to tear up the ship, embracing it with terrifying flames.

He came awake drenched, his heart pounding. There had been a final vision of charred pieces of metal tumbling all the way through the atmosphere. He didn't remember the rest, just the falling pieces.

He waited for the pounding of his heart to subside. Damn it! He couldn't keep his thoughts from the dream and the plunge through the atmosphere. In his mind he saw a shooting star, the streak of flame from a chunk of rock plunging downward, a needle-thin flame reaching all the way down to . . .

There it was. The key. He tried to stay with what now moved within his grasp.

No other astronaut or cosmonaut had ever contracted what stalked the living creatures in *Epsilon*. Humans, test animals, plant life. They existed in a clinically hygienic world, sealed within the confines of a the great S-II tank that made up the station. Into that world had been brought specimens from a dust cloud rushing through space—the same kind of cloud that existed as debris between the planets. It was a cloud made of the same stuff as meteors—and a hundred million of these whipped into the atmosphere every single day. Meteoric material. Most of it dust. *Dust*.

Some of that dust, imbedded deep within rock, survived the plunge and came to rest on Earth. Heat, cold, pressure, all manner of forces eroded the rock—and released what lay within.

He rubbed his knuckles against his forehead as if the physical pressure might release the answer. How many meteorites were there, on and imbedded in the soil? How many had fallen into the ocean to sink to the bottom of the liquid depths? How many giant meteorites had there been, like those that had torn open part of Arizona, ripped monster craters in Canada, flattened millions of trees in Russian forests?

Meteors were always exploding in midair, showering debris for hundreds of thousands of square miles, then coming to rest on the land surface, or sinking into the ocean.

The microorganisms they had brought with them in the station came from meteoric debris—*dust*— whirling through space. That same debris, that same form of dust, those same microorganisms, were in space and had been there for time unknown.

Men had walked the moon, had put samples of the lunar surface into sealed containers. Rock. Dust. Dust formed by the erosive forces of heat and cold, the impact of debris from space, from radiation coursing unchecked against the lunar surface.

There was dust falling into laboratories on Earth, dust from meteors exploding in the air, from meteorites striking land and water, dust carried by men from the moon. . . .

There was something else. He tried to force a memory into mental focus, to snatch it from the swirling thoughts that nagged at him. Something from—from . . . *Gemini!* That was *it!* One of the later shots in the two-man program. As he struggled to pinpoint his thinking, vagrant pieces began to fall into place. Gemini—a rendezvous mission using an Agena as a target. Something had happened *after* that mission. Something that held a vital, overwhelming sway over what was taking place right now.

Harder spun about in his chair, stabbing at the communications switch for Houston StatCom. Since the emergency, Houston had maintained an open line with *Epsilon*. Automatically the communications computers ran the signals through the comsat system to sustain the link between Earth and space. In the few seconds it took for StatCom to acknowledge him, Harder was running additional details through his

mind. The pulse of excitement began to beat in him.
Maybe. . . .

Atkins was on StatCom. "Get me Stubby Dolan,
fast!" Harder barked. As an afterthought he added,
"Emergency priority." Wherever he was or whatever
he might be doing, they'd get Dolan on the scene
without a wasted moment. Harder wanted Dolan
specifically. He'd made one of the Gemini flights,
and had stayed on as one of the key men for Apollo
and *Epsilon.*

It took ten minutes to raise Dolan. He'd been
asleep. He lived near the communications center,
and when his face appeared in the video-screen,
Harder guessed that the astronaut had sped through
every red light, to make it so fast. As soon as he saw
the expression on Harder's face he knew something
was up. Harder started to speak, but Dolan cut him
off with a curt motion. "Mike, is this hot?"

"What the hell—"

"I know what I'm doing," Dolan broke in. "Go to
code niner-six."

Harder stared at Dolan. A moment later he punched
in the numbered code that would route their exchange through a military scrambler. The moment
the screen cleared Dolan explained: "We've got a
flap on our hands down here, Mike. Our frequencies
are being monitored and the fanatics are screaming
to stop all space programs. We're routing the niner-
six channel through military scrambler systems. Okay,
shoot."

For fifteen minutes the two men talked. In the
clearest terms he could use, Mike Harder spelled it
out to Dolan. A tense excitement grew between
them during the exchange, Dolan sharing Harder's
thoughts, agreeing with the possibilities. Abruptly
the station intercom sounded. Harder ignored it.

Dolan was more important than anything else at that moment in the station. A few moments later the message call went to emergency. He couldn't ignore that.

"Damn it, hold on, Stub," he yelled to Dolan. He flicked on the intercom transceive. "This is Harder. Whatever you've got, spill it fast."

"Colonel—Dr. Sanborne here."

"Get with it, man, I'm—"

"Colonel, I don't know how to say this—" In that momentary pause Mike Harder went cold. He knew what was coming before the doctor said the words.

"It's June, Mike. She's got it."

Chapter XVIII

Harder clasped June's hand trying to find something to say. He looked at her and choked up. The moment he'd gotten the word, he had left Dolan, asking him to hold on, while he rushed to the dispensary. The rash had come with appalling swiftness, breaking out along the entire side of her face and neck, almost as if it had waited inside her body before cutting loose.

"I love you, June." He hadn't planned the words.

She looked up at him. "I know," she whispered.

She closed her eyes for a long moment, squeezing his hand. Her lids fluttered open. "I was thinking of home," she said, her voice so low he strained to hear. "I was thinking about us, Michael, and Norway, and . . ." He felt the spasm as she shivered. "It is forever away." She turned her head to look directly into his eyes. "There won't be any Norway, will there, Michael? Not any more."

Quit holding her hand, damn it! You can't help her this way.

"Maybe," he said, finally. "Maybe." He released her hand and left to return to his quarters. June wasn't as helpless as the others had been. Sanborne and Gunner were able to do more for her, and for Page and Luke, than for the three who had died. Massive plasma transfusions, new antibiotics, new drugs. Maybe it wouldn't do any good. Maybe it would. Either way, there wasn't any time to waste.

Dolan's face was still on the screen. "June?" he asked. "Is it bad?"

"It's bad," Harder growled. "Let's get with it, Stub." He forced them back to where they'd left off. "I want to find out more about that Agena. Isn't that the one that was left in orbit from an earlier mission?"

"Right the first time. We used it for rendezvous and some burn time with one Gemini, then powered down the systems to be used for the next shot."

"Didn't you run a trap test with that bird?"

"Yeah. We left a trap open. Gave the bird a slow spin while it was up there. We despun when the next ship went up. In fact, I handled the test."

"How long was it up?"

Stubby Dolan thought back. "Ten weeks, at least."

"Remember what happened with it?"

Dolan's eyes widened. "Christ," he breathed. "Of course! We had it up there for ten weeks, picked up some stuff in the trap, *and we brought it home with us in the Gemini.*"

"You said 'stuff.' What kind?"

"Hardly enough to see with the naked eye. Looked like dust. I remember it had the jokers in the labs all excited, and—" Suddenly he stared into Harder's eyes. "Mike, are you thinking what I'm—"

"Damn right I am," Harder said with a fierce intensity. "Didn't one of those guys in the lab come down with something?"

Dolan nodded vigorously. "Jesus, *yes!* We didn't know what it was. Guy broke out all over with bumps, if I remember. Thought he had hives, until the swelling started. I remember it now. The doctors said it looked like poison oak, and they gave him some pills and told him to put some sort of lotion on it. He went home and it was gone in a couple of days."

"Are you *sure* it was poison oak, for Christ's sake?"

"I'll damned well find out. Stay close to the line. I'll keep this on open monitor." He left the screen.

While he waited for Dolan, Harder made rapid calculations. What was the difference between what had happened after that Gemini flight and what was happening right now in *Epsilon?* In the answer to that question, Harder knew, might lie the solution to beating the life spores that were multiplying wildly inside their bodies. One answer was obvious. Never before had human beings existed for so long under the clinical conditions of *Epsilon*—and then, still under those conditions, been exposed to the microorganisms they had brought into the station.

Harder pounded a fist into his palm, keyed up, impatient for Dolan to return. Maybe things were finally starting to fall into place. "Maybe, maybe," he whispered to himself. Maybe he was right. Maybe the answer was that simple.

Maybe Norway wasn't really "forever away."

His reflections were interrupted by Dolan's return to the line. The latter didn't mince his words. "It was a waste of time, Mike," he said quickly. "The doctor who treated the man isn't around."

"What about the guy himself?" Harder snapped.

"Out of the country. Research trip in New Guinea."

He held up his hand. "I've already started it, Mike. As soon as they can be reached I'll talk to them directly. But at this moment there's no way of checking further. For all we know, it could have been poison oak or—"

"Or anything," Harder persisted. "We don't know what. Okay. But we *do* know that he worked with the dust, that he was sick, and that he *recovered*. Christ, we know *that* much!"

Dolan recognized the signs of Harder's wearing thin. "We know all that, Mike. As soon as possible I'll get to either the doctor or the guy who was sick, or both of them. Now, let's have the rest. You've been holding back."

"Okay, okay," Harder said impatiently. "I've got an idea. It's going to sound way out, maybe, but I want you to listen to me carefully. If you agree with me, you're going to have to stick your neck out. But if I'm on the right track, they won't be chopping everything to the ground."

Dolan kept his face expressionless. "Let's have it," he said.

Harder discussed with Dolan the special procedures for astronauts returning from a mission to the surface of the moon. The steps taken during and after atmospheric landing and entry were strict. The fear of alien organisms had been around a long time. For years the probes sent from Earth to the moon, and to Mars and Venus, had been meticulously sterilized. The object was to prevent terrestrial organisms from contaminating the other worlds and jeopardizing later scientific observations. It was also obvious that there might be something on the moon that could be returned to Earth.

The procedures for a return mission required the astronauts to remain within their spacecraft after landing. They carried with them up to fifty pounds of lunar surface materials in sealed containers. But they also had dust on them. Despite disposable boots, static electricity would cause dust to adhere to their suits and helmets. They left the moon in the two-man bug to rendezvous in lunar orbit with the waiting Apollo. Then the two astronauts who'd been on the moon floated through the airlock into the command module. They couldn't help but bring with them particles from the lunar surface. Recognizing this fact, they were under orders to remain sealed within their suits and to keep the command module sealed after it had landed.

The entire spacecraft was picked up and moved within a huge, hermetically-sealed container. It was like a giant thermos bottle. The trick was to make certain the container was airtight. Then, within the container, the cargo of spaceship, men, and lunar materials was rushed to Houston where the entire contraption was inserted into an even larger pressure capsule—a building, the size of an airplane hangar. For at least thirty days no one who entered that capsule was permitted to leave, including the doctors, scientists, and engineers who went inside to make their analyses. For at least thirty days there was absolute quarantine.

"We can do the same thing, Stubby," Harder said, his features creased with concentration. "We can come back in the lifting body. Everyone would be in suits, and the ship sealed. The lifting body lets us land out in the desert. No complications with a recovery force like for Apollo. If we come down near Edwards, we've got this thing hacked. There's a full quarantine station there, a duplicate of Houston."

Dolan nodded, still not speaking.

"Once we're down, we wait," Harder rushed on.

"Nobody moves. Nothing opens up. We have enough internal power for cooling, and everything we need until you get a chopper to us with auxiliary power. We sit there and wait until we're in your pickle jar."

Dolan agreed with everything Harder said. But they hadn't solved all the problems. The pressure was on to keep the astronauts and their plague right where they were—four hundred and sixty miles above the earth. As far as most people were concerned, their expected date of return was couched in one word: never. *Epsilon* must be sacrificed for the protection of the race. Not everyone agreed with this position, but those who were most vocal screamed it. Both Harder and Dolan knew this couldn't be accepted. Sooner or later the problem had to be faced squarely—and overcome. *If we knuckle under now, we're finished. The program is dead. We'll never see it started again in our lifetime.*

"Getting you back here, even in quarantine, isn't enough," Dolan said slowly.

Harder thought that one over. "Why not?" he asked, his manner brusque.

"Well, there's precious little down here we can do for you people that Sanborne and Gunner aren't doing for you right now," Dolan explained. "They're the best we've got."

"I know that," Harder snapped, "but what's that got to do with the plan?"

"Hold on, Mike. The quarantine doesn't help you. It just seals you off. That's all. What I mean is that the quarantine keeps whatever you may bring back with you from getting outside the chamber, and—"

"That's the whole damned trouble!" Harder shouted.

His outburst caught Dolan by surprise. He studied Harder through narrowed eyes. "How do you mean that?" he asked carefully.

Harder took a deep breath and spoke slowly. "It's the quarantine, Stub. It works both ways. Sure, it keeps anything that's inside from getting out. *But it also keeps anything that's outside from getting in.*"

Chapter XIX

There was an awkward silence. Dolan stared at Harder as if hoping to gain understanding from the electronic image before him. He jabbed his finger at the screen.

"Now wait just a minute, Mike. Maybe I don't hear you right." Dolan gestured with exasperation. "You said the problem of quarantine is that it keeps anything from getting in? You mean, from getting inside *to* you? From the outside?" He stared at Harder as if he couldn't believe any of it.

"Hell, *yes!*" Harder shouted. He leaned forward and his features filled the screen on Dolan's console. "That's the whole ball of wax. *Listen* to me, for Christ's sake!" He could scarcely conceal his agitation. "You can rig up that giant thermos bottle of yours so that if we're in quarantine, we can have an intake of ambient air, can't you? Of course you can. I don't mean filtered air, or bottled, or pressurized, or cleaned, or anything else," Harder ran on, breathlessly. "Stub, it's got to be *ambient* air. And at the same time, you can take off what comes out of the chamber, recirculate it or bottle it, I don't care, just so long as we have that continuous intake of ambient."

Dolan thought for several moments.

"Well, damn it, answer me!" Harder insisted with a shout that rattled the speaker.

Still Dolan hesitated before replying. "Sure," he said finally, "we could rig that up, all right. It'd be a bit tricky, but not too much trouble. But *why*? Why would you want that kind of a setup, Mike? The whole idea is to seal you off from. . . ." His voice trailed away as the thought hit him.

Mike watched the face with hawklike intent as Dolan scratched at the side of his chin, then heard the words, "Mother of God, I never thought of that. You mean—?"

For the first time in many hours an honest grin creased Harder's features. "Yeah," he said, his voice falling to a normal level. "How about that, Stub? We can swing it. Nobody worries about catching cold from us, right? It may be the answer, Stub, so help me!"

For the next several minutes the two men conversed rapidly in an exchange of excited words. Finally Dolan leaned back in his chair, groping for the cigar he'd forgotten for so long. He'd made his decision. "All right, Mike," he said in words chosen with care. "I'm going to stick out my neck. Like you said, way out. Just hang on up there, fella. I think we might just swing this deal, after all." His face sobered. "I can't promise anything, but—"

"I know that," Harder broke in.

"—but I sure as hell am going to make the dust fly," Dolan went on. He rose from his seat, almost out of range of the console scanner that carried his picture to Harder. "See you soon, hero," he said and disappeared from the video.

For a long time Harder stared at the set. Finally he reached forward and turned it off. Engrossed in his thinking he sat motionless. After a while he glanced through the viewport. Well off in the distance, rolling slowly in drifting mode, was the graceful, arrowhead shape of the lifting body spacecraft. Jack Dexter was still out there, still alone, hoping for them.

Harder switched the VHF equipment to the spacecraft frequency. He reached Dexter by radio.

"Get your lazy ass up," Harder said with a levity he couldn't control. He laughed at Dexter's startled response. Maybe we'll have some work for you sooner than you think, was his pleasant thought.

Chapter XX

The light reached out beyond the curving dark horizon of the planet stretching hundreds of miles into heavens that had come aglow. They hung suspended in space. Mike Harder watched shifting, formless bands of light rippling silently through the sky palisades.

They were coming around the downswing of orbit, farther south than the lowest extremities of Africa or Australia, crossing the southernmost tip of South America. Before them the southern lights were flung upward from the Antarctic, now visible as a golden crown along the flanks of the world. The light pulsed in a hypnotic fashion, reflecting from the metallic prow of the lifting body. The ribbons faded from sight and the heavens abruptly filled with rapidly twisting, shifting, moving bands of light. In an instant, tremendous streamers ran toward them from above the horizon, their colors riffled by an invisible space wind. The celestial vault filled with a kaleidoscopic pastel green, yellow, pink, red, and purple. Far beneath them the intense gold of Antarctic reflection flung its own hues to mix with the electrical display.

Jack Dexter poised, half-in and half-out of the cockpit hatch. He looked at the lights, overwhelmed by the display. Without turning, he spoke into his helmet mike. "Do you believe in omens, Colonel?"

Harder knew his meaning. "Maybe," he said. "We can use all the help we can get."

It took time and patient effort to transfer the three patients from *Epsilon* to the lifting body. Dexter pulsed the arrowhead spacecraft in close, just above the upper airlock of the S-IVB tank. That way he wouldn't have to chase the locks that rotated. It reduced their work and brought less pressure to bear on the three helpless astronauts.

Sanborne and Gunner prepared them carefully. Parsons, Page, and June were injected with sedatives to keep them unconscious for several hours. Working with the doctors, Harder and Guy-Michel encased their friends in emergency pressure suits. These weren't as binding or restrictive as the work suits. Semi-rigid materials replaced the screw-on-and-back helmet. There was more room inside the emergency suits, and that meant better oxygen flow and temperature control. The backpacks were hooked up, and the connections examined with meticulous care by Harder and Guy-Michel. Finally they were ready. They attached harnesses to the suits and hooked up safety lines. Parsons was to be first.

They carried the inert, suited form to the central corridor of the space station. Hal Gunner was in position at the upper airlock waiting for them.

"Henri, pull in the line," Harder directed. Guy-Michel reached into the corridor to grasp the safety lines extending from above. Harder snapped these to the harness of Parsons' suit.

"Careful, careful," Sanborne said, his words unnecessary but instinctive.

Guy-Michel slipped into the corridor and braced his back against the guidepipe. Harder lifted Parsons in his arms to carry him into the corridor where he and Guy-Michel changed his body position to vertical. The Frenchman climbed alongside Parsons, who was now being hauled upward by Hal Gunner. They transferred Parsons from the upper airlock through the long tube extending to the S-IVB tank. Gunner remained with Parsons while Guy-Michel returned to help with the others. It took twenty minutes more to bring them into the S-IVB airlock. Now they were ready for the transfer to the waiting spacecraft.

"Check suits," Harder ordered. They inspected each other's equipment. "Okay, let's vent," he said, nodding to Guy-Michel.

The Frenchman turned to the airlock controls. The three figures, lying prone, swayed as the air vented, the suits tugging gently at the safety lines snapped to bulkhead rings. The hatch swung open. Thirty feet away loomed the spaceship.

"Let's go—" Harder snapped, anxious for the transfer to be over with. He wanted them all in the lifting body and the hatches sealed. If anything went wrong now with Luke, June, or Page, there wasn't a thing they could do in vacuum. The ship afforded some safety.

It took only ten minutes to transfer the patients. While the doctors and Guy-Michel strapped them into the deceleration couches and hooked their life-support systems to the spaceship, Harder returned to *Epsilon*. He drifted slowly down the corridor, opening all airlock hatches leading from the long central tube to the different compartment levels.

Finally he returned to Engineering on Level 5.

He entered the compartment, looking around, studying the instruments and gauges. One by one, he went along a bank of master switches: oxygen mix, forced-draft, the separate power feeds, communications, water. One by one, he pulled down the switches, shutting off the flow of life to the great cylindrical ship in which they had lived for six months. He stood before the main power console that controlled the nuclear reactor in the second S-II. Harder positioned the guides to Low Standby and pulled the main switch. The power flow from the reactor ebbed to a trickle. Harder worked his way back into the corridor and drifted again to the lower airlock where he opened the hatches. The last vestiges of air from *Epsilon* sighed away from the station. Vacuum had taken over.

Harder began to work his way upward through the long cylinder. The lights that had gleamed so brightly were gone now. No glow came from the compartments as he eased his way through the tube. The viewport hatches were dogged, and darkness had returned to the station. Harder's flashlight stabbed ahead of him, reflecting in silvery trickles. He felt as if he were gliding through an endless tube of shadows.

The station was nearly dormant, its only life the barely perceptible energy flow from the powered-down reactor. It seemed too soon for memories, but they surrounded him in the tube, followed him, a phantasmagoric bustling without sound. Harder reached the upper airlock. He paused and for a moment looked back, then slipped into the tube that would take him to the S-IVB tank.

His light stabbed through the yawning space where they had performed so many times in weightlessness. He smiled as if he could hear the shouted cries and laughter of Bill Jordan: "I'm gonna cream your ass, boss." And then the delighted shout of Werner Koelbe: "Time! First fall. . . ."

Quickly Harder left the tank. He didn't stop as he went through the top airlock and drifted free above the station. The arrowshape waited for him. It could wait a moment longer. Harder thrusted, to turn himself about until he was looking down, facing the center tank of *Epsilon*. The Earth loomed dazzling and white, with a great spread of clouds covering most of the planet. Harder didn't look beyond the station where Bill Jordan, Tim Pollard, and the still form of Werner Koelbe rested. He had the fleeting thought that Werner was free forever of the ghosts that had pursued him.

Abruptly the astronaut's hand came up. His gloved fingers touched his helmet in a final salute.

An hour later, the ship's timer rushed through the final seconds of countdown. Dexter punched to automatic mode, ready at any moment to take over manually. The count and sequencing went perfectly. The thrusters tweaked final corrections for attitude-hold. Dexter counted the dwindling time aloud, giving them the chance to brace for the retrofire.

A muffled explosion boomed through the metal structure. Almost at the same instant pressure squeezed their bodies. Retrofire lasted sixteen seconds and the shutdown sprang them from their couches, back into weightlessness. Sanborne and Gunner paid no attention to the sensations of their deceleration. They kept their eyes riveted to the three unconscious people in their care.

Dexter thrusted to reverse attitude. Now the arrowhead shape fell along its low slanting path with the nose pointing ahead to the approaching world. Their fall would carry them a third of the way around the planet before they reached the atmosphere.

"Jack?" The pilot couldn't turn in his bulky suit. He glanced into his panel mirror. He saw Sanborne motion to him. "What's cabin pressure?" the doctor asked.

Dexter glanced at the panel. "Three point five. Anything wrong?"

Sanborne nodded slowly. "The retrofire," he explained. "It wasn't easy for Page. Raise the pressure. I'm going to open her suit."

Dexter reached to his left to work the controls. "Coming up to five psi," he said.

Sanborne removed the zippered helmet covering. A thin line of blood trickled from Page's nose, pooling by her lips. Guy-Michel took the absorbent swab from Sanborne's hand, then reached down to Page. The doctor watched silently.

Fifteen minutes went by, the horizon expanding to each side as they slid closer to the planet. Now they were in the upper reaches of the atmosphere. Another minute, and a panel light flashed brightly.

"We've got point zero five-g," Dexter said crisply. "Get set for the loads."

The long plunge through atmosphere—the nose raised high to take heat along the belly of the spaceship—took another thirty minutes. Six of those minutes imposed a steady force of three and a half times normal gravity. Easy punishment for re-entry— only half that of Apollo. The arrowhead vessel threw off a brilliant corona of ionized air, heated to several thousand degrees. Finally the intense orange light deepened to a dark glowing red-black flame.

For the first time in months, Harder heard the sound of air rushing past the sleek shape. He listened to it absently, twisting around as much as he could in his seat beside Dexter. Sanborne and Gunner were huddled over the still form of Page. Harder saw Sanborne slump back suddenly. The next thing he saw was the white face of Henri, lips working soundlessly.

"I'm sorry, Mike," Sanborne said at last. "The g-loadings were too much. Massive hemorrhage. She didn't make it."

Hal Gunner reached over to close the helmet. Harder heard a snarl. He saw Henri push away Gunner's arm. The Frenchman reached out for absorbent swabs and bent to wipe the blood from her face. Sanborne shook his head slightly at Gunner. The doctors turned away to leave Henri with Page.

Harder didn't have to ask about June and Luke. "They came through fine," Gunner said, answering the unspoken question.

Losing June would have been too much even for him, Sanborne thought.

Atmosphere transformed their spacecraft into a high-speed glider. Dexter watched the altimeter needle slip past 30,000 feet. He used aircraft controls now, and eased back on the stick. The nose went up and they climbed again as Dexter killed their forward speed.

The pilot flipped away a safety cover and pulled down a bright red handle. "Hang on," he said tersely.

Within the bowels of the arrowhead shape they heard a muffled roar, and then the strident bass cry of compressed gases. On both sides of the ship long wings began to bend forward. Tucked in securely during all operations except for this final descent through the thickening air, the wings transformed the arrowhead into a straight-winged glider, capable of slow speed and responsive control.

Harder watched thin vapor trails of the chase planes knifing toward them in wide curves. "Contact!

Confirm visual contact!" The voices sounded in his earphones, a message from the chase frequency. Dexter acknowledged calls from ground radar. For the next several minutes the pilot exchanged flight and course data, taking up a new heading in response to ground command. They were on their way home, following the invisible electronic paths leading them to the desert floor landing sector. Moments later a shadow fell across the canopy. Harder looked up and saw two great sharklike forms escorting them down.

He watched mountains leaping into prominence. Harder knew this country as well as his own name. He'd flown it countless times. There, in the distance, were the dry lakes surrounding the flight test center. Beyond it stretched the greater lake—off to their left, isolated from the world. Smoke pots and brilliant flashers beckoned to them. The homing needles were smack on their pegs as Dexter glided down smoothly. The world stretched out, the horizon lifting higher into the sky as they dropped. Across the desert, directly ahead of them after a final turn, ran the black-and-orange line, the final pointer.

Dexter reached out to the panel, and the gear came down with a burbling, thumping roar of wind. With those wings extended, approach was—as Tim Pollard would have said—"a piece of cake." Dexter brought her in smoothly, easing the nose up, flaring her out. The airspeed read 110 as the main gear sighed onto the hardened desert floor. The nose came down, and the forward gear passed its vibration back to them. They came to a halt in a great cloud of dust.

Silence. Harder couldn't believe it. He glanced into the mirror and caught Sanborne's eye. The doctor nodded. "They're fine, Mike."

"Bandit One, Bandit One, this is Snatch Five. You guys reading me?"

Dexter grinned at the call. He pressed down his transmit button. "Snatch Five from Bandit One. Got you clean."

The voice that came back was cautious. "Everything okay? You still holding pressure?"

Dexter flicked his eyes over the gauges. "Affirmative, Snatch Five. We're sealed tight."

There was a pause. "Keep it that way. We've got a chopper coming down next to you in a minute, and they'll plug in for auxiliary power. Over."

Dexter acknowledged the call moments before a chattering roar buffeted at them. A helicopter dropped to the ground. Through the front windshield they saw several men leap from the machine, dragging cables behind them. Muffled bangs and thumps sounded through the spacecraft as the technicians unsealed plug covers and jammed in the umbilicals.

Another light flashed on the panel. "Snatch Five, Bandit here. We're hooked up, and on outside power."

"Mike?"

Harder recognized Stubby Dolan's voice. "Where are you, Stub?" Static rattled in his earphones.

"Right over you and on the way down. Be there in a minute."

Another chopper dropped to the desert floor. It was still rocking back and forth on its gear when the stocky figure of Dolan emerged from the front hatchway and trotted across the sandy surface. He waved as he caught sight of Harder's face through the spaceship windshield.

Dolan threw up a thumb, and Harder returned the gesture. Dolan disappeared from sight as he moved to the lower side of the spaceship and plugged in his communications umbilical. He didn't waste time or words. Too much had to be done quickly.

"Pickup is only a few miles out and coming straight

in," he snapped to Harder. He leaned close to the side of the machine and stared in. He couldn't see much, only shadows and suited figures in the aft part of the cabin.

"How are they?" he barked. Until a few moments before, the only communications had been between Dexter and the landing controllers. Dolan couldn't know, of course.

"Not good," Harder replied. "Page didn't make it. She couldn't take the g-loads."

"The others?"

"Holding up," Harder said. He saw Dr. Gunner nodding to confirm his words. "Hal says they're okay."

"Sorry about Page, Mike." Then he added brusquely, "Can Hal and Ken hear me?"

"They're listening."

"Good." Dolan addressed the doctor. "Ken, pickup will be here in a minute. Everything's aboard whole blood, all the supplies you need. We've got Zystra also."

"Mike, ask him if the pickup is sealed so we can open up this can." Harder relayed the question from Sanborne.

"That's affirmative," came the reply. "The pickup is mobile. We'll stick you inside and seal it off and move you that way into the main chamber."

"Got it," Harder said.

Sanborne looked at him. "I never thought the old goat would go for this behind-the-bushes scene," he said. "He's strictly by the rules. He's also the best man there is." Sanborne glanced at June and Parsons. "I'm glad we've got him."

Harder's glance behind him caught Guy-Michel, his face screwed up tightly in pain. Zystra was too late for Page.

* * *

A huge skycrane chopper descended in a clattering dust storm. As the flurry subsided, a trailer van inched to the ground beneath the helicopter. Moments later it backed away and was driven directly in front of the spacecraft. The doors in the van opened wide. Men ran forward to hook cables to the nose gear. The machine lurched forward slowly. Abruptly they stopped as a technician signaled frantically to Dexter.

"The wings! I forgot the damn wings." He reached to the control panel and pushed up the release. "Can you hear me out there?" The technician nodded. "Okay, the wings are free. You'll have to push them manually."

The man waved his hand and shouted orders. Helicopter crewmen rushed forward and slid the wings back into their slots. The lurching motion began anew, and the cables winched the spacecraft into the van. Overhead and side lights shone brilliantly on them.

More thuds and clanking sounds followed. There was the muted whine of generators. They heard commands shouted from one man to another. Then Dolan's voice came to them.

"That's it," he said. "You're inside and covered from view, and you're sealed in. You can open up now."

Dexter worked the safety releases and the canopy moved. Hands grabbed at it to haul it away. Harder saw the face of Dr. Richard Zystra. The doctor nodded briefly as he climbed into the ship.

"Mike, I'm in the chopper right above you," Dolan said. "We've got the chamber at Edwards all set."

Harder felt another lurch and a steady vibration through the machine. The helicopter was lifting, carrying them to the waiting chamber. Suddenly he didn't care any more. Fatigue sluiced through his body like icy needles. It was all over for him now. He had done everything possible. Let the others worry about anything else—

"Mike!" Sanborne's voice was urgent.

"June's out of it," the doctor said.

Harder twisted his helmet free and handed it to Dexter. Awkward in the suit, he turned in the seat and pushed closer. June stared with eyes still drugged. She didn't know where she was or what was happening. Sanborne freed the twistlocks of her hand gauntlets and removed the covering. Harder reached for her hand.

"Mike?" She tried to focus on his face.

"I'm here, June."

"What—where, I mean. . . ." She couldn't form the words.

Harder squeezed her hand gently. "It's all right. We're home, baby. We're home."

Chapter XXI

Ben Blanchard cast a critical eye over the press auditorium. *Maximus Circus.* The fourth estate out for blood. *Not this time, you bastards.* He still smarted from that last episode when he'd been left standing before them all with his pants figuratively down around his ankles. From that moment on, Blanchard had declared his own private war with the press.

He'd called in their top representatives, and he blew his cool. They threw angry words back and forth until the TV networks got smart. Blanchard couldn't stop them from getting what they wanted, but he could screw up the works until he made their professional life unbearable. He swore he would do just that. As a starter, he invoked a security classification for *Epsilon,* and Garavito backed him up. He placed heavy thumbs on the identification badges by updating them without warning and refusing admittance to key conferences without a valid badge. He raised hell in seventeen different ways until the press leaders declared a truce.

They rebuilt the press auditorium. TV crews went

into closed booths that gave them better acoustics, camera control, and a direct microphone link to the officials presented to the press. It cut down the noise. Blanchard ruled out individual lights for the auditorium. The unions screamed, and Blanchard told them to shove it. He was going to have built-in lights, and that was that. The networks settled their grievances behind closed doors.

Blanchard thanked his own personal deities for his decision to act the son of a bitch. Because today was the cropper. Today he'd need everything going for him. He called another secret session with the power boys of the press and they came to an agreement. They'd work together.

Blanchard looked out into the packed throng, wincing from the lights, but more confident than he'd ever been. Today, by God he'd knock them clear out of their seats. He noticed his assistant giving him the high sign. The public affairs chief stepped out from behind tall curtains and walked briskly to the end of a long table. He stood by a microphone, expecting silent attention—and got it. The members of the press were like bloodhounds hot on the trail of a fresh scent. They had plenty of leads but no one knew just what was going on. Blanchard and the others made certain that radio traffic kept up between Houston and the space station although they alone knew the sham that was being enacted.

What the press couldn't figure was NASA's hardnosed attitude toward the *Epsilon* disaster. After the last debacle, with the announcement of Pollard's death, NASA had floundered. Then, suddenly, NASA's back had stiffened. No one could figure it. They sensed it would come out in the wash today. Blanchard had virtually promised them just that. They leaned forward hungrily. Blanchard played it like a maestro, his pauses and hesitation carried through with perfect timing.

The expected lineup of officials appeared. Three men were familiar. David James Heath, NASA administrator. Dr. Emanuel Garavito, *Epsilon* Project Director. Dr. Richard Zystra, *Epsilon* Medical Programs Director. Where was Thayer, the boss of the Manned Spacecraft Center? What about the Vice President? The rumors had been thick that Harrison, as Director of the National Space Council, would be there.

Blanchard had fought desperately to keep Harrison out from under their feet. He hadn't been there when they needed him, and no one wanted him around now. The fewer the people on that stage the better. The fourth man brought raised eyebrows and exclamations of surprise, a murmur that swelled like a sudden breeze through the auditorium. Dr. Anton Kustodiev of the U.S.S.R. Academy of Sciences.

What's he doing here? . . . I told you, goddamnit! They're going to cancel the whole space program! . . . Boy, I thought Blanchard had run out of tricks. Hey, that's Stubby Dolan over there. . . .

Dolan took his seat next to the Russian scientist. They'd come to be good friends, and Dolan was looking forward to this session.

Four seats remained unoccupied. The newsmen strained their eyes. There were no nameplates. Members of the press looked at one another in mild confusion. The lights dimmed. That was another ploy by Blanchard. They wanted a show and he was giving them one. He'd convinced the others that Garavito should run with the ball to open the conference. Heath was NASA's big gun, but this wasn't NASA—this was *Epsilon*, front, rear, and center. Heath represented the United States; the world accepted Garavito as international representative. Heath agreed—indeed, he favored the proposal.

Blanchard announced Garavito's name. There was immediate silence as Garavito rose and moved forward. Slowly he clasped his hands and cleared his throat. He tried to prevent a smile but could not. At the last moment he switched his plans. He had been prepared to talk to the press. Suddenly he knew that would be a mistake.

"Ladies and gentlemen—people of the world." He liked the sound of that. Then he hit them with the planned impact. That was the best way. Tell the whole world—right out.

"People of the world," he repeated slowly. "It is my great pleasure to inform you at this time that we have brought back to Earth the members of the space station, *Epsilon*."

He leaned back in his seat, knowing that for several moments anything more would go unheard. He was right. For an instant there was absolute silence. Then an explosive roar from hundreds of voices spilled over them. Blanchard smiled to himself. *They'll knock it off in a hurry. Manny's got 'em by the short hairs.* It didn't take long. The hush that followed the outburst seemed even more deafening.

The significance of the four empty seats slammed home to them all. Garavito hadn't said *survivors*. He didn't need to. They knew several men had died in the station. But wait a minute! Three were known to have died. Someone else? *Who* else . . . ?

In that first, immediate impression, they missed the true significance of what had happened. What about the plague? Could they possibly have taken such a chance? Could they have brought back to Earth the infected survivors? And what about Kustodiev? His presence meant there would be no loud screams from the Russians. It signified a solid front by the United States and the Soviet Union. They waited for Garavito.

"We have effected a complete cure."

He paused to let his words sink in . . . *a complete cure.* How nice that sounded! He made the most of his opportunity.

"A complete cure," he repeated. "The crew of *Epsilon* who are with us today are fully recovered." Master that he was of such occasions, Garavito waited again until the silence had become almost painful.

"Colonel Michael Harder . . . Dr. June Strond . . . Dr. Henri Guy-Michel. . . ." His words intoned the death sentence for the names he would not call. "Astronaut Luke Parsons." Again he fell silent. The long pause made it all too clear. Dr. Page Alison had died.

Garavito was not through yet. What was said in the next several moments would be critical. It could well determine the future of man's space explorations. Garavito had the key moment, and wanted to avoid the critical questions that would come later. Garavito raised his hand. "People of the world," he said slowly, "I am honored—" he turned slightly and nodded to the Russian—"to introduce Professor Anton Kustodiev, one of the world's great scientists. He has a statement to make to all of you."

It was superb timing and it achieved maximum effect. Kustodiev rose to his feet. In his deep rumbling voice, his words accented, the Russian scientist made his critical statement.

"We, my staff and I, were honored to help in solving this problem that faced us all. We came here with our best doctors. We were welcomed. We worked with Dr. Zystra, with the others." He seemed to straighten, to change his words from an announcement to an edict. "I confirm . . . that the cosmonauts from Station *Epsilon* . . . are completely cured of the disease. There is no question of their recovery."

The murmuring had begun anew, the demand for details filling the auditorium. Blanchard gave the signal, and at the side of the stage a door opened.

They walked in one at a time—Harder, Strond, Guy-Michel, and Parsons. They did not take their seats immediately. The press wouldn't have it. For five minutes bedlam reigned.

There was wild applause—a thundering roar from eight hundred voices. Emotion overwhelmed them all.

The tumultuous, spontaneous reception ebbed slowly. As silence resumed, a man in the front row rose to his feet. Hank Marrows stood quietly, eyes turning to him. Blanchard looked at him, suddenly angry. Marrows knew there wouldn't be any questions until. . . . Something about the look on Marrows' face stayed Blanchard's words. Marrows glanced directly at Blanchard, and the latter nodded. He signaled an assistant to take a microphone immediately to the newsman.

Marrows looked at Harder and then at the others. "I believe I speak for all of us," he said. "Colonel Harder, Dr. Strond, Dr. Guy-Michel, Astronaut Parsons. It is very good to have you back with us." He sat down.

Stubby Dolan told the story as only he could—as the man who had initiated with Mike Harder the chain of events that had brought the survivors home. When he had finished his brief résumé, and everyone was waiting with growing impatience, he turned the microphone over to the surviving members of the space station. Henri Guy-Michel sat quietly, his face impassive. The death of Page had left him within a shell of his own pain. He did not want to be here, having agreed to appear only because his absence would have caused rumors. By agreement among them, Harder fielded most of the questions, acting as their spokesman.

The crisis within the station, he explained, had been created by the clinical nature of their environment. It was this unnatural situation, as we think of environment here on Earth, that had brought on what easily could have been a total disaster.

"You see, the microorganisms we brought into the station were nothing new to Earth." Harder wanted to be certain they understood this fully.

"There's no question of that," he went on. "Not now. We've had space dust impacting our atmosphere for millions of years, long before our first ancestors walked this world. Every day thousands of tons of dust and meteoric debris hit the atmosphere. Much of it survives entry and filters down. It mixes with the air we breathe. The organisms sometimes carried with this dust end up in the ocean where conditions are perfect for their reproduction. Men, animals, and plants have long been exposed to these organisms that reach us from space.

"Yet, there's never been an epidemic of any kind that we couldn't understand—or, if it ever did get started, that we couldn't handle ourselves. Or that just died away, without our knowing why, or even that it was here in the first place. The point is that nothing has ever spread completely beyond our control. That is the key."

They waited for him to go on. At Houston, throughout the country, around an entire planet people hung on his words.

"I thought about that for a long time. And then,

before I talked this over with Stubby Dolan, I remembered something. A story. A story I read when I was a boy. It was a science fiction story—one of the classics. I'm sure many of you have read it, that some of you have already guessed what it is."

A newsman stood up. Harder nodded to him and a microphone appeared. "Colonel Harder, could that be the story by H. G. Wells? You know that one I mean. *The War of the Worlds?*"

Harder smiled. "That's the one." He looked directly into the television cameras.

"For those of you who aren't familiar with Wells's story, I recommend it stongly. In fact,"—the smile broadened to a grin—"all of us up here are terribly fond of it right now."

A ripple of sympathetic laughter met his remark.

"Wells wrote about an invasion of Earth from Mars. The machines of war the Martians brought here overwhelmed all our defenses. We couldn't stand up to them. The Martians swept victoriously across the whole planet. Earth was doomed.

"Then, when it seemed that everything was lost, the great war machines of the Martians faltered. Finally, they ground to a halt. Inside those machines— the most terrible Earth had ever faced—the Martian invaders were dead or dying."

Harder paused, calm and assured, the hardened astronaut many of them knew. His voice picked up again.

"They were struck down by the deadliest creatures of this world. The most dangerous forms of life that exist anywhere.

"The microorganisms of Earth. Our own bacteria. We have them in our system, in the air, in the soil, in plants and in the oceans. Everywhere. We've lived with them for millions of years. And that's why, despite alien organisms always drifting down through our atmosphere, we have never been decimated by disease we couldn't understand, or that was so great it might overwhelm us completely.

"We're *protected* by the bacterial life of our planet. This is what Stubby Dolan and I talked about before we came back to Earth. We didn't take any chances. We were sealed within a pressure compartment. Hermetically sealed. Nothing could get out. No one was endangered."

He leaned forward, intense. "But we needed something we could never get in space. Something that could save our lives. We made certain that the normal air of this world was brought in for us to breathe. We ate fresh food, drank unfiltered water. For six months we had been breathing purified air, eating sterilized food, drinking sterilized water."

He gestured suddenly. "Not any more." Again he grinned at them. "Now we were breathing the unfiltered, unpurified, wonderful dirty air of the Earth." He laughed. "We ate fruits, vegetables, meat—every kind of food—that hadn't been packaged or sterilized. The water we drank came straight from an open well—and it *was* touched by human hands, you could say."

He looked out at them and into the cameras, and knew he was speaking to an entire planet. "We ate, drank, and breathed in bacteria. Germs of every kind and size and shape. They're deadly. Nothing on Earth can stand up to them.

"Except," and his grin flashed around the world, "*us*."

**Real people, real problems, real science and
no compromises:**
New Destinies delivers everything needed to satisfy the science fiction reader. Every issue includes hard sf and speculative fact written by scientists and authors like these:

-Harry Turtledove   -Charles Sheffield   -Dean Ing
-Poul Anderson   -Spider Robinson   -Larry Niven

New Destinies: the quarterly paperback magazine of science fiction and speculative fact. *The Washington Post* called it "a forum for hard sf." This is *the* place to go for exciting, new adventures and mind-blowing extrapolation on the latest in human inquiry. No other publication will challenge you like *New Destinies*. No other publication will reward you as well.

And, it's the only place to find
Jim Baen's outrageous editorials!

Why worry about missing the latest issue? Take advantage of our special ordering offer today—and we'll send you a free poster!